Rescued Hostage
Chris T. Delarmy

Rescued Hostage

Chris T. Delarmy

Chris T. Delarmy
Rescued Hostage. A Camsted Adventure

Creative-Story
Safferlingstr. 5 / 134
D-80634 München (Munich), Germany
Tel.: +49 (0)89 / 12 11 14 66
Fax: +49 (0)89 / 12 11 14 68
info@creative-story.com
www.creative-story.com

Cover design and layout:
Creative-Web-Projects, München

ISBN: 978-3-95964-100-5

Acknowledgement
Special thanks go to my parents and Andru, who always
believed in this story, endured its pre-versions and encouraged
its creation.

– 1 –
University of Camsted, Office of Prof. Benning

Waiting normally was something Sophia did quite well, letting her mind wander and entertaining herself with fantasy stories. But today, she sat nervously, almost hopping off the chair at every sound. Waiting this time meant torture for her, especially when so much depended on the outcome of the meeting with her professor. Prof. Benning was a demanding tutor, but so far had promised to be supportive of her intended research topic. The feedback of the assigned co-corrector, an independent second professor needing to countercheck her work, so that she could receive her degree, was still missing.

Sophia knew, it would be hard to offer a research topic which both of the world's leading professors in the area, Prof. Benning and Prof. Lynford, would be supportive of, and on which they could agree on. As they were competitors, if not open opponents, to please both was a hard thing to achieve. And the meddling of Prof. Benning's new assistant, Dr. Stewart, a man she could not stand, certainly did not help in the matter. Caught in between the three, with no money or time to spare, Sophia was at her wit's end how to proceed in her studies and reach her heart's goal, to work for her idol, the elusive Prof. Lynford.

Exhausted after just finishing her final exams and trying to get into the graduate program, she was almost at the state of losing hope entirely to ever start her studies for her degree, which was a requirement for her dream-job. She feared her latest topic offer might have been rejected once again. It was the first her supervising professor, Prof. Benning, had even deigned worthy to show to Prof. Lynford for his appraisal, and only because Dr. Stewart had re-formulated and transformed it out of recognition of her own initial suggestion. Sophia still found the new topic ludicrous and not likely to enable successful research results, but what was a poor student to do, when she was glad to have secured the support of Prof. Benning in the first place. She just wondered, why Prof. Benning was letting himself be dominated by the obnoxious Dr. Stewart so much lately, when in her opinion, that man had no knowledge or inspiration at all.

Trembling, Sophia sat waiting to be called in to her professor. His secretary, Mrs. Farndale, snubbing her like a recalcitrant child, had gone back behind her desk and no longer took note of her presence, while furiously writing on her computer keyboard.

When the door to Prof. Benning's office opened, Sophia let out a breath of relief. Finally the waiting was over and she would hear the result to her topic suggestion.

The severe face of her professor did not give her much hope and indeed, his words immediately confirmed her fears.

"Prof. Lynford rejected your latest topic of choice."

No coddling or talking around the hard truth. Prof. Benning was not a man of nice words. That had been one of the reasons she had chosen him as her supervising professor for her exams in the first place. So now was not the time to lament about it.

She wanted to know exactly how she was doing and covering the facts with disguising words in her opinion would not help her academic progress. She had intentionally studied with the professor with the reputation of being uncompromising but fair.

So far, she had done well. Working hard, she had managed to accomplish her goals and additionally doing research-work for her professor had gained her the points for him to consider her as a research student for a doctoral degree program.

But now, getting her research topic granted proved to be more difficult than she had anticipated. It had already been the tenth project suggestion and the first the professor had even considered to offer to the sole adequate co-corrector for her subject choice about bio-photons, Prof. Lynford.

The two professors did not always see eye-to-eye and the financial success Prof. Lynford had with his research results and his own company certainly did not help to gain him acceptance from the academically ascetic Prof. Benning, who abhorred the morally polluted world of the economy outside the gilded tower of academic research.

"Why?" Sophia could not help but ask. "Did he say anything that I could do better to get his approval?"

"No. He is not in a good situation lately and it is a wonder he even gave feedback at all. He didn't come back to me about your earlier suggestions."

That was news to Sophia and in her astonishment, she kept silent. She had, like Dr. Stewart had told her, presumed Prof. Benning had not forwarded her earlier suggestions at all.

"Perhaps, you can try and do some more research to find an adequate topic or to focus on one of your earlier approaches. We could try again at the end of the semester holidays, to get you in for the next semester."

"But that would mean two months of doing nothing for the thesis."

Sophia did not hold much hope that Prof. Benning would understand her objections. He came from an affluent background, where money was no objective, while she struggled to pay her expenses. Two months without even having a chance to apply for a grant and without time to work to earn money to pay her rent, but having to do more honorary work for her professor to eventually find a new angle to her intended research topic? That would financially bring her to her absolute limits. She already had to take a break from her part-time job during her exams. If she did not get a well-funded scholarship soon, to which she could only apply if her topic was accepted, she would have to give up her studies and move back home to her parents. She would be forced to rent out her little flat she had bought with money her grandmother had given her for that purpose. She would not be able to keep up regular rent-payments to live here otherwise.

Indeed, the further arguments of her professor confirmed that he was completely unaware of her financial problems.

"Prof. Lynford has no time to spare on your thesis right now anyway. His wife is taking this murdering bastard apart."

"What?" Sophia blurted out her astonishment unguardedly. Seeing her hero Prof. Lynford, the man who had been the reason this line of scientific research had awakened her interest in the first place, being dragged into the mud so rudely, especially by her always so polite and well-spoken professor, made her forget her inhibitions in the presence of her strict and demanding tutor.

"Oh, nothing," Prof. Benning conceded. "It just might take a while for him to come back to …, well, anything, really."

"But that is not fair. He's not …" But the intense gaze of her professor stopped the words in her throat. Thinking again, Sophia blurted out: "I can't afford that long a wait. I need to earn money to pay my living expenses. If I can't apply for a scholarship, I won't be able to stay here for research."

"Oh!" Prof. Benning seemed really surprised about her argument, looking as if it had just burst his bubble of contentedness. "That would be a pity, a real pity. We can't let that happen. No! – I'll look into it. I think I even have a job for you right now. I'll send you the details by mail and you can start immediately, let's say tomorrow morning. Yes, that will do nicely. Tomorrow."

Astonished by this sudden turn of events, Sophia needed a moment to collect herself, before she could utter her thanks.

Almost distractedly, Prof. Benning waved her gratitude off and sent her on her way. Sophia had the impression that his attention was far away already, no longer on her case, though he handed her a sheet with suggested different angles she should try on her earlier thesis approaches, when he opened the door for her, always the polite professor.

Even his absentmindedness played into making him the utter prototype of a university professor; though with being no more than about 35 years old, he was still astonishingly young for having achieved his reputation in his field. Admittedly, his dry and stiff behavior made him appear older than his mid-thirties.

Sophia smiled, walking through the corridors, unable to contain her happiness. They had not talked about her salary, but everything coming in would be a heaven-sent relief after months of draining her accounts. Bubbling with happiness, she took out her phone and called her parents, to tell them, her most loyal supporters in her studies, the good news. They in turn would have nothing more urgent to do, but tell her older brother and sister, so the whole family would know about this favorable turn of events in no time at all.

– 2 –

6 Months Later – An Apartment House in Camsted

Working relentlessly at her desk in her tiny apartment in the early afternoon, Sophia looked wistfully out of her large window in front of her writing desk. The view was not beautiful, just the apartment building on the other side of the street, but at least a change from always looking at her computer screen, either in the tech-lab or at home.

Taking a deep breath, she wished for a little more freedom in her life, to research what she wanted and to breath in fresh air, feeling the wind on her skin, dreaming of salty cool air and the rushing sounds of waves of the sea crashing onto the shore.

But that had to remain wishful thinking, Sophia mused. She was just glad that she did not have to pay rent, but only the running costs for her apartment. That was burden enough right now.

Her work for Prof. Benning in his new research-lab had worked out as the professor had announced, though her thesis topic still had not.

None of her topic-suggestions had been accepted so far and the unresponsiveness of Prof. Lynford, her intended co-corrector, had not even played a role in that. Though his being continuously 'unavailable' lately posed a major obstacle in her plans for her future.

But the more pressing hindrance on her way to graduation and her dream-job was her strained relationship with Prof. Benning's newly proclaimed first researcher, Dr. Stewart. This man made working on her own research in the university-lab hard for her every step of the way. Whenever she tried to do some extra tests following her own ideas, Dr. Stewart was breathing down her neck, wanting to know exactly what purpose and results her experiment had. As if she could give him the exact outcome he wanted before she had even had a chance to do the experiment. Why even do a series of tests, when you already knew the result?

She now tried to go to the lab at hours she expected Dr. Stewart not to be there, like early in the mornings or late at night.

At least, not spending all her time in the lab gave her some spare time to work on extra work assignments she had acquired online.

Now, at 2 o'clock in the afternoon, she sat at home, doing work for extra money she could well use, as the pay for her research position in the lab was decent, but only for a few hours a week, while she needed much more time than she was paid for, to actually complete the test-constellations expected of her.

At least, Sophia did not have to worry about someone else depending on her. Living alone, she enjoyed the possibility of working whenever she needed to, without others making demands on her time. Yes, she knew, that made her rather appear like a recluse, but she enjoyed the freedom of it. Her one-room apartment was big enough for her alone, but she would not like to have to live in this space with others, like many of her neighbors did. Even families with children lived here, in apartments the same size, having to share such a tiny space.

The building her gaze rested on, situated on the other side of the street, had much larger apartments than hers. It was the shiny, newly renovated project of a real-estate company in town, with large, expensive flats.

Smiling, Sophia thought about the concierge of the neighboring building, Mr. Arnestone, who had been so annoyed about all the technicalities now included in the building. The technical gimmicks were fine when they worked, but a real bother when they did not. And they had not the day she had met Mr. Arnestone for the first time. The older man, not too far away from his retirement, had been grumbling and angry, standing in front of the house, looking helplessly up the front facade, where the sun mercilessly burned down on the large glass window front. But none of the newly installed sun shields rolled down, something which they should have done automatically.

Sophia had not been able to walk past him, leaving the man alone in his helplessness. She had asked him, if she could be of assistance. The company that had installed the system had remotely done their check-up and told the concierge with an air of superiority that all was working fine. But it obviously was not. And Sophia, after an exhaustive search with Mr. Arnestone, had found the culprit. An unplugged cable to the main master-switchboard. In her opinion, that problem should have easily been revealed by the company's check-up. But their error had made her a dear friend, so who was she to complain. Now, every day she went to work in the lab, she stopped by to talk and chat with Mr. Arnestone, who was one of her most loyal customers for her software repair & help services she now offered as a result to her unexpected success with his problem.

Software and technical gadgets were Sophia's favorite occupation. At high school, she had long thought to go into software development, when she finished school, but the research results published by Prof. Lynford had changed her course. She had rather researched the photons, the 'system behind the system', as the euphoric young professor had called it in the first of his articles she had read, than computer programming.

All flow, all energy, depended on the rules the photons determined. But what determined the way of the photons? What could influence it?

Sophia had been fascinated as soon as she had heard about it and had read up every article by the professor she could get a hold of at her school and town library, which to her annoyance had not been many, back then.

That she later had not studied at the university Prof. Lynford taught at, was solely the result of him withdrawing from his university courses by then and starting a private lab, where he did most of his research. He had still sporadically done a few university courses at the renowned MIT, but Sophia had never had enough money to attend one of them, as the fees were exorbitant. Her choice had fallen on the state university on the other side of the country, where Prof. Benning was teaching that same subject.

But that did not keep her from hoping, that one day she could work for Prof. Lynford and get to be part of his bright ideas and innovations.

Still looking wistfully at the neighboring apartment building, Sophia envied them being able to let down their sun-screens and open more than one window, letting in a breath of fresh air, instead of having to sit in the abominable heat of her little apartment, where the large windows absorbed the heat, but did nothing to bring in some much-needed cool air. Never even having thought about installing an air conditioning in the northern region the university was situated, she was rather surprised by the suffocating heat of this year's summer. Resigned to her fate, Sophia grabbed the wet towel she held ready over the armrest of her office chair, to wipe the sweat from her face.

At least, now in the afternoon, the sun had moved to the back of the building and was no longer burning down onto her side in full force.

The sun instead basked the house on the other side in sheer light and Sophia changed position to avoid the beams, reflected by the window from the apartment one level below her own. The windows of this apartment were neither covered nor open to let a breeze in. As Sophia knew, they had ventilators in each apartment, some even in each room, but no air condition, she was certain the air must be stifling in this certain apartment, when they were using neither of the options to get relief from the boiling heat.

She had seen men moving in this apartment some days ago, so it must be occupied at present. But while all the other windows on her side had their sun-screens extended, this one let the sun burn down full force in the greatest heat of the day.

Sophia did not think further about it for the moment, just that the occupants must be out for the day and had forgotten to activate the sun-shields, she herself had repaired to properly work.

In the evening, the shields were still not extended, so Sophia had a good view into the room across the street. At first, she reluctantly averted her gaze, when she found a man lying on the bed in the room in there, with all his limbs stretched out, spread eagled. But reluctantly, her eyes had their own mind and came back to him time and time again.

He never seemed to move and Sophia wondered, how he could hold the position for so long. It must be uncomfortable to lie like that.

When the daylight faded, the man still seemed not to have moved even a tiny bit. Worried, that the man might be dead, Sophia now kept an even closer eye on him and was no longer able to concentrate on her own work.

Later, the light in the room came on for a short moment and she saw a man standing with his back to the window, but only seconds later, the light was turned off again. If she had not kept constant watch over this room, she would not have noticed the light at all.

At least, now Sophia was relieved, that the man couldn't be lying dead on his bed, as she had first feared. The one man standing at the window would surely have found out and helped him, if that was still possible. She went to sleep with that hopeful thought still in her mind.

The next day in the morning, when she turned on her computers, she could not help but look over to this man again. He was still lying on his bed, not moving at all, as far as she could detect from her position. When the sun came around in the afternoon to directly shine on the windows of the house, the shield once again did not go down and the heat burned into the room unhindered.

Sophia wondered why nobody activated the shields. It would have been just the turn of a switch on the electrical board of the apartment. As far as she could tell through the glimmer of the sun in the opposite window, the man was still on the bed. It must be torture for him, as he must feel all the heat, not able to get relief in any way.

Like the day before, the light was turned on in his room for mere seconds, otherwise everything remained dark in the room and Sophia wasn't able to make out, if the man on the bed was still there.

She wondered, why they bothered to turn on the light at all, when the man in front of the window did nothing discernible in the room, just standing with his back to her.

But this night, following the procedure, Sophia, glued to her window, discovered that the lights were turned on again about half an hour later, also for just the mere blinking of her eyes. She was quite certain that the man standing in front of the window could not be the man from the bed. His clothes were different. But Sophia also wondered, how the man turned the lights on and off, when he was standing in front of the window. Seeing a foot still on the bed of the first man she had detected there, she deduced that there must be at least two other people in the room with him.

Curious about the strange behavior in the apartment across from her, Sophia suddenly remembered her video camera, a Christmas present from her parents two years ago, which she had not used for a while. But the camera had a night-view mode. Estimating the distance to the opposite apartment, she thought that the night-vision sensors might still work over the width of the street and penetrate the dark of the room at the opposite side. The only downside was, that she would not be able to see a preview picture in the camera's display, so she would only see the result after the recording was done. With the suspicious behavior of the men across the road, Sophia was not plagued by a bad conscience for even a moment for interfering with their privacy. Her curiosity and pity for the man on the bed immediately won out and overrode all her potential concerns.

Taking out her camera, she put it on a tripod and directed it at the window of the room, starting the recording. Stopping it right away, she tested the result and though the picture was very grainy and vague, she saw immediately that the man was back in his usual position on the bed. His form was clearly discernible on the bed.

That can't be natural or healthy, Sophia thought. No person can remain in the same position for so long without feeling stiff or his muscles to weaken. Wondering about the man and the reasons for his strange behavior, she put up the camera again, to record what was happening with him in the other apartment.

At the end of her recording disk, after about twenty minutes, Sophia took the camera down and watched the recording. Fast forwarding it, she discovered that the man really did not seem to move at all. Only almost at the end of the recording, did another man enter the room in the dark. The legs of the man on the bed were pushed down and the man was turned around and made to kneel in front of the bed, his upper body remaining on the bed and his arms, as far as she could detect, still in some way bound to the bed, as they were awkwardly twisted up over his head, which surely must hurt or at least be a very uncomfortable position to remain in.

Not wanting to overwrite her discovery with a new recording, but urgently needing to know what was going on in that apartment across the street, she fished out a new formatted disk from her desk-drawer and restarted the recording immediately.

But the next twenty minutes of recording came as a shock to her. The man she had seen coming into the room, had taken out his belt from his trouser loops, folded it in his hand and slapped the kneeling man with it over and over again. The man still half laying on the bed had squirmed in agony at first, but finally had just sunk onto the bedding, taking the punishment without any more outward signs of the pain he surely must feel.

But that was not the end of the punishment. The man standing above him finally threw the belt onto the bed next to the bound man, then opened his trousers and slipped them down. Kneeling down behind the other man on the bed, his hips pushed forward and Sophia could only imagine what had gone on over there just minutes ago.

Utterly shocked by the actions, she grabbed her phone and dialed the police, reporting what she had seen over there, giving them her details and the address of the other building and apartment.

It did not take long, before she could see a police car stopping in front of the opposite house. When the two police officers entered the other building, Sophia breathed a sigh of relief, watching the windows of the other apartment.

But only a few minutes later, the two officers left the building again and drove off without arresting any of the men in the other apartment or even entering the apartment at all.

Instead, a quarter of an hour later, Sophia got a phone call from the police, severely chastising her for her false alarm against a film-crew, recording adult material. She should immediately stop stalking them, or they would consider taking legal actions against her.

Stunned into silence, Sophia could only mutter weak protests and offer to show them her recorded material, but her suggestions were pushed aside. The officer on the phone even instructed her to immediately delete all recordings she had taken or he would send a team to her which would do it for her.

"No, no. I'll do it – right away," Sophia meekly conceded, though even at that moment, she did not have the least intention to really go through with it. Still, to convince the officer on the other line, she clicked some buttons on her computer keyboard, to make it appear that she was doing as ordered.

"So, there. See – all done. All files are gone now. You need not send someone over. It is all gone and extinguished."

"Good. And keep away from the window. Do you hear? It's not going to happen under my watch, that people are spied upon in their own homes. There are severe punishments for stalkers. Only as it is your first time, is this treated so leniently. It will not be so in the future. Do you hear me?"

"Hmm, yes. I'll keep away from the windows. I have enough work to do anyway, officer. Thank you, officer. Sorry for raising the false alarm."

Sophia put down the phone with relief, but also shaking her head. What had just happened there, she wondered. Could it be that the police were in lieu with the rapist in the apartment over there? The officers had been there only mere minutes. They had not even entered the room she had told them about. What story had the men, holding the other one on the bed captive, spun to get rid of them so quickly and easily, she wondered. Could it be a film-team? But a film-team filming in total darkness? Who had ever heard of such nonsense? No. Sophia dismissed that option right away.

Whatever was going on over there, now obviously with the help of the police, did not bode well for the man on the bed.

Not being able to help herself, Sophia put up the camera with a new disk again, careful that no light from the streets would catch in the lens and give away her position.

After twenty more minutes, she played the new recording. The man was back on the bed, unmoving. This recording, she overwrote with the next twenty minutes, observing the man throughout the night in his unmoved position.

Only in the early morning hours, when she was able to see without night-sight again, though with the morning reflections in the window-glass not all too clearly, did someone seem to come in and raise the man from the bed. The one man standing with his back to the window took up his position as usual. She could not see much of what was going on in the room, just the part of the bed she could see was empty, so the man must have been allowed to leave it.

This time, the man she only knew from his back to the window, turned around and pushed a chair to the window. Stepping up, he pushed the wings of the window open and stepped on the window-sill. He tried to pull down the sun-shades. But Sophia knew how futile that effort was. Those screens did not work manually. They only worked when attached to the main temperature-regulating-system of the house and were automatically rolled down and up again when the computer behind it saw fit. She knew that, not from her efforts to help Mr. Arnestone, their concierge, but from various people complaining in the nearby bakery about this user-unfriendly technology, allowing no individual regulation.

If the men in that apartment did not know that, their landlord must have forgotten to hand over the description or access instructions to activate that system. Did that mean they were in the apartment illegally or just that they had a negligent landlord, Sophia wondered.

Whatever their reasons, Sophia felt uncomfortable, leaving that man, who so obviously suffered as their captive over there, to his own fate. If the police did not want to help, she needed another way to free the man. Sophia could not, with good conscience, leave a man in a situation where he was beaten and raped. That part of his captivity was the most horrible nightmare to her. She just had to help that man.

Missing her next intended lab-time on campus, Sophia spent the early morning checking all options, even thinking about friends, who could give her at least some advice on what to do. As the semester had just ended, most of her friends had left the town after their finals and had gone home to search for work over the semester holidays. Even those remaining, had taken the hottest time of the year to go on holiday and leave the burning heat of town. Not one of her friends from university, who would be willing to help, was still in town.

Sophia was still not ready to give up. She just resolved that she would have to take this on alone. That meant careful observation and planning and treading lightly.

'Treading lightly! – That's it!' Sophia thought. The other building had installed new fire-exit ladders. At least during a fire alarm, that exit would be accessible.

'No,' Sophia thought, 'that's not the way to go.' She feared, the men would rather kill the man than risk detection or reveal their crimes and intentions, if they heard her coming over the iron steps of the fire-ladder. She would have to rescue him another way, but how?

The fire-ladders were at the opposite side of the apartment building, so would be hard for her to access anyway, without arousing attention.

'But – yes! That was it.' Sophia beamed with joy over her new idea. They wanted their sun-screens down and she knew how to get them working by connecting them to the central system. That would give her a reason to request entering the room facing hers, where the man was held. But how would they react? What would they do with the man and how could she get a hold of him and leave the apartment with him unhindered?

At least, for now she had solved the issue of how to get access, but she would have to hurry, to convince Mr. Arnestone, their concierge, to let her handle this request, before he got news of it and handled it himself. He was overworked and certainly would not mind her help. She would also show him the video footage. Sophia did not want to directly get him involved and risk getting her friend injured, but eventually he could help with raising the fire-alarm in time for her to get the guards distracted, while she was in the apartment.

Packing her camera, Sophia resolutely went over to the entrance hallway of the other building, where she was sure to find Mr. Arnestone. He had a booth with monitors there, surveilling and checking the whole building.

– 3 –

Luxuriously Renovated Apartment Complex in Camsted

Mr. Arnestone greeted Sophia from the entrance of his building, even before she fully crossed the street towards him. "I have been waiting for you to come by today in the morning. I have a new computer problem for you to help me with." His voice indicated, that he knew how much Sophia liked to solve those riddles the computer posed for him.

Sophia swiftly detected the source of his printer problem and everything was settled in mere minutes.

"I am coming with my own problems today," Sophia told him. "You see, I have some suspicions about the people on floor eight of your building."

"So it was you who sent the police?"

"Yes, that was me. But the officers didn't do anything."

"Because the entire floor is empty right now."

"No, it isn't. Men, at least three, are living in the apartment to the left."

"Ah yes, the police went up and found a film crew up there. They were setting up a scene for a low budget film. – Sex, if you know what I mean."

"Oh, that is what the police told me, too. But they are holding a man in there against his will, I am certain of it. And if the police are not willing to help, I need to do something about it."

"Now, not so heated. What can a young girl and an old man do?"

Sophia was glad, that Mr. Arnestone immediately took her side and included himself in her off-kilter rescue mission.

"We need to do something! We have to," she begged.

Pulling out her video camera, she showed him the footage of the imprisonment, stopping when the rape came up. Sophia felt strangely reluctant to reveal that much about the unknown man and show him in that weak state of being used by the other, bulky man. She just had to help him, to get him out of the clutches of the men who abused him.

The concierge sat in a shocked silence after seeing the treatment of the man, though she had left out the worst part of it.

"And the police wouldn't help you?"

"No. They made me swear to destroy the footage. Though I begged them to have a look into that room."

"That means, we need to have a closer look ourselves then. You say their sun-shades are not working?"

"No, they are not. The connection must have been deactivated, as all the other apartments on that floor work correctly."

"That must be, because in the system, the apartment appears to be empty. I already wondered where the police had met with the film crew. The flat is not unlocked and hooked into the central panel. That is sometimes done to apartments, when they are not rented out and no tenant currently pays for the expenses."

"That is an opportunity for me to get in, but how can I get the men away from there, to get their hostage out? They won't even let me enter and I can't think of a way to get to the man unobserved."

"A gas-leak! That's it. The alarm system in the kitchen will catch it. I'll call my friend Tom at the next fire-station to come over and evacuate the floor for us. As the other apartments on the eighth floor really are empty, they won't recognize that they are the only ones being evacuated long enough for us to act."

When Mr. Arnestone's friend Tom arrived in full fireman-uniform only a short while later, he wanted to see her video footage as well, cringing, when the muscular man bent down to prepare for the rape of the other man, as if knowing what would happen next, though Sophia once again stopped the video there.

"We need to help. Let's get on with it." Tom fiercely joined in their ruse to help this unknown man.

Going through their plan in detail, they set up their mobile phones.

The girl activated hers and leaving the conference-call app to the two numbers open, so that the two men could follow how things turned out with her efforts to get into the apartment and react in time.

Going up the elevator, she repeatedly rang the bell. When this did not show any results, she went on to knock at the door of the apartment. Finally, the door was opened by a burly, balding man with light hair in his early forties. He only opened the door after she had called out that she had come to repair the sun-shades and was sent up by the concierge.

The man looked at her with an empty stare out of bright blue, almost translucent eyes, his gaze wandering up and down her entire form repeatedly, before letting her enter when she explained that she had to get access to their electronic panel. From his size, Sophia was not certain, if he was the one who had punished the man they kept hostage. He was bulky enough, though seemed too stocky to be the man she had seen on her camera screen. Trembling none the less, Sophia took a deep reassuring breath, to calm her nerves and try to outwardly appear unmoved by the presence of this frightening criminal, who looked more like a contract killer to her than a guard or a member of a film crew.

Working at the switch-panel in the hallway of the apartment, she fortunately had a clear view into the empty kitchen.

"Do you smell that?" she asked the man who was not letting her out of his sight for even a moment.

"No, what?"

"The gas. It smells like gas." Walking into the kitchen, she looked under the hearth and with one grip pulled the gas valve wide open, which before had been securely closed and switched off.

"Can't see a thing wrong here. It must come from somewhere else," she stated and tried to distract the man at her side. "We now need to check the shades."

Stepping out of the kitchen, she went towards the door she knew the bound man was in, but immediately, a firm hand on her arm held her back.

"This way." The man opened the door to the room in the back of the building, which she could not see from her apartment. Not resisting, she let him lead the way.

The shades in this room were up as before. But that was not really a surprise, as the sun now, in the early afternoon, was shining on the other side of the building.

"We need to see the other side of the house to determine, if they are working. Here, with the sun on the other side, it won't show one way or the other."

"No," the man answered gruffly.

"No? Are they working or not?" Sophia did not give up so easily.

"I go. – Stay."

That was a man of few words, it seemed.

But at least it appeared that the man she wanted to rescue was still in that room, as this bulky guard so strictly kept her away from going anywhere near.

When she came out into the hallway, the smell of gas was quite discernible. Sophia was only a few steps along, when the man stepped back out of the room and stated angrily.

"Not working. Get to it."

"I need to have a look at the shades. They might be blocked somehow."

"Go."

Surprised that he no longer prevented her from entering that front room, she did not have to wonder for long. The man, now in a more natural sleeping position than she had seen him from her apartment, lay motionless on the bed. She could not see much under the arranged pillows, but she suspected that the brute had knocked him out.

Taking the single chair in the room and stepping up, she took an exaggeratedly extensive look at the rolled-up shades outside, tearing and rattling here and there to appear busy, while desperately waiting for Mr. Arnestone's fireman friend Tom to appear.

She did not have to wait long, before a loud ringing indicated that the alarm system had finally detected the leaking gas. To great effect, the fireman came up to the apartment door only moments later and called out: "Gas leak! Evacuation. Leave your apartments immediately. It's urgent. Gas leak!"

Sophia stepped up to the man on the bed. "We need to wake him up. He is sleeping so deeply that he can't hear the alarm." But the man who did not leave her out of his sight, to her horror, just took the man and threw him over his shoulder as if he weighed nothing.

"Took sleeping pills." He threw him back over his shoulder and confidently stepped out of the room into the hallway, where the fireman Tom was waiting for them. The doors to the next two apartments were open, as if their occupants had already left their homes and had been evacuated.

Tom swiftly went into the apartment and out of sight of the guard closed the gas valve in the kitchen again. Rummaging around a bit for effect, he stepped back out and announced: "All found and cleared. You can come back in."

The man with the other still over his shoulder immediately turned back from the elevators, which Mr. Arnestone according to plan held on the ground floor, and came back into the apartment with his burden. The waiting fireman knocked him out with a well-placed surprise hit on his chin. Tom did not try to hinder the man's fall, rather tried to catch the unconscious hostage, but instead went down with him under his weight. Stumbling, he sat up, righted the unconscious abductor and gave him another knock for good measure. Taking the hostage over his own shoulder and stepping out of the apartment, he waited for Sophia, who had nervously been observing the whole scene and now stepped over the unconscious man on the floor towards the electronic board and switched on the sole button necessary to solve the problem with the disabled shades.

Leaving and locking the apartment behind her with Mr. Arnestone's master key, they hurried into the elevator Mr. Arnestone had sent up for them.

"We have him," the girl spoke into her phone.

"Hurry down and leave on the first floor. They are coming

back." Mr. Arnestone's voice could be heard as a desperate murmur via her phone.

"Back? Who?" Sophia wondered aloud.

"The others. Get out of the elevator. Over."

Mr. Arnestone ended the call, leaving her hanging without any more information. But as they were already going down with the elevator, she hectically pressed all the buttons in between she could manage. The lift had the unfortunate setup of working on the 'first come first serve'-principle. She hoped that all her buttons could somehow override that and stop their progress down into the arms of the unconscious man's captors on the ground level.

They descended without a pause and Sophia had almost given up hope, but on the second floor, the lift finally stopped, not because of her clicks, but because an old lady had pressed the button for the elevator on that floor, waiting in front of it and had saved their rescue mission and potentially their lives that way.

Sophia wanted to embrace the woman, so full of happiness was she, but refrained from doing it and settled for a bright smile and greeting, meeting the disapproving stare of the grouchy old woman bent over her walking-aid.

Stepping out, Sophia and Tom crossed the corridor and took the staircase down, intentionally taking their time and listening out for any unusual sounds. Only when they heard the elevator going up again, did they dare to get out into the open entrance hallway.

As the police had not been of any help and the unknown man in their midst was still unconscious, Tom and Mr. Arnestone agreed it would be best to bring the man into her apartment swiftly, to hide him out of sight. Tom, practical and efficient in his help, disguised the man in a large fireman's blanket and so effectively hid the content of the heavy load he carried over his shoulder, changing into his civilian clothes in her bathroom, to get out unhindered and without being noticed as the fireman involved in their scheme, should the men upstairs start looking for him already to find their hostage.

Tom was reluctant to leave her alone with the unknown man in her own apartment.

"We don't know anything about him or the reasons for why he had been held prisoner. He might want to hurt you when he wakes up. It would be best if you kept him bound in some way," he argued.

But Sophia refused to bind a man she just had rescued from his shackles. She could not possibly do the same thing to him as his captors had done.

Sophia let Tom put the man onto her bed, before he left. She would take the couch, but this man, after his ordeal, needed every comfort he could get. And the bed was just a small price to pay for getting him better again.

– 4 –
Sophia's Apartment

She was worried that her involuntary houseguest might have a severe concussion, because he remained unconscious for so long. Carefully, she searched his head, stroking her fingers through his soft hair, but could not detect any wounds or bumps. Only now, she became aware, that she was touching a rather good-looking man. Strong features, relaxed in sleep and enhanced by the dark stubble of his beard. His dark-brown, almost black hair was short and straight, but with a light, enticing wave to it. Somehow, she had the feeling of having seen the man before somewhere. Perhaps, he was a film-star or a model, Sophia mused. He certainly had the looks for that. His strong jaw and cheekbones were commanding and even his relaxed pose in sleep did not lessen his attractiveness.

Not finding any indication for the cause of his long unconsciousness, Sophia concluded, that the other man must have injected him with something very strong. It at least gave her some relief that he was breathing normally and so could not have been poisoned, but was only sleeping off whatever he had been given, while the length of his unconsciousness from a knock out would have worried her and she would have had to call for a doctor or ambulance and with that would have had to reveal his hiding place.

As it was, she tried to roll him into a more comfortable position and covered him with a light blanket. She thought she heard him sigh with relief, but could not be sure she had heard correctly.

Turning around, she sat down in front of her computers,

where she could keep an eye on him, as her bed was, like her couch, placed opposite her working desk, which effectively separated the small one-room apartment into a relaxing area and a working space.

But though back in front of her work, she could not concentrate on it. She even found herself scrolling the missing persons' page on the internet, but she did not come across this man's face. The missing persons; she was stunned about their enormous number in her town, and that they were almost entirely women. The only missing man at present had left the senior citizen's home where he lived and most likely had not found his way back. Sophia still had no clue who the man on her bed could possibly be. Was he from out of town or from another country?

But for Sophia, all that did not really matter. What did matter, was the connection she felt to this man. The bond that had not allowed her to look the other way when she had thought him to be in danger, though the police had demanded her to leave the case well alone. She strangely did not feel threatened by his presence in her apartment, though she was not used to having someone, especially a man, around so close in her private quarters. Her emotions concerning him were rather of curiosity, of joy to have him around, someone to help and care for.

That thought threw her out of her musings abruptly, by reminding her that she hardly had any groceries left. With all her work and avoiding Dr. Stewart, she had totally forgotten to do her shopping. She would have to go to the shops, but she did not want to leave him alone, so she opened the website of the grocery chain she usually went to and put in her order online. Fortunately, they had a cheap home delivery service, which had already come to her rescue repeatedly, especially when she had been ill or feeling unwell. Being single and far away from her caring family had its disadvantages, but not wanting to bother any of her friends, the shop's service had come in handy.

When the doorbell rang some hours later, the delivery man stood in front of her, handing the boxes and bags over to her. She paid and the deliverer went on his way again. But from inside the apartment she heard rustling and moving. Nervous at every sound, fearing the gangsters from across the street, who had kept 'her man', as she in her mind called him, could somehow have found out about the whereabouts of their prisoner and invaded her apartment, she hurried back into the main room.

'Her man' had managed to sit up on the bed, looking at her when she entered.

"Where am I? Who are you?"

Smiling at him, she carefully put the heavy bag of groceries down, which she had not let go of in her hurry, but instead had planned to use as a means of defense against potential invaders, as it contained the cans of food and jars of her purchase.

"Can I help?" he politely offered, but the girl jumped up from her kneeling position, to prevent him from over-exhausting himself after his ordeal.

"No, thank you. Please just lay back down. You need the rest. After all you have been through."

"What do you know? How did I even get here?" His voice was rough and the fatigue clearly audible.

"Don't worry. You are safe here. They don't know where you are."

"Are you working for the police?"

"No. They did not want to help me."

"The CIA then." On the shake of her head, he continued, when she did not elaborate further. "FBI, NSA, MI5, BND, FSB, …?"

"No. You can stop guessing. I am just a normal neighbor. While working from home, I saw you in your room on the opposite side of my street."

"You watched me? And what did you see that caused you to jump in and rescue me, even when the police told you to stop?"

Disappointed by his cold assessment of the situation and of him so clearly not appreciating her effort and risks she and her friends had taken to free him from his tormentors, she barked back at him in anger: "I rather should have left you there."

"Come, come, now. I don't want to appear ungrateful, but what in my motionless form on a bed caused you to singlehandedly storm an apartment full of criminals?"

"It was not only your unmoving form. I saw …, I saw …" Her voice drifted off. The ugly images from his punishment and rape raising unbidden in front of her eyes again, she could not continue. Ashamed of what she had witnessed, she tried to avoid his piercing gaze.

"What did you see? Tell me," he demanded with the authority of a man used to issuing orders and expecting them to be obeyed immediately.

When she hesitated to answer, he started to get up from the bed.

"Don't! You need the rest. And … – And, I can show you what I saw, as … – I can't say it. I just … – I can't."

When she turned around to where she usually kept her

camera, she did not find it. And only then remembered that she had taken it to show her footage to Mr. Arnestone and his friend Tom and so still had it in her handbag she had taken with her.

Going back to the corridor, where all her groceries lay in bags and heaps, she jumped to retrieve one and hurriedly hastened to the fridge.

"What's that? Do you store your devices in the fridge?"

"No, of course not. I just thought you might like some ice cream and so had some ordered."

"What kind?"

"What kind of material I have? A video."

"No. What ice cream."

"Oh. Chocolate and vanilla and stracciatella and mango sorbet. You see, I didn't know what you would like and so ordered a variety."

"How long do you plan on keeping me here?"

"I? Keeping you? Not at all. You are free to go any time you like."

"But you ordered food like you expected a cohort of visitors."

"Oh, that's just in case. And I heard men eat more than women."

"You heard? So you have no firsthand experience with it? You live alone?"

"Not at the moment," she snidely responded vaguely to his accumulation of questions, immediately recognizing the strategic error she had made, being alone with an unknown man in her home. "Besides, I ..."

"Besides me? Anyone I should be warned of in advance, before a jealous boyfriend or lover appears in the doorway?"

"No."

"So, what? No, no boyfriend or lover or, no, no reason or intention to warn me?"

"You are obnoxious. – I have a caring boyfriend, who looks out for me."

Once again going back to her bag, Sophia searched for the camera, no longer so reluctant to embarrass this man, who so rudely questioned her and her motives. The camera had slipped down to the bottom, so she had to rummage through all her contents in the enormous bag. She wondered about her usually so reserved and quiet self. How easily she had fallen into arguing and nitpicking with this total stranger, as if they were old friends. With one uttered word, he could get to her. His opinion strangely mattered a great deal to her, though she knew nothing about this man. Still, she wanted to protect him. Strange, just strange, she thought.

Fishing out the camera and turning it on, she was so focused on it, that she let a gasp escape, when she bumped into the stranger in the doorway to her room. Silently, she handed over the camera to him.

"Delete it. All of it," he said after mere moments, when he realized what was about to come in the recording.

Ignoring his outburst, she defended herself: "You see now, why I had to act?"

"But why did the police not help you? Did you show them your material?"

"They refused to watch it and told me to stop looking, or I would get a restraining order."

"Who was on duty?"

"Who? At the police station? I have no idea. The two men they sent introduced themselves as Officers Charlie and Leonard. No second names." Sophia had this information from Mr.

Arnestone, who had let the officers into the building.

"Ah, I see."

"You know them?"

"I know about them. Which is close enough for my liking."

"You mean, parts of the police would not be willing to help you? Why?"

"Because they have larger goals than my freedom."

"What could that be? You have a right to your freedom, like everybody else."

"Not when I should be locked up in one of their prisons anyway."

"Anyway? Why? – You, a prisoner? An escaped prisoner? A criminal yourself?" Sophia had difficulties to adjust to that thought and strangely, she still did not feel threatened by his presence, but rather curious.

"Why do you care? Keep your nose out of my things."

Not knowing, where her bratty attitude and bravery came from, Sophia still could not help but answer: "Oh, you are a grateful chap, aren't you? Who ever heard of a freed man, biting the hand that freed him."

"It's none of your business. Be glad that I don't want to embroil you in it."

"I am already involved in it. I freed a freed and re-imprisoned state prisoner. – What, by the way, did you commit? Murder?"

"That's really none of your business, nosy lady."

"Oh, good. Then it's none of my business, if you are hungry or have nowhere to go, now that the police and the criminals are both searching for you."

His gaze, serious after their heated argument, looked her all over. For the first time, he closer inspected the girl who had singlehandedly freed him. Looking at her stubbornly raised chin, he knew she meant trouble. The girl was slim and fragile looking, but from what she had done, he knew she could be determined and did not give up, even against severe opposition. Her small breasts covered by a crinkly software-convention t-shirt, heaved in anger and indignation.

Though boyish and tiny breasted, clear interest for her stirred in his loins. Was it the long spell of forced celibacy due to his court process and prison sentence, that caused him to be attracted to this nosy and self-righteous girl? Whatever it was, he was determined to suppress any rising feelings for her. He did not have time or energy left, to cope with romance, when all his energy now had to be focused on the mere deed of surviving and proving his innocence.

A naïve and inexperienced girl would only hinder him on his way to real freedom and would be a further burden with her emotions and clinginess. From his ex-wife, he knew that one could not trust a pretty face and their fake promises of love, which had only one goal, the control over his purse and possessions, nothing else.

When he did not answer her implied question for so long, Sophia snidely commented: "If you are not hungry, that's your choice. I am and will now prepare something for me. Much cheaper for me, if I don't have to feed and host you as well."

She turned around and left him standing in the doorway.

Picking up a bag with vegetables and another one with further groceries, she tried to push her way through the doorway, which he still blocked, to reach the tiny kitchen, a minimalistic room, which hardly did justice to that term.

Her arm, still holding the bag, slipped along his firm breast and stomach and a ray of electric static sizzled between them. He stood up straighter, jumping back from her. After what she had seen of him in the video, he very much doubted she would want him anyway. What woman would be interested in a male fucking toy and a sex starved criminal. He wondered, why she had even bothered to get him out from there and not just turned away in disgust at what she had seen, like most people would have done. She certainly was an unusual girl.

Deliciously smelling food was simmering in her tiny kitchen in mere minutes. He went back into her room and sat down on the bed where he had woken up. Dizziness still plagued him, the effect of the drug one of his guards, Andrew, the thug from the Irish mob, had injected him with, which was the last thing he could remember before waking up here in the girl's room.

The meal was not ready yet, when a phone rang on her work desk. Taking it up, she smiled into it, as if the person on the other end would be able to see her. Astonished about that girl, he shook his head in wonder.

"No. Everything went fine. No. – I didn't call earlier, because he was drugged and still sleeping on my bed. No changes from the start or news. I didn't want to wake him … No. Everything went fine. They have no idea who took him or where he is now. – No! You need not come all the way up here. No, I assure you, I really am safe with him. He would never do anything to harm me. – Of course I am sure. – Yes, he is awake now. – Hmm, if you insist."

Taking the wireless phone with her, she pushed it into his hands.

"My parents," she stated and turned back into her miniature kitchen.

The first moment on the phone was awkward.

"Hello," he tentatively spoke.

"If you do anything to my girl, you will have to answer to me, do you hear?" An angry male voice spoke at the other end, while a female voice in the background encouraged the man to first ask him, who he was.

Smiling, he answered: "I have no intention to harm your daughter. You can rest assured that I will do nothing to hurt her."

His words did not appease the man on the other end in the least.

"But you'll bring her in harm's way, I am certain of it. I told her to stay out of it, let the police handle everything, but she wouldn't listen to me. When the police left the case alone, so should she have done. But no, she had to make certain you were all right. And who are you, to deserve her effort? Risking her life for a stranger, just some criminal scum."

"So she really was alone in her decision to help me?"

"Fortunately not. She had the concierge across the street on her side. Don't dare to think she is helpless and without protection. I'll move heaven and earth if you even come near my little girl. She is much too good for your kind."

"And what kind am I?" he could not help but further tease the man on the other end of the line.

"That's of no importance. She is too good for anybody. Helpful and kind, so don't dare to exploit her caring nature or you'll have to deal with me."

"Dinner is ready. Oh, I forgot, you are not hungry," came her shout from the kitchen.

"You see, she is by far not as good as you think she is. She wants to let me go hungry, while preparing a deliciously smelling meal."

"Serves you right, for playing around and not giving me

straight answers. So, who are you? Sophia did not say."

"Merton C. Lynford. Professor of neuro-technology and optical fiber-transmission."

"What? Never heard of such a subject. Professor, you say? Where?"

"At the MIT, lately."

"Not currently? Where are you employed now?"

"Not at the moment, at least as far as I have heard in the latest news that reached me. They took my company."

"Oh, a company? Financially solid then?"

"When it has not been confiscated, potentially. Eventually."

"What now?"

The girl interfered and took hold of the telephone.

"Papa, please don't worry. Everything is all right here. You need not worry about him. He is harmless. He just woke up from being heavily drugged. He really needs rest and not an interrogation by you and mom. Please don't worry, he really won't harm me. Right now, I even doubt he could, as weak as he is." She could not tell, where her certainty came from, but she did not say those words just to appease her parents, but was convinced the man did not wish to really hurt her.

"I'll keep you up to date and let you know as soon as I learn more. We haven't had time to speak yet, or to plan what to do now. – Good night to you and mom. – I promise, I'll call as soon as possible."

When she put back the telephone, he spoke from the bed, still calmly sitting there.

"You so callously lie to your own parents?"

"I never lie to them. What are you talking about?"

"Me just being 'harmless'."

"You are … you were. Oh, just stop. You yourself told them

that you won't do me harm. I just wanted to calm them. Otherwise they will jump into their car this minute and will drive all the 500 miles up here in one go. I don't want them to do that. The journey is exhausting to them at their age at the best of times, much more so driving the whole night, burdened by all their worries."

"So, you are the good daughter then. The good Samaritan, taking in stray criminals and care for your family."

"And what is wrong with that? You yourself are the beneficiary of my help and a rather ungrateful one, from what I can tell so far. And I don't even know your name yet."

"Yes, you do. I told your parents."

"What? That Prof. Lynford crap? That fairy-tale you only dared to tell my parents, as they have no way to verify that? But I do. Prof. Lynford is a great man whose greatness you could never reach. So tell me, who are you truly?"

The girl her father had called Sophia agitatedly marched to the small coffee table in front of the couch and decked it with two sets of plates, clearly having forgotten her threat to let her annoying guest starve.

He watched her every move and calmly, with a superior air, answered: "It's of no importance to me, if you believe me or not, but I usually have no need to introduce myself twice."

"As arrogant as you are, you well could be Prof. Lynford. They say that he is very hard to get along with. My professor warned me, when I asked to get him to co-correct my dissertation. So, if you indeed are Prof. Lynford, what happened to get you into such a heap of trouble?"

"Now you pretend to know about me. What do you expect as a recompense? A good grade? A good lay?"

"You are insufferable. I really should let you starve. But from your appearance, you rather need food quite urgently. Get to it, even if you don't deserve my help at all."

"Thank you, my unknown gracious host."

"Oh, sorry." Sophia was suddenly reminded by his words, that she had never bothered to introduce herself to him. He had been so obnoxious, that he had immediately embroiled her in a war of words, completely forgetting, that they were indeed strangers.

"I am Sophia, Sophia Warren. Sorry, I didn't mean to keep you guessing." Though after her introduction slipped out, she thought she should have let him guess her identity from her topic suggestions. But what professor paid any attention to the identity or names of mere students whose work they co-corrected. So that would be no real proof anyway. But his next words surprised her.

"Oh, Prof. Benning's girl. The one insistent enough to get him to bother me."

"You do know Prof. Benning? Then you must be who you say you are."

"I thought my arrogance had already been sufficient proof of that."

"No. Arrogance is not such a rare trait, unfortunately. But the more I learn about you, the more I understand, why you are reputed to be such an unbearable man."

This time, her words seemed to have hit a nerve. He silently sat down on the couch in front of her little table and took up the napkin and placed it on his lap, before he started to help himself to her food.

When he did not speak for a long while into their meal, Sophia regretted her words.

"I'm really sorry. I shouldn't have been so harsh with you. You had a hard time and need some rest. You'll surely be much more pleasant, when you feel better again. I am really sorry."

"Why are you sorry, when you tell me it is my own fault? You can't make me be any different."

"But I shouldn't have judged you so harshly."

"You only repeated openly what you had heard about me."

"Well, yes. But … You surely …"

"I surely am not. Did your professor not tell you what I answered to his latest request to take on your research subject?"

"You didn't like my choice of topic." Sophia did not really mind so much whatsoever. She herself had not liked Dr. Stewart's topic suggestion.

"But did he tell you my exact words?"

"No, I don't think they were important. You rejected my last subject choice, ignoring all others. That's all I know."

"My words, my exact words were: 'Bullshitty idea by a dreamy girl with her head in the clouds.' – Do you still want to feed and help me?"

"You surely had your reasons not to like the topic. Prof. Benning told me that it was a very inconvenient time for you, when my request came in," Sophia replied stiffly.

"Did he? – That's strange. It hadn't been public knowledge back then."

He fell silent again, his eyebrows creased in intense concentration. Sophia let him eat in peace and prepared some more of her mixed fruit juice for him to drink. He took it without acknowledging her effort, but she had the impression that the information she had given him just now, had caused him to rethink some events of his past and she wanted to give him time. After all, she could not fault him for not liking the lunatic idea of Dr. Stewart, though Prof. Lynford thought that the idea for the nonsensical topic had come from her. At least, contrary to her own ideas, it had triggered a response by him at the time. And she herself had had much more juicy words for Dr. Stewart's suggestion he had forced upon her, though she had not dared to utter them in front of the doctor or Prof. Benning.

She was sure Prof. Lynford would come around to tell her, if he thought she needed to know, and she was reluctant to press him. After what he had gone through, he deserved some time to cope.

Finally, she put some of her favorite stracciatella ice cream in two bowls and placed one before him. He took the spoon and tried some and a contented growl erupted from his throat.

"Good, isn't it? It's my absolute favorite."

"Thank you."

"It's nothing." Sophia was reluctant to accept his gratitude.

"It is. Thank you for the meal and thank you for saving me. It's a remarkable thing you achieved."

"It's o.k. – Really. You needn't thank me. It's not why I did it. I only wanted to help you and hope I didn't put you into any more danger than you already were in before. – What are your plans for now? Perhaps I can help you with them, too?"

"No! That's out of the question. You have done more than enough already." He spoke with abruptness and Sophia was not sure if his words showed gratitude or rather criticism of her actions.

"But you are in danger outside, are you not?"

"So are you. You went in there, so you must have met at least one of my guards."

"Yes, but the one I met, bulky, blond hair and light blue eyes, thinks that I was just someone from the technical repair service. He can't know what happened to me afterwards."

Sophia now retold the events, leaving out no detail.

"You may be right, but you still might be in danger, when they detect that you were plotting this together with the fireman and the concierge," Prof. Lynford concluded.

"That may well be, but from what you mentioned beforehand, the criminals and the police are both searching for you. How come, the police are on the hunt for you, but did not take you, when they thought you safely in the hold of those criminals? What interest do they have in you, to overlook the law so blatantly?"

"Financial gain. – Always the motivation of all mean things. If it is a woman, a criminal or a corrupt policeman."

Sophia did not fully understand his allegation, but recognized, that his enumeration had a deeper meaning to him.

"Why did you say 'a woman'? You know, I didn't rescue you for financial gain."

"And what did you expect from me, if not a reward?"

"Nothing, I presume. Perhaps a bit of gratitude for being freed, but I recognize by now that this is beyond you."

"Perhaps you saw the video and thought you could get an easy fuck toy for your suppressed sexuality." He knew he was intentionally cruel to her, but he did not want her to interfere with his plans or involve herself in the dangerous path he had to take any further than she had already done. And to alienate her seemed to be the swiftest solution to reach this.

"You are cruel. I am not sexually suppressed. I have a boyfriend, as I have said before. And besides, that is none of your business. And the sexual partner I chose is a nice guy, someone who cherishes me and not someone like you, alienating everyone around, thinking himself the only one worthy to judge. I would never demean myself so much as to sleep with you."

"We'll see, how long you can keep your suppressed sexual desires in check and before you realize what you really want." Sparring with her was surprisingly invigorating and he found himself enjoying their verbal encounters. The angry red, now suffusing her cheeks, somehow made her even look more enticing. How was that possible? He shouldn't really be allowing himself to play with this angry, spitting little kitten in front of him at this moment, though admittedly, to tease her was surprisingly a lot of fun for him. He would not have expected that after the experiences with his ex-wife.

"Not you, for sure." Sophia, unaware of the direction of his thoughts, shot back at him.

Sophia turned around and took the empty plates back into the kitchen, where she grumblingly rinsed them. When she came back into the main room after a while, she found the man spread out on top of her bed, sleeping. Taking up the blanket, she covered and wrapped him in it. He looked so peaceful and helpless like a little boy, when he was asleep. Nothing hinted at the intelligent mocking gaze, which scorched her skin whenever directed at her. Her heart leaped just thinking about it and she feared he was right. She could easily develop deeper feelings for this man, especially after admiring him and his extraordinary mind from afar for so long, but she mustn't, under no circumstances. He did not want her, as he clearly had expressed. And what future would her feelings have, being in love with a fugitive, hunted by both criminals and the law. Not even his reputation as professor and ingenious inventor could save him from prosecution now.

Was his rough rejection just an effort to keep her away from him, to protect her from eventually being hurt in the dangerous circumstances he faced? She had never before felt so comfortable with a man, freed from her usual shyness, to so easily fall into a cat-fight or even bother with his opinion enough to want to correct his perception of her. But with this man, his every word strangely mattered to her. She wanted to help him, though his words tried to push her away at every turn and mocked her every move.

For now, she let him sleep, as that was the best way for him to regain his strength. The criminals seemed to have barely fed him, though they had obviously wanted him as their sex toy and must have had an ulterior motive to break him out of prison. But for them keeping him alive had not necessarily meant keeping him healthy and well.

– 5 –
Research and Information – Sophia's Apartment

Knowing her guest's name now, Sophia went to her computer and searched the internet for the projects he had last been working on.

When she put in his name, articles about a Prof. L. popped up. With the knowledge of him getting a prison sentence, she finally made the connection between Prof. Lynford and the mysterious Prof. L., who had been in the news some months ago.

Sophia found articles about his court hearing, his divorce – so indeed, Prof. Benning's comment about the marriage crisis had been right; Prof. Lynford had been married. She had been so focused on his research work, that she had never bothered to research his private life. Was his ex-wife the reason, why the man on her bed thought so badly about women in general?

At least, he hardly seemed to have spent time in prison.

After the condemning reports by his wife and two of her doctors, he had been sentenced and sent to prison for attempted murder quite quickly. His company had been put under state custody, while keeping its name out of the news because of the military importance the company held. To her utter astonishment, it dawned on her that her own professor, Prof. Benning, was the only one capable of taking over the vacated lead of Prof. Lynford's tech-laboratory. The research she had been working on for the past six months, had it been Prof. Lynford's and not a new project of Prof. Benning, as she had presumed?

Prof. Benning had never said a word to her about it. All the extra work he had given her and the contractual work she had taken on to earn some extra money, as her applications for scholarships still could not be filed without her own research topic being accepted, had made her totally miss most of the reports and their implications about this mysterious Prof. L. and his imprisonment. To her vindication, the articles in their entirety did not mention his full name, but only used the shortened form of 'Prof. L.' and in her haste to get back to work, she had never made the connection or had heard anything about Prof. Lynford and his fate at university. The only thing she had heard about him in the lab had been, that he had no time to make a decision about her research-topic right now.

As her work on her own topic had been repeatedly blocked and hampered by Dr. Stewart, to get in contact with Prof. Lynford to hand over her new suggestions had never come up lately anyway, as she had not been able to fully prepare and underpin her new ideas. She had never learned that Prof. Lynford had not been just his unavailable self in his laboratory as usual, but had been sentenced to prison in the meanwhile. Now, with all the news swarming around her, she wondered, how she could have missed all the media upheaval his imprisonment and escape had caused.

Thinking of it, her parents had mentioned once, that they were glad that she was safe and far away from that professor up-start 'L', who had thought himself clever enough to commit the perfect crime and had attempted to kill his wife. But she had not paid much attention to it back then, thinking it had nothing to do with problems to get her thesis-topic through, to finally be able to apply for a scholarship and not having to work all around the clock any longer to finance her studies.

Sophia was glad, that fortunately her parents seemed not to have made the connection between the man they had talked to and the escaped murderer Prof. L. They certainly would be in their car by now, if they had. But she did not take the risk and not to wake her 'guest', sent them a reassuring e-mail instead of a call.

The strange reaction Prof. Lynford had shown when she mentioned the comment of Prof. Benning at her topic meeting half a year ago, had raised her curiosity. Scribbling down a timeline of events from the newspaper articles, she recognized, that indeed her professor had mentioned the murderous Prof. Lynford some time before the first court hearing or published article in the media. She had not believed Prof. Benning back then and had just filed his comment under his dislike for the vast success of Prof. Lynford. But now in hindsight, it seemed strange that at a time when the public was not yet informed about the accusations Prof. Lynford's wife had thrown at her husband, Prof. Benning had already seemed well aware of them.

Another point that astonished Sophia in all of this, was the haste, with which the court trial and imprisonment of Prof. Lynford had been handled. As normal cases took years longer, she wondered who could have had an interest to push this case through court so quickly.

But her own professor, who largely benefitted from the demotion of Prof. Lynford, raised her suspicions most of all. How could he have known about what was going on between Prof. Lynford and his wife, when he was not involved in the intrigue in the first place, Sophia wondered.

Her next research no longer centered around Prof. Lynford, but Prof. Benning and his contacts. From his research, she clearly saw his involvement with certain companies and state organizations. Sophia suspected that he must have had an agenda to want his successful colleague gone. But what was his motive?

Sophia printed out some of the reports about Prof. Benning and his connections to companies. Fortunately, companies want to make the most publicity of their connections to famous researchers and so their press material gave her a clear idea about his involvement. He had been working on the security-system of the state resources and its mint.

Prof. Lynford had worked on a similar topic, which might have been of interest; proof that biometrical systems were not as secure as they were reputed to be.

Was that the reason he had been discredited? Was that why the criminals wanted him, to get into security vaults like Fort Knox and rob the national banks of all currency?

Sophia suspected, that his worth to the criminals, who had held him captive, lay somewhere in that area, though she had no idea how they would want to execute such an outrageous plan. The banks were secured by more than just biometric security locks. They were already guarded by an almost unbreakable protection by guards and surveillance. What could the criminals' goal possibly be?

"Busy bee," a voice directly behind her uttered and made Sophia jump up in her seat in surprise.

Prof. Lynford stood directly behind her, the blanket still wrapped around him.

"Do you have to surprise me so? I am not used to having someone in here, so please don't do that ever again or I can't be held responsible for the result."

"What would you do? Kill me?"

"Potentially," she snapped back, taking up the large letter opener from her desk, which was formed like the Excalibur sword with two sharp blade edges.

"Oh, peace then. I won't do it again. But it seems, you did research me in the meantime. Why is it, that you did not follow my court trial? It made top news, as did my divorce."

"First, I had final exams and then, I had to do extra research projects for Prof. Benning, to keep him supportive of taking me on as a graduate student. I also had to do contract work from home, as without my accepted dissertation topic, I could not apply for a scholarship and somehow had to earn money in the meantime. And second, I never thought you would be the 'murderous Prof. L.' and your case was never mentioned in the research-lab."

"For one reason or other, Benning and his associates must have wanted you to remain unaware of the current developments. – Perhaps I should take a closer look at your initial research requests once again."

"Why did Prof. Benning want to get hold of your company?"

"Did he?" That news seemed to come as a surprise to him.

"Didn't you know? He is now the leader of research for your state supervised company. He controls the direction research in your labs may go."

"When did he get the position?"

"The day you were put into prison. So, three months ago."

"Good."

"Why 'good'? He had three whole months to do research with your whole team."

"But he only knows about the official team and that won't help him much."

"How do you know? He now has access to all your company files and all the research you had already done. They even got hold of your ex-wife. She must have lead them to everything you knew."

"She doesn't know," he drily commented.

"You kept secrets from your wife, even in times when you must have thought her to be trustworthy?"

"Those were things she didn't need to know. Her interests in me lay in other areas."

"How so?"

"Did you not see images of her? Then you would know."

"No, I didn't want to ..."

"You didn't want to what?" he prompted.

"Not poke into your privacy. She still seems to be an open wound for you."

"Only because I was so stupid to fall for her at all. Not that there is any more love lost between us. That scheming bitch sold me out for money, the sole thing she was interested in right from the beginning."

Clicking on her computer, Sophia searched for images of his wife, not to hurt or further enrage him, but because she was curious about the woman, who had been able to catch the interest of this grumpy good-looking professor. The image results took her breath away, and not in a good way. The woman was beautiful, more than that. She was stunning, traffic-stoppingly gorgeous. But what really took Sophia by surprise, was something else.

"I know her."

"What? How? – She was never here in Camsted, as far as I know."

"She is the girlfriend of Prof. Benning. She visited his lab repeatedly. The first time I saw her, was almost a year ago and on various other occasions since."

"A year ... – That was ..." Prof. Lynford fell silent.

From the timeline Sophia had been able to put together, that was the time, when the first accusations against Prof. Lynford had been raised, that he was conspiring against the nation. Those insinuations had been discarded at the time, but had still played their part in the unholy rush to pass judgement, when further accusations of him trying to murder his wife had been strategically placed in the media. The court, prejudiced by the reports of two doctors of his ex-wife, had hastened along his show-trial, which surprisingly suppressed images of him and the use of his full name, but had been quick with committing him into custody. With unheard of speed, he had been tried and sent to prison a bit over three months ago, where he was sprung out of only days earlier.

The reports about his prison break were of a single opinion, that his escape was a confirmation of his guilt regarding all the previous accusations. Though Sophia did not share this conviction. If someone as ingenious as Prof. Lynford wanted to murder someone, that person in her opinion most certainly would be dead by now. That his wife could still utter accusations against him, of being beaten and of him trying to kill her by hand, just did not ring true for a man who had other options available to get whatever he wanted. His wife still being alive in Sophia's logic was proof enough for her that Prof. Lynford was innocent.

She was convinced that something entirely different and underhand was going on, where Prof. Lynford conveniently had been made the culprit and forced to leave his high-profile research alone. But what was going on and to whose advantage was it, that his efforts and research were stopped?

Prof. Lynford had wandered back to her bed, sitting down on it in thought.

Sophia did not want to disturb him at first, but when he remained in this position and had not spoken for almost an hour, she could no longer stand his silence.

"What is it?"

"What?" He came out of his train of thoughts distractedly.

"What is it you think is going on?"

"Nothing of your concern."

Angrily, Sophia rolled her eyes. "Are we back in that stage? I thought we had established that we are bound together in this case."

"We had established nothing of that kind."

"Oh, come on. You can't leave this room without being caught again. I at least have a chance to do that. You need me, if you acknowledge it or not. But what is even more important, you have been framed and we need to find out who did it."

"Why do you not think I have been behind everything from the start, like the court and media believe?"

"Isn't that obvious? No guilty fool would run into a trap like that. Only if you are innocent of their accusations, your unpreparedness against all their accusations would make sense."

"And if there is a bigger game played here?"

"What do you mean? Tell me more about what you suspect. Please."

"No!"

"You can't undo my involvement in your case. You better tell me what is going on, or I'll go out and find out myself. The chance of stumbling into the wrong guys then is very likely. But give up the notion that I am not involved already. Either you tell me, or I go to discover what's going on all alone. Your choice."

"I'll take a shower, if you let me."

"Is that all you have to say?" Sophia was much too shocked about his abrupt change of subject to vent her anger adequately. But when he started for the door of her tiny bathroom, she jumped up and got there before him.

"Wait a moment. I'll prepare towels and things for you."

To his surprise, she did not hinder him taking the shower he wanted. She had even laid out soft towels, shower gel and to his utter surprise an assortment of different healing salves and creams against bruises and injuries and a big, fluffy bathing robe. He had not expected the nosy and upfront girl to be so caring and thoughtful about his needs.

She did not speak about the abuse she had seen him endure, but she did her best to help him heal. Her father was right. She deserved a much better man than he was. His efforts to push her away had completely gone unheeded, as she perceived him in need of help. It was as if she thought he needed a punching bag, after what he had had to endure, in prison and afterwards. He did not deserve the trust and bonus she had tried to give him. He had intentionally tried to make her push him out and stop her involving herself in his business and endangering herself.

But as it was, he had a hard time going through with his initial plan to make her hate him and leave him alone.

His rising dick was urgent proof, that his body wanted something his mind tried fiercely to resist.

Sophia was a vivid, desirable package he would not mind

exploring more deeply. With her curvy figure in his mind, he tried to take care of his desire for the fragile looking brunette with the big, soft brown eyes. But his relief was only temporary.

Already, drying himself and treating his body to the pain relief she had provided, brought his desire for her back full force.

He chastised himself. He could not mistreat the good Samaritan she was, but his body clearly did not follow his reasoning.

With a dent at the front of his bathrobe, he left the tiny bathroom, realizing that his experiences in prison had not shorn him off sex entirely.

– 6 –
Ancestry & Family –
Sophia's Apartment

"Prof. Lynford, I think I've found something," he was greeted, when he stepped out of the bathroom door.

"You can call me Merton."

Color spread over her pale cheeks, clearly showing him how nervous and uncomfortable the girl was about the informality he offered.

"Are you sure?" she squeaked in surprise.

"That my name is Merton? Quite sure, yes."

"Oh no, I mean, about me calling you that. I mean, …" Breaking off, he had effectively distracted her from her discovery.

"What is it, you have found?" he had to remind her.

"I've found a connection between your wife …"

"Ex-wife!" he interjected.

"… and Prof. Benning."

"And that is?" he prompted impatiently, annoyed that she had brought up his ex-wife again, who he would rather forget as quickly as possible.

"She is his cousin."

"And how did you find out that nonsense? Vanessa is not related to Prof. Benning. She herself told me so."

"Oh, but she is. One of the newspaper articles mentioned her age and birth place. So, combined with her full name, instead of 'Prof. L.'s wife', I went on and did a local search of her and her family. As it turns out, one of her relatives is an obsessive ancestry researcher and with my father's account, I accessed the family archive files. They are first cousins. Their fathers were brothers. Though the one strange thing is, that the family tree mentions an early pregnancy for her when she was only eighteen years old. But I thought you didn't have any children."

"You must be mistaken. My ex-wife didn't have any children."

"There was no marriage mentioned, but the named father of her child is Prof. Benning."

"What? Prof. Benning indeed has a child, that much is correct. A daughter about thirteen years old. He is a single father. Though from what he told me, his wife died in a car crash before he had even finished university, when the girl was still a baby," Prof. Lynford for once came forward with information.

"From the data in the family tree, which is assembled by his great-uncle, a man who had married one of his father's aunts and who should know, he was never married. When the child is from his first cousin, it would explain why they, both Catholics, did not marry, though in some states, they could have."

He felt bile rise in his throat, though he had thought himself over the state of anger over his former wife's betrayal. Had he known this woman at all? In hindsight, he supposed that she had him fooled completely. Nothing of what she had made him believe had been true.

He even doubted the results of Prof. Benning's research in the last years. They had clashed quite a few times with identical results, and he had graciously given him precedence, when their research seemed to go in a similar direction, even though he doubted that Prof. Benning had the ability to achieve those conclusions in his lab. But now, it seemed that Prof. Benning had not just arrived at similar results through his own merits, but had had access to his, Prof. Lynford's, own research materials.

Whatever those thieves thought they had found in his notes, must have brought them to the opinion that he, Prof. Lynford, was now expendable.

Sophia had been watching Prof. Lynford intently. She could not bring herself to think of him as Merton.

"What is it?" she finally brought him back to the present. "You do believe me now, don't you?"

"Yes. That would explain quite a lot of things."

"For example?"

"His research results without adequate laboratory setups. He always seemed to be a step ahead of me in the last three years, though I never found his actual laboratories impressive or sufficiently equipped."

"Equipped for what?"

"For biometric nano-transmission."

"That does not work. It is a fantasy, a utopia."

"And that from the girl who wanted to prove the retina security scan validity by analyzing the differences of retinal imprints."

"Not really. I wanted to prove the connection between the imprint to the human emotional system and health. The retinal reaction of the human being to the image one sees and the electron transmission process of the image to the body is the thing that would really interest me. Those were my earlier suggestions you never gave feedback to. But for the last suggestion, Prof. Benning's new assistant Dr. Stewart changed my topic. He made me do a lot of tests for it over the summer and made them a requirement for me to stay in Prof. Benning's official project."

"And do you have any idea who is funding this new research?"

"No, not really. I'm not involved with the financial backing of this project, just the research part. I did not even know that it was initially your research project and Prof. Benning just took over after – wait! He gave me the position, when you rejected my topic suggestion half a year ago. That was even before they sentenced you and put you into prison. How could he have even had information about your project back then?"

He did not answer her statement, but looked at her intensely, as if evaluating what best to reveal to her. That made Sophia feel very uneasy in his presence, though when speaking about her research topic with him, some kind of understanding between them had been established and she had begun to feel less insecure in the presence of her long-time idol.

"Are you currently doing any lab-work for Prof. Benning?" He seemed to have reached a conclusion what to divulge and his words were clipped and decisive.

Unsure about the role he had now given her in his mind, Sophia answered with unease still clouding her voice: "Yes, he wants me to assemble my current results and put them together in a presentation for him."

"Would your work allow you to get into his laboratory again tomorrow, perhaps, to straighten up some facts for your report, to eventually do some further search of the lab?"

"I don't know. My access codes should still work, though they are changed on a regular basis and I wasn't in the lab today, so I don't know. Perhaps I should do whatever you deem necessary quite quickly, before they change the entry codes as a precaution because of your escape."

"So they did see you and can potentially identify you as my accomplice?"

"No. I'm sure they can't. But for one, they could have had hidden cameras I didn't detect. Second, they could indeed be working for Prof. Benning, as you seem to think – which, by the way, I can't ever believe he would countenance, or for a third, they could make the connection to my police report and get my details from the corrupt officers. Better to be safe than sorry. It's not as if you have many more options besides me."

"What are you now, my rescue squad?"

"Something like that." Sophia looked sternly and a bit recalcitrant at Prof. Lynford, angry with him for treating her help so lightly, as if it was foisted upon him against his will.

With an enraged sniff, she turned around and began packing her rucksack, which she normally took to university with her.

"What are you doing? Are you planning to break into the labs in the night? That will certainly get their attention."

"No. The labs are open till 11 p.m. And as my usual research time is always in the late evenings, nobody will blink an eye, if I turn up now."

It was almost 8 p.m. by now. That would leave her almost three hours to look around the lab.

"You can't go just like that. You don't even have an idea what you are looking for. I need to go with you."

"Are you crazy? The security team around the lab will immediately report you."

"A security team especially for the laboratory? How unusual. Or is it just campus security? You could tell them I am your brother."

"No. They are specially there to secure the lab. They register anyone entering and leaving. If you are unknown to them, they will take your fingerprints and identification and check them with their database. No way will you get near the lab that way."

"Did it never occur to you that this amount of security is strange for a normal university laboratory?"

"Prof. Benning explained it with his work for state security."

"Ah, and that made you feel important in getting access to such a secure area and you immediately stopped asking any further questions."

"Do you want my help or not? If you continue to annoy me so much, I will gladly let you wade through all your enemies alone."

"So I hit a nerve?"

"No, well, yes. But I did ask further. Just my every attempt to learn more was blocked. Prof. Benning told me I would learn more when I finally became a full member of the research team next semester, when my scholarship was granted."

Prof. Lynford sat down in her desk chair in front of her computers and murmured distractedly: "Why the wait. Why not utilize an able work-force to its full potential right away, when he had you working there already?"

Though his words seemed more to himself than a question to her, she answered anyway: "Prof. Benning is not here most of the time at the moment. He would not have been able to supervise my work, should I continue on my own right now."

"But where is he and what does he fear you could find out without him around, that he can't let you work on your own? You must be close to something. – Where are your notes for your research reports? Show me." He ordered her around, expecting her to follow promptly, but she remained where she stood near the door.

"What are you waiting for?" he grumbled impatiently.

"For a polite request, perhaps? Not that it would be part of your vocabulary."

"What? Don't waste my time."

Sophia lifted her nose and looked away from him as if she had not heard him.

"Please, Miss Sophia. Please show me the finished parts of your research findings."

"Wasn't so hard, was it?" Sophia promptly walked over to her desk and from one of the drawers pulled out her neatly bound and finished report.

"I thought you hadn't finished it yet."

"I haven't handed it in yet, but I finalized it last night, before I accidentally observed you."

"So my rescue is due to a research you did for Prof. Benning on a project of mine? How strange things can get."

He opened her report somewhere in the middle and immediately seemed to forget all about her presence. Sophia once again grabbed her rucksack, picked up her jacket and slipped into her shoes to leave the apartment.

"Be careful," he called after her, when she opened her door, thinking him lost to the world.

"I will. Take care yourself and don't go close to the windows. With light in the room, you will be easily visible from the opposite house. Though you should be alright with just the desk-light on." Only a distracted grunt followed her statement. Sophia slipped out, wondering about her strange house guest. His last comment had surprised her. It had almost sounded as if he really cared about her. But she shook her head. No, she was just his last resource for any kind of help he had any longer. He was most definitely not interested in her personally. What kind of woman did that make her, she wondered, immediately falling for his pretty face and snide arrogance. Though face might not be entirely correct. He was more than a pretty face. His features were rough and very masculine, fascinating more than beautiful, intoxicatingly drawing her to him. But his lithe body, the strength and bodily presence he emitted, pulled her in as much as the workings of his mind had, before she had even met him.

Her bratty comments and rebuffs, she recognized, were more efforts to hold him at arm's length. Sophia was honest enough to admit to herself, that this man was very dangerous for her peace of mind and she planned on doing everything not to let him know about her attraction to him. His arrogance certainly would know no bounds, if he should ever detect her weakness and she had no doubt that he would try to use her like a trained puppy for his advantage, if he knew the effect he had on her.

She would not let that happen and the stroll through the cooler summer breeze on her way to the university helped clear her mind.

Though on the footpath to the university laboratory, she could not help but daydream about how it would feel to be held in his strong arms. Would it make him forget about his own experiences with that criminal raping him? That thought effectively tore her out of her comfortable and cozy dream-world.

She had to be careful, if the criminals were on the lookout for her and not daydream about the attractive professor, who was much too snobby to take a look at her, much less deem her worthy of his attention. He was freshly divorced, even his separation from his wife making top news in the press, not only his prison sentence and certainly now his escape …

'Wait!' Sophia thought and abruptly stopped in her tracks on the dark path in the park surrounding the campus area. Reports about 'Prof. L.'s' escape from prison were completely absent from the pile she had accumulated about him. She had only found a tiny message about a prison break four days ago, with some escaped unnamed prisoners and had just assumed that was his. Why had his escape not made top news, when he indeed was the dangerous, subversive scientist earlier reports had made him out to be? Did they want to avoid a mass panic, or were there other reasons behind this expertly and quietly staged prison break, which had nothing to do with his earlier sentence? Had she perhaps broken him away from a secret service unit, using him for their own purpose? 'No,' Sophia immediately answered her own question in her mind. What agent had ever abused his prisoner, when wanting information from him. 'Well,' Sophia admitted to herself. That was not the best argument against it, she conceded to herself, her mind busy as usual. With all the reports about waterboarding, that fact not immediately relieved her mind. Whoever his guards had been, he was certainly better off with her, whatever side paid them or had ordered to hold him prisoner.

How could she have left him in a situation like she had seen him in? No man deserved that, not even her adored and at the same time so confrontational Prof. Lynford. Well, she would have to keep her adoration in check somehow.

– 7 –
Camsted University Campus

Her mind still buzzing with all the rivaling thoughts, Sophia was almost at the entrance of the laboratory, before she saw the moving shadows inside. She had presumed the laboratory on the ground floor would already be empty at this advanced time of day.

Hiding in the shadows of the bushes, she was glad that it was already late in the summer and it was almost completely dark, to hide her suspicious behavior from eventual passers-by. Moving backwards, she tried to get a look into the elevated windows, to see who was inside.

But her hopes to easily get access to the lab and search it were dashed instantly. The person roaming around inside, was clearly searching for something. Noises like carelessly pulled open drawers and furniture pushed around, could be easily heard outside where she was standing, the searcher inside taking not the least care of remaining undetected.

The face appearing at the window for a short moment, belonged to one of the men who had held Prof. Lynford captive. Not the rapist she had on video, but the one standing with his back to the window mostly.

Sophia was out of options now. She doubted she would find anything in the laboratory after such a thorough search. But what did it mean that one of the criminals was in there, without the least fear of detection? Was he perhaps in lieu with Prof. Benning, as Prof. Lynford suspected? 'No,' Sophia shook her head, though nobody could see her reaction. She could not believe that of her calm and focused professor. He was much too idealistic and engrossed in his research, that she could believe anything like that of him.

Withdrawing from the window, Sophia searched for an even more secure hiding place with diverse escape options and moved deeper into the park in front of the lab, before taking out her mobile-phone. Dialing the saved number, she let it ring. After the sixth ring, Prof. Benning took up the phone. He seemed to be at home, a TV sounding in the background and she heard a female voice, if the call was for her.

Either he was intentionally fabricating an alibi for the time his lab was being searched by his cohorts, or he was not involved with them and innocent of any connection with the criminals. Sophia still did not know what to think, after Prof. Lynford had raised her suspicions against anyone, leaving everything she had so far thought safe and settled under renewed scrutiny.

"Prof. Benning here. Who is there?"

"Good evening, Prof. Benning," Sophia made her voice sound more agitated than she really felt. "I didn't know whom to call this late – but – there's someone in the lab."

"Yes, it's a lab used by all professors on campus. So, what's the matter?"

"Someone's searching it, throwing things around. Certainly not a researcher. I was just coming here, wanting to ascertain some facts, before I finished my report for you, when I heard strange sounds coming from the inside."

"Stay there! I'll call the police."

"Are you sure that's safe?" Sophia wanted to make certain that she had heard the professor correctly.

"Yes, stay there. We need you as an eye-witness."

"O.k." she murmured hesitantly.

"I'll be there in ten minutes. Stay."

He disconnected the call.

Sophia could not believe the words of her professor. He and an ominous 'we' wanted her to observe a potentially dangerous man breaking into their lab, all alone and without a weapon to defend herself? Could that really have been her usually so professional and caring professor?

But only moments later, she saw the man in the lab taking out his phone. He had received a call and instinctually looked out of the window, when answering it. Was it her professor, who had alerted him to her presence outside?

Did that mean that he knew about her rescue of Prof. Lynford, or did he just want to get rid of her because she, like his rivaling professor had got too close to some mysterious research he wanted kept a secret?

Seeing her chances to search the lab gone, as well as her trust in Prof. Benning, Sophia silently took the dimly lit route through the campus greenery, not waiting for the criminal to find her, though she heard him come out of the lab-building behind her. Rounding the corner of a fraternity building on campus, she got into a run, hiding from streetlights wherever possible.

When she neared her own apartment building, she watched out for strange signs. A look up to her own windows confirmed that all was dark inside, just her normal lights from her computer screens. Still, she was nervous, not wanting to be seen from the other house, so she went in as she had left, via the back yard, entering her building through the underground garage.

– 8 –
Sophia's Apartment

Not trusting that her apartment was still safe, when the workspace in her lab had been invaded, Sophia took the elevator up, but stopped one floor below hers and got out there, walking up the last flight of stairs, listening for unusual sounds or the presence of others in the barely used staircase. But everything seemed all right, though from the stink, she presumed that quite a few of her fellow inhabitants had been using it as their smoking area, lately.

The hallway looked abandoned and trying to make no sound on the gray old linoleum floor, she approached her door, but almost at it, she detected that it was slightly ajar.

She was so surprised, that she could not hold back an audible gasp.

"Come in. Don't catch flies." The voice of her 'houseguest' sounded from directly behind the door.

Sophia threw off her shocked immobility and almost ran into her apartment, carefully closing the door behind her, while still watching the hallway.

Turning around, she angrily glared at him. "Why did you do that? You almost shocked me into running away. Leaving the door open like that was just mad."

"That would have been a pity and completely unnecessary, if you had run. Your friends came just over for a visit."

"What? Which friends?"

"Your friends, my guards."

"You can't mean that. And you let them in? Letting them know your whereabouts? Have you gone completely crazy in my absence? – Or perhaps you were that all along and I should not have sprung you out …" She added the last words in a murmur more to herself than for him.

"Yes, the ones you saw on your video tape. They questioned your neighbors about the repair woman. The concierge must have given them a tip."

"Then why are you still here?"

"They left, when they heard the voices coming from in here. The subterfuge worked perfectly. Now, are you still angry?"

"What voices?" Was this man dense somehow or intentionally playing with her?

"The voice of you so prettily begging not to be shot."

"What? But I was not here. How could I … – Oh!"

"Yes, that exact recording." The wicked gleam in his eyes hinted that he had found the audio-file of the recording she had once done as a contract work for a friend writing steamy erotic novels. The beginning of this sex recording held an abduction sequence, where the heroine begged the hero not to shoot her.

Embarrassed, she gave up grilling him further, as she slowly began to understand why the men had left so easily.

She had done the recordings for a friend, who needed them at first for her creative writing classes, but the author herself had gone mad with the technicality and the voice modeling to present her own writing. Sophia had been quite sure that embarrassment about her writing had been part of her problem, why she had not been able to read her stories aloud herself. But Sophia, getting her friend to promise that she would not tell anyone who had read her audio-stories, had done it willingly, especially as her friend, coming from a rich background, had paid her well for the audio-recordings of her extreme-sex erotica. They now had a deal that Sophia would read all her rich friend's stories and to her astonishment, the audio files did well in sales.

Finding that her surprise house-guest had discovered her secret occupation, being here for only a few hours, did not sit well with her. How had he even been able to find it in time to use it, she wondered and could not stop herself from asking the question aloud.

"Why, it was the first file I opened, as it was stored under a strange name and while listening in, your friendly concierge from across the street called and spoke on your answering machine, warning you that the men were on their way over in search of you. They had called the service company to find out your address, which in turn had contacted the concierge."

"Mr. Arnestone, yes."

"The idea with the open door, as if one of the men had already got to you, just came in handy."

"But won't they find out, when none of them …?"

"No."

"How so?"

"One of them did. Michael, my friend from prison."

"Your what? You trust him to keep mum? One of them was already searching the lab, while the others were here. And you, goading them with such petty tricks, while Prof. Benning wanted me to wait at the lab, to potentially be caught and killed by them?"

"Don't be so melodramatic. They are criminals, but no contract killers."

"How do you know? After what they did to you, you should know better than to underestimate them."

"I am far from underestimating them, when I tell you they

need me alive for what they have in mind."

"They might need you, but that does not guarantee my safety – wait, I don't want them to do to me what they did to you either!" Her thoughts were back at the disturbing pictures of his torture she had caught on camera. She had never heard about men doing that to other men, well, yes, she was not so naïve not to have heard what was going on in men's prisons. But outside of prisons, the reports were always about cruelty between men and women, not men raping men.

"They won't. The men are gay through and through. They would rather beat you up than touch you."

"Well, that is rather a big relief," Sophia answered with irony dripping from her voice. "Thank you for reviving all the vivid pictures in my mind. How could you so callously play with those men? They are dangerous."

"Before you go completely ape-shit about it, though your embarrassment is quite cute, I joked about your recordings. To watch your reaction was just priceless."

"Thank you for making me your entertainment." Sophia wanted to turn away from him snidely, but he continued:

"They left because of the sounds coming from the neighboring apartment. The open door just conveyed that you were over there, involved in the argument. And as the men left, it worked out perfectly."

"Oh, well. I understand now. Surely, Mrs. Grantham was on the telephone with her son again. They never get along, not for one whole minute. – Why didn't you tell me that before? You are so mean to string me up like that. It is not as if I am used to rescuing escaped convicts and then be followed by criminals. There's no need for you to be a liar as well."

"What, you still see me as a criminal? I thought we had

established that I was framed. Are you now willing to help me or not?"

"Oh, so now you want my help? I thought you wanted to leave and did not want me to get involved, not wanting to tell me anything at all, something incriminating, I'm sure."

Sophia did not know, why she was arguing so harshly with this man, especially now that he was willing to involve her. She was normally known to be quite calm and able to soothe waves in the conflicts around her, but with him, she was enraged in mere milliseconds. Their further argument was interrupted, though.

Prof. Benning's number appeared on her mobile phone. She immediately went to answer it, holding her hand out to keep Prof. Lynford silent.

"Hello, Prof. Benning …" she started, but was immediately interrupted by an urgent whisper.

"Where are you? I need to see you, to give you some material. – It's urgent. Why did you leave?"

"I thought it wasn't safe. He came out and it seemed like he knew I was there. I had to run, to avoid being seen by him."

"Good," he conceded. "But it's urgent I give you those documents. I am … – later. Can you come to your favorite spot off campus right now? I'll meet you there in as few minutes as you can make it in. Hurry."

The line went dead.

Sophia had always really trusted her professor, but his demand that she should stay close to a criminal and then find that man looking for her had shaken her trust severely. But his voice right now had sounded so desperate, so urgent, that she just didn't know what to do. After what she had learned about Prof. Lynford, she didn't know any longer, if it was safe to go to

Prof. Benning and meet him in her favorite café, because that was what he had hinted at without naming the location.

They had seen each other there a few times when buying the excellent coffee or ice cream, so he knew she liked the place. She had swapped campus lunch, to get some of their delicious ice-cream sometimes.

Picking up her bag again, Sophia went to the door.

"Keep the door locked this time. You can enjoy the rest of the sex-recordings in the meanwhile."

"Where are you going? – Meeting up with your boyfriend?"

"No."

"Your lover?"

"None of your business."

"It is mine, when you are leading my abductors back to me. – And you talked to Prof. Benning without even telling me."

"I can talk to whomever I like. I owe you nothing."

"Not so, when my safety is concerned. You have no idea what this is all about. Giving him information about my whereabouts will bring the thugs over there back to your doorstep. Think about it, you are not only risking my, but also your own safety. Do you trust Prof. Benning that much to risk that?"

"I have no choice. If I don't go to him, he will be suspicious. As far as we know, he has no idea yet that you are with me."

"Then keep it that way."

"I intend to. But I will see him, you can't prevent me from going to him. He said it was urgent. And yes, I do trust him." Sophia said the last stubbornly, almost as if in contrast to her feelings for him.

Did she trust the man standing so angrily in front of her and so easily able to play with her emotions? Sophia really did not know, but she had no choice. She could not throw him out after rescuing him. Somehow, she believed that he was not guilty of the crimes he was accused of. Even after their short acquaintance and after teasing her so mercilessly and getting her angry without showing any sign of remorse, she didn't think he was capable of trying to murder his wife. There must have been another motive or reason to pack him away into prison so quickly.

She knew he was a clever man, able of elaborate subterfuge, but deliberate betrayal and embezzling money from the government, the reason his wife had given for his attempted murder, was too crude a crime for this intelligent man. He would have other means to get what he wanted and he would not make his thievery so obvious that his wife would accidentally find out about it. Sophia was sure that even now he had his own agenda, like keeping her in the dark. His ability to play his elaborate games could easily make his thievery untraceable. With his dealings, nobody would be the wiser about what had happened, she was absolutely certain of it.

That was how she saw him, but not as a petty thief, going in for the money. That just did not sit right with her, when all his research and scientific results must already bring him a fortune.

Prof. Lynford saw the conflicting thoughts chasing each other on her creased brow, but did not try to hold her back or convince her of his trustworthiness. He awaited her judgement patiently and with unbroken arrogance, as if her throwing him out would not have any effect on him.

But Sophia's thoughts went on. 'Perhaps, her opinion would not have an effect on him, if he overpowered her and …'

He must have seen the growing fear on her face, because he

immediately intervened.

"I'll be waiting for you till you come back. If you need a security guarantee for your meeting, call your landline here and I'll rush to your aid, when you tell me where you are going."

"This whole generous offer, just to find out where I am going?" Sophia tried to shake off the fear that had grown in her and answered him more harshly than she felt comfortable with.

"No, to keep you safe. I can't do that, when I don't know where you are supposed to be. We can't expect that apartment over there is their sole hiding place or that they are the only interested party. I won't necessarily find you and be able to return the favor of freeing you, if someone took you."

"Well then. I am going to Marty's Café at the corner of the campus area, main entrance. If I'm not back in an hour … – Oh, I have no idea what to do then. Call the police?" She really doubted that would help her. "Take over my apartment for your own purposes? – You'll do that anyway, even if I don't allow you. So, just stay safe and if I am not back in an hour, you can start to worry about what happened to me."

She did not see the determined look in his eyes, but rushed out of the door and to the meeting place with her professor, using her disguised route again.

– 9 –
Marty's Café

Sophia was deeply worried, because Prof. Benning had only referred to their meeting place in code only the two of them would understand, which made her certain that he had believed others were listening in on their conversation. Was it the telephone connection he suspected, or had he not been alone at the time of the call?

Sophia was at the meeting place in record time and found Prof. Benning in one of the hidden booths in the back of the little café. She did not want to draw attention to them and slipped into the seat opposite him, whispering her greeting. Looking up at him, she found his worried gaze searching their surrounding, checking if she had been followed.

"I came alone. Nobody followed me."

"It's just … – I am worried. – What I am going to ask of you, is not something to take lightly. I wouldn't entrust it to anyone else."

"Has it to do with my thesis topic and Prof. Lynford?"

Sophia had rushed in with her question, wanting to see the effect of mentioning the other man's name on Prof. Benning. But his reaction surprised her. Wincing and almost squirming in his seat, Prof. Benning shook his head in irritation.

"More than that. We need to find out what he had been working on before he disappeared. His break-through must have been so imminent, that diverse interested parties already sent out their emissaries to get it and get rid of their rivals and eventually him. It would be catastrophic, if his research fell into the wrong hands."

"But how do you know about all that? Why can't Prof. Lynford help you?" Sophia feigned ignorance about the man's imprisonment and escape.

"I always forget that you don't know." He did not specify what he thought she didn't know, but she suspected he meant the trial and the omission of Prof. Lynford's name in the press and especially in their research laboratory.

"They made me supervisor of his laboratory, after Prof. Lynford was arrested."

Sophia made an obligatory gasp, to feign surprise, but fortunately, Prof. Benning was too wrapped up in his own message to pay much attention to her reaction, as Sophia was aware that acting was not one of her talents.

"And now the vultures are all circling around me," the professor continued. "I need to get the information out of my hands, to somewhere safe where they won't expect it. And that is where you come in."

"But what can I do to help with that?" All of Sophia's former doubts about his honesty had evaporated at his words. She just could not believe it of him, that her stiff and overly correct tutor would do something wrong.

Prof. Benning brought up a backpack from under the desk, inconspicuous in its looks, as it was one of the materials freely handed out to all students on campus at the beginning of their studies. But he put it back down and pushed it towards her side under the desk with his foot.

"Take it and look through it and see what you can make of it."

"Material from Prof. Lynford? But he found my topic choices ludicrous and didn't even bother to comment on them. How would I be able to make sense of his notes?"

"I think that in your topic choices you came too close to his solution, so he wanted to distract you, or had some other reason to hide his interest in your line of research. – It must be something like that." The professor said the last engrossed in his own thoughts.

"But wouldn't it be better, if you looked through it?" Sophia intervened. "You have much more experience and resources. I am not yet accepted with a doctoral thesis topic, I only have limited access to the university labs."

"You can't use them!" Prof. Benning was utterly disturbed by her mentioning the university labs. "They are off limits to you. They are watched. This material must not leave your hands and never come close to the campus. They are watching my every step. Even now, I am not completely sure that we are safe. – Empty your backpack and switch it with mine. I don't want them to think I deposited something somewhere."

Under the table, Sophia pulled her almost empty backpack towards herself and took out her wallet and necessities, placing them next to her on the seat, then taking the similar backpack of the professor and filling it with her things, the large bundle of documents in it not leaving her much space. Finally, she took her cardigan and stuffed it in her now empty backpack to fill it up and disguise the swap and pushed it over to her professor.

"And what if I find something? How can I reach you without alerting the vultures, as you call them?"

Her professor handed her a website address, scribbled on a tiny sheet of paper.

"Write it here. The site is secure and locked down, so only I will see it and I will check every day. Don't publish your writing, just leave it in the drafts. – But now we should leave. It's already late and I have early summer-classes in the morning. They will know my routine that on those days I am always home early."

"Yes, professor. Good night."

"Good night, Sophia. And good luck. We'll both need it."

"Is it so dangerous?"

"You have no idea. Be careful. Don't trust anyone and don't let anyone see those documents."

"But couldn't Prof. Lynford help with their meaning?"

"If I just knew where he is. But that can't be helped. He had to look out for himself to survive."

That did not sound as if Prof. Benning wanted to harm or outsmart Prof. Lynford to get his position. Her professor looked rather scared. Looking over his shoulder and also keeping an eye on the windows to the street outside, he declared: "It's better we don't leave together. Stay here for a while and leave through the back doors."

"Yes, professor. Good night and good luck."

Sophia waited some more. She was nervous during her wait, because with having to hide on her way home, avoiding the well-lit streets running along campus, she would not make it home in time. She hoped Prof. Lynford would not immediately call the police or do anything to find her as he had suggested. But when she slid out of the back doors of the restaurant, she quickly discovered that Prof. Benning had been right. Men were sitting in cars on the front street, vaguely illuminated by the street lights above, watching the restaurant. Fortunately, they did not see her slip out in the dark, surveilling her surroundings from between the garbage containers in the back of the kitchen, and hiding in the undergrowth of the walkway to the park, overshadowed by thick, old oak trees.

Stumbling over the uneven ground of the unlit park-way made bumpy by the tree roots, Sophia got on her long way home, not encountering any more suspicious looking gangsters in suits, trying to hunt for information she still had to figure out herself.

– 10 –
Back in Sophia's Apartment

Sophia once again stole back into her own apartment complex via the car garage, taking the stairs up to her floor, though she knew she was already late. But after the near miss in the elevator during the escape with Prof. Lynford, the enclosed cabin gave her the creeps.

Letting herself into the apartment, she found it dark and seemingly abandoned.

"What the…" she exclaimed. But then the door to her tiny balcony opened and, bent down and out of sight, Prof. Lynford came back into the apartment, holding her video camera in one hand.

"So you are back from your little rendezvous with your lover," he flatly commented, not showing any of the worry she had anticipated after being more than an hour late from the time she had anticipated to be back.

Unreasonably, that made her strangely angry with him and without thinking, she lashed out: "Missing your own lover so much that you now must stalk him?"

Prof. Lynford looked her up and down haughtily, put the camera down on her desk and without words went into her tiny bathroom, completely ignoring her comment.

When he came back out, she heard the toilet still flush and she entered after him, to give it a hard shove to stop it from running. The mechanism had a glitch, but she knew how to live with it.

Prof. Lynford still wore the big white bath-robe her sister had given her as a Christmas present last year and she had been reluctant to use, as it was much too valuable for every-day use. He had it cavalierly closed in the front and it threatened to fall open any moment, when the heap of his old clothes next to the shower made it abundantly clear to her that he wore nothing beneath.

"Do you have anything for me to wear from your absentee boyfriend?"

"He doesn't leave his things here." Sophia did not want to confirm his correct suspicion, that she was alone.

"Because he doesn't exist. Something else from one of your lovers that might fit?"

She could not think of anything, but finally found a big t-shirt she had received at one of the computer conventions. They had only had one size for all attendees and it was much too large for her small frame, but she liked to sleep in it. She took it out from her wardrobe and wordlessly handed it over to him. He took it and threw it over. While it came to the middle of her thighs, it barely covered his genitals, which now, as he had slipped out of the bath-robe as if she was not there, were on full display, showing an impressive package to her inexperienced eyes.

Uncomfortable, Sophia turned away from his uninhibited display of nakedness. Did he just do that on purpose to make her feel embarrassed in his presence?

Pulling the shirt down, he turned to her. "Where am I to sleep?"

"In the bed. I'll take the couch."

He took up the camera from her desk and went to the bed without hesitation, as if nothing untoward had happened. No 'thank you', no hint of what he had found out in the meantime, while she had the distinct impression that he had discovered something in her absence, but with his comments about her boyfriend had intentionally tried to push her away once again. He did not even show the least interest in her own progress.

Instead, her remark about his boyfriend had angered him and he had now completely cut her out, as if she was not even there. How funny was that, in her own apartment. 'Not at all,' Sophia answered her own question in her head. She felt even more angry with him that he took her help as if it was an overdue reverence by one of his deeply indebted subjects. She was in no way obliged to help him, nor did she even begin to trust him.

Grumpy, she turned away from him, making herself a cup of tea, when she heard him order her around.

"One cup, milk, without sugar."

"Argh …" Sophia suppressed further comments and made him a cup as well, before sitting down at her desk and carefully hiding the bag Prof. Benning had given her. She wanted to take a look once Prof. Lynford had fallen asleep. But her fidgeting under the desk had not escaped his notice.

"What do you have there? Something Prof. Benning gave you? – Let me see."

"That's none of your concern."

"Whatever you do is my concern, after unexpectedly coming into the loving care of a desperate single woman."

Sophia angrily looked up into his face. "You have no right …"

"I have every right to demand your undistracted attention, my sweet green girl. Now come over and hand me the backpack."

"I'll do no such thing. My boyfriend will not allow you …"

"Yes, yes. Your boyfriend again. The mysterious man that doesn't exist."

"How can you say that? He'll defend and protect me."

"And where is your wonderful, loving boyfriend now, when you need protection and defense? Did you even think about involving him in your mad scheme? Or are you finally ready to admit, that he is just a figment of your dreams? Now, hand me over your backpack and let me see what you got from Prof. Benning."

"No!"

He came to her with surprising speed and agility, reaching her with just one threatening step, catching her with one hand by the neck and pushing her back into her office chair. Sophia was much too stunned, to even attempt to get up and run away.

"Let's make one thing clear. I'm not a patient man. Either you do as I say, or I'll bind and gag you, to get some peace."

His hand holding her by the neck squeezed, to get an answer out of her, but only made her look up at him in silent terror.

Shaking her by the neck, he repeated: "What is it, cooperation or being my prisoner?"

He watched her reactions intensely, before his second hand lifted, ignoring her hands trying to fight his hold around her neck, and softly stroked her lips with his thumb.

Shocked by the electrifying intensity shooting through her body, Sophia could not look away from his mesmerizing gaze. Her hands remained ineffective around his, holding her in place.

"Or, …" he said as if disinterested. "There is another way." An ugly, knowing and still so sexy smile appeared on his face, before he bent down and his lips softly touched hers, teasing her, licking, breathing on her, making all her senses go on high alert.

Her first kiss. Sophia could not breathe, only sense and feel. The soft movement of his lips on hers sent her over into a dreamy sphere, making her close her eyes, never wanting to leave this state of elatedness.

When he pulled away from the kiss, Sophia slowly regained her senses, her eyes blinking, as if not believing what had occurred or just refusing to come back to reality.

Prof. Lynford softly chuckled, nuzzling her neck his hand had released during the kiss, licking her sensitive skin and sending flames throughout her body.

Unaware of her own moans of enjoyment, the sound drew her out of her haze of pleasure.

"What the hell …," she started, but his finger over her lips stopped her, more a sensual touch than preventing her speaking.

"You want me, my sweet. And I am willing to give you what you want, when you let me see what you have there. It will be to our mutual pleasure."

His casual words tore her out of her bliss with full force.

"You arrogant prick," she almost screamed at him, pushing him away fervently. "You are so full of yourself that you honestly believe I will fall for that? – How could I just be so stupid to rescue the dumbest man on earth?"

"Nobody asked you to," he countered, not showing how annoyed he was by her straightforward refusal of his seduction methods, which so far had always gained him what he wanted. But he was not ready to admit, that he had really looked forward to sleeping with the girl, not just for the sake of gaining the information he wanted.

But the bubbly and talkative girl had remained silent about her meeting with Prof. Benning, rather wanting him to reveal something to her before telling him anything. That had alerted all his caution towards her. Just another woman trying her tricks on him, but he was no longer the trusting fool he had been during his marriage. He had gone through a hard school to learn the truth about women.

The coincidence of her being a student trying to get him to co-correct and supervise her research. He did believe in strange things in this world, but this? And she even had the audacity to think he should show gratefulness to her? Not in this world. He would find out what she held back and would make her his willing toy. All his previous lovers before his short marriage, had begged him to sleep with them and so would she, a mere girl, thinking an invented boyfriend would hold him back in making a move on her. If she thought that would save her from him, she had to think again.

The storm she had unleashed coming her way would leave her begging at his feet. He would enjoy the experience of bringing her to her knees.

The foreboding smile hushing over his features, made Sophia shudder. Why ever had she felt it to be a good idea to let a stranger into her home, a domain no man except her father had been welcome in so far? Now, she had made herself vulnerable to this attractive man, who by his many successes had been made so arrogant that he could not believe anyone could resist him.

Well, she certainly would, she promised herself, though a quiver in her stomach made her aware that maybe resisting him might not be as easy as it had been with all the other men in her life trying to date her. Her fellow students had been easy to discharge and she had never felt anything for any of them. Even before she had met the professor, he had held her full attention and admiration. Since the first time she had laid eyes on him in the other apartment complex, he had stirred feelings in her she was not used to. Protectiveness, as if such a big and strong man would normally need that, though he had, she admitted to herself.

But now, any sign of his weakness or needing her was gone. He wanted to force her to obey him like a brainless puppy. If he thought her hormones would make her his willing tool, he had to think again.

Shaking off the effect of his touch, she pushed his hand away. "Don't touch me, you bully."

"Oh, does my touch affect you too much, my dear? Has your latest lay been too long ago?"

"If you think you get me to do what you want by insulting me, you need to think again. Brainless fool. How could I have been so mistaken in thinking him to be intelligent …" She murmured the last words to herself. "Sitting around in my t-shirt and thinking he can order me around."

Slowly, one side of his mouth began to quiver, before he broke out in a full-hearted laugh.

"You are a curious girl," he stated, turning around and walking back to her bed, leaving her and the backpack he had wanted to inspect behind without a fight.

Outstretched on top of her bed, giving her a full and unhindered view of his body, exposing all but his dick, he found her eyes on him, as if she was unable to tear her gaze away.

That was what he needed. Her fascination of him, keeping her on her feet, not letting her get comfortable and spiting him.

When her gaze wandered up his body to his face and she recognized that he was observing her, she blushed feverishly. Like an innocent little virgin, seeing her first almost naked man, he thought, but dismissed that idea immediately. She must be around 24 or 25 years old, at the least, when she was applying for her thesis. No girl these days kept her virginity that long, he thought. So much for her appearing innocent. Just another vile woman, like his ex.

Pretending to be comfortable, he threw her blanket over his lower body. Her room was still hot from the day and any more than that would be stifling. After a few moments, he forced his breath to slow down and pretend deep slumber.

As he had expected, the girl settled in her place in front of her computers, after a short trip to the bathroom, where she must have taken the backpack with her, as coming back, she held it in her hand, placing it on her chair and rummaging around in it.

He let her be for a while, sensing her uneasy looks shifting over to him ever so often.

So he was right. Whatever she had, she didn't want to show him. That made him just the more determined to see what Prof. Benning had given her.

He would let her find out for herself that she no longer was in a position to keep secrets from him. He would not allow her to play him like his wife had done. No, he would keep an eye on her, never leaving her out of his sight again as long as he needed her.

When she became fully engrossed in the material she had, he from time to time heard her surprised breath. He wanted to make sure that her full attention was taken up by whatever she was doing so that he could approach her in silence, not alerting her to him slowly trying to leave the bed without making a sound. He had prepared his final move already by throwing off his blanket and turning to the side of the bed. She had not even given his last movement a flicker of notice. Well, he was about to approach her. He could have taken and read the material, when she had fallen asleep, but he wanted to show her his dominance. He relished the coming fight with her.

But what happened next took him entirely by surprise.

The girl jumped up from her chair and almost ran over to him, roughly shaking his shoulder to wake him up, papers still held tightly in her other hand.

What was that all about? What surprise did the annoying girl hold now? He had some problems in faking his slow awakening, when all he had done was watch her all along.

Grumbling and murmuring, he sat up, angrily looking at her. "What is it now?"

"You need to see this."

"Couldn't it wait till the morning?" He could hardly believe himself that he spoke those words, after plotting how to overthrow her and get hold of those files she now held under his nose.

"No!" she contradicted with vehemence. "I need to know what you think of this. I can't wait."

Jumping up and down in front of him, she reminded him of a child getting the promise of a large birthday cake, unable to hold back the enthusiasm.

Strange girl, he thought. Hadn't she learned the ways of the modern socialites? Could she really have gone through university having remained unaffected by them? His wife at her best, would only lift a brow, when she was curious. Later in their relationship when she was annoyed, would rather take his credit card to get back at him in her way, for whatever slight she felt he had committed. But showing unrestrained emotion as the young student so unabashedly did in front of him was not something he was used to.

No wonder all his usual seducing and dominating tactics he had used so far had not shown the least result.

Making a big gesture of rubbing his eyes before fully opening them to her, he grabbed the papers in her hand immediately. Only hesitantly, she let them go.

– 11 –
Prof. Benning's Documents

Patience did not seem one of her strengths. Almost jumping from one leg to the other, Sophia could barely contain her euphoria, while she studied him reading the papers.

When he looked up, she couldn't keep silent any longer and burst out: "Isn't this great?"

"What? – What are you referring to?"

Grabbing the sheets to look where he was in the document, she pushed her finger on the page. "Here, see. – Nobody can gain, as it seems to be a universal weakness of all systems."

"And so what?"

"None of the companies or countries so determinedly looking for it, will have an advantage …"

"I don't see your point," he interrupted, when he could not get any sense out of her words.

"The weakness of the biometric data transfer is so universal, that they wanted you out of the way not to reveal it. And now they are after Prof. Benning, because each one of them wants to gain access and get a head-start against the others to run the competition into the ground. All we have to do is to make it public knowledge."

"That's not how things work, my dear good Samaritan."

"But you must see …"

"What? That you are a naïve child, having no idea what is going on? The human meltdown that is going to follow this discovery? And what, after all, do you think the discovery is at all?"

He slowly saw the euphoria on her features vanish and

disappointment take hold.

"You think there is no way out of this?"

"There is, there has to be. And if you don't mind and let me read what you have here, I might find out what you think is the matter."

"But are they not your papers all along?"

"No." He would not admit to her, that they were from his laboratory and he knew what they told. But they did not contain the solution, or even the way to go to get into all digital systems.

He just wanted to make certain that she had not come across any real information in them, not just the general statement that the break in might be possible.

As far as he could see, the papers did not contain any implicit details on how to gain access. This part he had intentionally kept completely away from his 'official lab' and they did not seem to have been able to work it out for themselves so far.

But by Prof. Benning handing over the information to his student, who had wanted a dissertation topic coming close to the solution, he must have some suspicions about how things might be able to work, as might have the girl herself.

"Stop fidgeting around," he rebuffed Sophia.

She seemed almost devastated that he did not think the solution she had found to be a viable way, where nobody had to be left the looser.

"But might it not mean," she slowly started again, "that Prof. Benning can't be all bad? – I mean, when he wants this to be held secure, he can't mean to sell it to the highest bidder, like we thought."

"Did we? What gave you that idea?"

His voice showed her that he was still angry with her, she had just no real idea why he would be. She had done nothing but help him. Now, thinking the files were initially his anyway, she had even given them to him, though she had promised her professor she would not show them to anybody. Now also angry, she grabbed the files and tore them out of his hands.

"What the hell …", he started, but seeing her petulant face, he got up from the bed.

"Oh, I see. You weren't supposed to show them to anyone. You just showed them to me, because you thought them to be mine anyway, and perhaps to get some more information out of me. But now, you are disappointed I didn't spill what the real breaking point of these files is. – Poor child, dream on and run back to your holy professor-daddy."

"He's not my …"

"Not your sugar-daddy and lover?"

She ignored his revolting allegations, but lifted her chin in anger, glaring at him.

"Why else would he give a woman the chance to get on board with the research?"

"You are obnoxious. No wonder they wanted you locked away, if you are always that nice to people who are trying to help you."

"Yes, help me they did. Fucked over my life is much closer to the truth, especially my well-meaning wife. Tell me, what is your real motive to get into this area of research? Unprecedented richness? Every lover you can dream of? Pleasing your professor-lover? Tell me what it is that motivates you."

When she only stared at him in anger, the fire burning inside her almost steaming out of her ears in clouds, he continued to drive her on to make her lose her reserve and finally spill the truth: "What secret desires can be fulfilled by absolute access to all knowledge?"

"You have no idea what it even means, you …, you …" The words failed to describe such a contemptible man. "What would absolute access really mean? Just a big cloud of bullshit. You seem to think what people share and do always needs to be important. But mostly it's a waste of time, things just to pass time. That would cloud your knowledge of everything so much, that you wouldn't be able to hear the truly interesting things."

"And what, if I could exactly orient the access-point and that is what all sides are after so feverishly, to get their hands on before anyone else does."

Forgetting her anger, she blurted out: "You mean, you are not only able to have the solution for opening up everything, but also can focus to one specific open portal to really get access? You mean you are not only one step further than anyone else, but many?"

Sophia sat down on the bed in astonishment. This news was too much to stomach for her to comprehend the entire effect it could have on the world, society, almost anything. She tried to picture a situation in her mind, where all information of all machines was available everywhere in the world at the same time. That was not possible. No way!

"You are leading me on. You think I am so stupid to believe a thing you say. You just want to manipulate me."

"Do I?"

"Answering me with questions won't help you. You are in no way so brilliant to outsmart the whole world. Though for the moment, even with your notes, Prof. Benning doesn't seem able to fully figure out what you are working on. He would never have handed over this material, if it already worked, or does it?"

"And what, if I could access the next bank vaults of whichever bank you like, without breaking out in a sweat, just by doing exactly what you think does not work yet?"

"Can you or can't you? Tell me outright and stop playing your elaborate mind games with me."

"You indeed are an impatient girl. No class, no style."

"I don't need class to come to the point. You just want to distract me, till I am so angry with you, your haughty majesty, that I'll stop asking questions. Don't depend on it. It won't work with me."

Sophia was impatient and stubborn, like a bloodhound, not letting its prey go once it had a scent of it, he thought. His tactic to annoy her would not work. Then indeed, he would have to swap tactics and have to resort to binding her to him with desire. But annoying her certainly was the first step to success. Women strangely craved what was hard to get. She would crawl and beg, to turn his supposed low opinion of her. That was what made women so easy prey for bad boys, and he had every intention to use what he had learned the hard way during his marriage to his advantage now.

When he still did not reply to Sophia's question, but kept looking at her musingly, she prompted him again: "What is it you can do now?"

Stepping towards her, he took the nape of her neck in one hand and leant down, silencing her lips with his own, pressing his mouth on hers, till he felt her gasp in surprise. Opening her lips as if to ask something, he took immediate advantage and slipped his tongue into her mouth, exploring, touching, stroking and effectively silencing her, making her lose any line of thought, scattering away any idea she had tried to hold on to.

Sophia's legs went weak. His touch made her heart quiver, her breath caught between them, the soft strokes of his tongue focusing all her senses on where he touched her, all the world around her forgotten.

When he finally lifted his head away from her, Sophia glanced up at him with glassy, unfocused eyes, unable to fully process what had just happened. Still looking at his hard and determined looking lips, she could not understand how they had been able to evoke such a multitude of feelings inside her, her heart still beating like after a marathon run, her brain a muzzy fuzz.

"So, silent now?" He asked her with a mockingly lifted eyebrow.

Shaking her head, trying to regain her senses, she felt embarrassed by his knowing look, feverishly trying to think of a way to hide the extent of the effect his kiss had had on her.

"What was that about?" she tried to counter nonchalantly.

"Exactly what you asked me to do," he countered snidely.

"No, I didn't …" Having no idea what he was talking about, Sophia shook her head still trying to clear her mind.

"Yes, you did," he interrupted her. "You asked me to show you what I can do now." He spoke like he was explaining something to a child, slow to understand what was common sense.

"What has that to do with …" Sudden understanding cleared her clouded eyes. "You did that just to distract me. You obnoxious, aggravating …" Searching for words, she added helplessly: "… man," as if that was the utmost accumulation of all things vile.

"But it worked, didn't it?"

"Oh, you! I won't let you win. I know you are hiding something. And I promise you, I won't give up till I get to the heart of it."

"Well, I expected as much, you little bloodhound. Now, what is it you think I am after?"

"I don't intend to let you know what I suspect, but rather want to know from you, why all those people are after you. So, if I am to help you, cut to the chase and tell me. No more distractions."

"But they are such fun. And you must admit, that I have no reason to trust you with my secrets, when you are trying to keep yours. You need to give me something, if you want to get anything from me in return. When you want to betray me anyway, I at least want something to repay me for my efforts."

"What do you want from me? I have no secrets that could interest you." Sophia was surprised what he, an experienced and successful professor and scientist, could possibly want from her, a mere aspiring grad-student. "I am not even rich, to pay you anything," Sophia added in an afterthought.

"Oh, it's not money I want. I want your body. For every piece of information I give you, I want access to your body."

"You are crude. I'm not a whore, to pay with my body." Though Sophia had to admit to herself, that this attractive professor even asking for this, strangely made her insides quiver. Did he really want her or was this just another of his little tricks to manipulate her?

"Oh, it's not only whores that use their body in such a way, my dear naïve girl. It's the way of women all the world over."

"Your world, maybe, but not mine. I won't give you my body for information."

"Then, no information."

"Oh, you didn't want to give it to me anyway, so no loss. Even if you had, it would not necessarily have been the truth. – And I'm even beginning to think that you don't have any information to begin with. You are just notoriously annoying, playing cat-and-mouse with all the parties that are interested in what they think you have found out, but in truth, you have nothing. You just play them, like you try to play me, to get whatever you want from them. That is it, isn't it? That is all you have."

"If it makes you feel better to believe that, when you so obviously crave to get the information, so be it."

"Oh no. You don't have information to share. That is, why Prof. Benning can't figure out what you are working on exactly."

"Whatever." Prof. Lynford nonchalantly lifted his shoulders and turned away from her, going back to her bed and lying down. On his back, the arms under his head, her t-shirt rode threateningly close up to his male parts. Sophia could not help but follow the lines of his well-formed anatomy up and remain at the dark shadow between his legs. Her eyes grew large round globes, when a bulge between his legs tented the t-shirt. She heard him chuckle from the bed and her eyes shot up to his face, just to discover that he had observed her every reaction to him with intent scrutiny.

"Come over here, and we'll both get what we want."

"No!" Sophia shot up from her seat at her desk and hurried into the kitchen, avoiding having to see him. She started to prepare tea again, just to keep her hands busy. When she came back with a single cup for herself, he mocked her. "What, no peace offering for your guest?"

"You are not my guest. And if it were not late at night, I would gladly throw you out right now."

"You let me stay, because you want to spend the night with me." He smiled at her with fake joy, as if saying 'you just don't want to confess your feelings honestly, but I still know'.

He could not know, not about this extraordinary desire of hers. It felt so unreasonable that this obnoxious man could evoke such feelings, when so far no other person had even come close to arousing her interest. But his closeness made her feel tingly, more aware of her surrounding, more aware of him and his male attractiveness, his scent, the timbre in his voice, resonating deep inside her body. His irritating behavior did nothing to distract her feelings, which were all focused solely on him.

Grumpy about his arrogance and for knowing how attractive she found him, Sophia stamped to her wardrobe and took out a further blanket and pillow for herself to prepare the couch as her night quarter.

"No stress relief then?" he commented drily from the bed.

At the end of her patience, Sophia snapped back: "If that is all sex is to you, no wonder your ex-wife left you."

He remained silent, after a while turning his back towards her and pulling his blanket over his body.

Sophia knew that her comment had been a cruel thing to say. She did not know herself any more, when being in his presence. Normally, she was so calm and always in the middle of settling all conflicts around her. What had caused her to lose her temper with him repeatedly now and strike out so harshly? The one thing she knew, she could not leave him like that for the night, thinking the worst of her.

Hesitantly, she stepped closer to the bed and reluctantly

offered her apologies.

"I'm really sorry I said that. I know that it's not even true, not in the least."

"What do you know how much sex was part of the reason for my wife leaving me? You know nothing at all about it. And you don't know anything about …"

"I know … – that I have no right to judge." She knew that he did not want to make things easy for her to apologize to him.

"… sex with me."

He gripped her arm and with a forceful pull, had her spread out over him.

Sophia shrieked in surprise at this sudden attack.

"But I am open for you to find out. To our mutual pleasure," he calmly commented.

Struggling against him, Sophia tried to get up, tangled in his blanket and attempting to avoid any intimate touch with him. To her astonishment, he did not try to hold her back when she finally managed to get up from her undignified position scrambling on top of him. She would have scratched and bit him, if he had tried anything. She glared down at him, from her position next to the bed, but was just too angry with him to form coherent words. Just fuming and spluttering about his arrogance, she offendedly marched to her makeshift bed, before realizing she still had to change for the night. With upturned chin, completely ignoring his presence, she marched to the bathroom for her nightly preparations, before going back to her couch. He did not comment on her behavior and she, attempting to erase his entire being from her senses, could not tell, if he even looked at her, as she tried hard to keep her gaze averted from him, not to allow him any more chance to annoy and taunt her.

Before being able to fall asleep, Sophia mused. What arrogance the professor had shown, to expect her to easily fall into bed with him, 'for their mutual pleasure' as he called it. Was that all he ever thought about? What pleasure would he give her? He was so arrogant that he just presumed she had to be attracted to him. She would rather die than to let him know that he was right.

But why did he think he was so very irresistible to womankind? Because of his good looks? He certainly had those in abundance, dratted man that he was, with his dark, brooding, well chiseled features. Her sister would describe him as a man no woman would push from the edge of her bed. Why else did he think he was irresistible? He could not have had very much opportunity to put his nonexistent charms into practice while he was married. Because now he was divorced? Because he was an ex-professor, an ex-convict, an escaped prisoner, a fugitive, from criminals and the police both? What woman in her right mind would find that attractive?

But what annoyed Sophia most was the fact that he did not even pretend to have feelings for her or try to seduce her and win her favors. No, far from it. He tried to annoy and offend her any chance he got. Pretending to come to the rational conclusion that sleeping with her would be for their mutual benefit.

What an oaf!

Sophia might have been a rational person in all things, but in love she wanted her feelings to dominate her. Well, they did and she had to admit, that if he had tried the least bit of real seduction and charm on her, he might have succeeded quite easily. With all the adoration she had stored up for him for so long, it would not have been hard for him to reach. But as it was, she was determined to lock away her attraction to him as securely as possible and throw away the key to those erring feelings. Perhaps, she re-thought, best keep the key, to put more attraction away any time in the future. An arrogant and unfeeling man like him did not deserve her devotion, thought right now, she seemed to be stuck with him. She just could not bring it upon herself to leave him alone with the problems he faced.

But Sophia would have been rather surprised to know the real motives for Prof. Lynford's strange actions, the reasons going around in his head, while Sophia turned restlessly on her unaccustomed sleeping position on her couch.

Because of the betrayal of his wife, his distrust for all women sat deep. Their apparent softness and weakness was just a show, while their cold hearts were not to be trusted. But his experiences, seeing all the abuse and violence in prison, made him crave to regain the rule over his own sexuality and exacting dominance over a woman, and an attractive and spirited one at that, made him lust for her in a way he had never felt before. Those deeply buried causes made him uneasy and withdrawn from his usual calmness and feeling of superiority.

The girl kept him on his toes with her fast switches between anger and lust. He could not bring himself to let down his guard enough to trust her, while wanting to sate his lust without engaging his emotions was certainly tempting.

Both deep in thought, turned around in their beds for a long while, before exhaustion made them fall asleep in the early hours of the morning.

Sophia was generally a slow riser in the morning, her alarm clock usually ringing at 7 a.m. She struggled to turn off the offending interruption of her sleep, but her swift touch to the position where her alarm clock should be, hit only air.

Opening first one then a slit of her second eye, she looked around, seeing her apartment from a totally unusual perspective. Only slowly did her brain start to function and work out, why she found herself on her sofa, while the alarm clock next to her bed rang relentlessly.

Jumping up to stop the ruckus, she detected too late that Prof. Lynford was patiently sitting in front of her computer and had been attentively observing her every move.

Suddenly uncomfortably aware of her old nightshirt, she pulled on its lower seams to hide her legs as much as possible, stumbling in her steps, before rushing into the bathroom after a mumbled 'Good morning', to hide from his intense gaze.

Only when fully dressed and after doing her morning routine, did she dare to come out again. Wordlessly she went into the kitchen and made breakfast.

Prof. Lynford had once again not asked for her permission to use her computer, but seemed to have already worked on it for hours, the files from Prof. Benning spread all over her desk.

Their information somehow seemed to have hit a nerve with Prof. Lynford, but it was hard to guess, because his demeanor gave nothing away. He should be a poker player in Sophia's opinion. No emotion showed on his face, and whenever it did, she was not sure if she could trust it or if it was a well-guarded attempt of the man to manipulate her.

The silence prevailed between them during their breakfast, till Sophia could not stand it any longer and directly asked her involuntary guest: "You do not seem happy with being here, but rather seem angry that I freed you from your captors. But that can't be, can it? Not after what I saw in the video."

"Why not? They at least would have supported me in getting the information I wanted."

"What?" Sophia jumped up in shock and nearly threw over her small breakfast table between them.

"You ungrateful… – Oh, you …" Lost for words, she once again stared angrily at him. "You just want to raise my anger. You can't mean you would prefer to still be with them, still bound to a bed and used by at least one of them."

"Michael, yes."

"What?"

"It was Michael you saw in the video. He was the one who protected me in prison and also the one who accompanied me on my prison break."

"And he kept you bound to a bed, so he did not seem all too sure about your gratitude. Why do you pretend you were happy there? You are acting more like a spoiled brat than an intelligent man."

"And what are you? Rushing into a mafia safe-house, unarmed and completely unprepared, to free a man you find attractive …"

"I don't," Sophia interrupted embarrassed.

"… and wanting to force me into being grateful to you. For what? For a foolhardy action you rushed into without thinking or preparation, not listening to reason, the police or your parents. No, what the foolish girl wants, she gets. Isn't it so?"

"No. You ungrateful idiot. I don't care what you think of me. I didn't do it to gain anything from you. I thought to help you. But if you so obviously don't appreciate it, you might as well go and not feed yourself on my expenses. – Go! I don't want to see you here any longer. Leave my apartment. You were obviously happy back where you were, so you might as well go back to it. I won't try to help you any longer. Why I even bothered to try, I can no longer fathom. I should have searched for a new job and at least would have done something useful. Instead, I foolishly tried to help you."

Angry with herself for even getting so angry about such a worthless and arrogant man, she took his unfinished plate away from him and started to put the breakfast dishes away. But he stopped her and took hold of his plate.

"At least, let me finish breakfast, you hotheaded Valkyrie."

"No. They can feed you, if they want to. If they are indeed mafia, they can better afford the food."

Tearing at the plate he still held, his toast slipped and he caught it with his other hand, putting the entire bit in his mouth.

"Oh, just finish and then go," she gave in reluctantly and let him have the plate back.

Sophia had never behaved so childishly to bodily fight for food, not even with her older brother and sister during childhood. She felt extremely unsettled and turned away from him, leaving her own breakfast behind almost untouched.

Instead, she went to the computer to have a look through the things he had done there, but he had meticulously erased his browser history. Even all cookies were deleted, so no hint about what he had done or seen remained. Her annoyance with him only rose and that somehow completely made her forget the fear she had felt of him last night.

At least the documents from Prof. Benning still open on her desk, gave her some hints to what he had found especially interesting in them. He had taken out some of the statistics and scratched out numbers he seemed not to agree with. While all the wrong numbers were again listed in a neat row on the side. Letters were associated to those and read in line, they gave a strange result: 'darkwood'.

Now what did that mean? And why did Prof. Benning's files contain a secret code she could not decipher, but which Prof. Lynford immediately found? Did Prof. Benning know about the secret message? Could he have placed it? Who was the intended recipient for it? Who had leaked or manipulated the data?

Sophia's head spun around with questions?

"What does 'darkwood' mean?" she finally gave up and asked Prof. Lynford, almost certain that he would not answer her.

For once answering her, he made her jump with surprise.

"It is the solution of the puzzle."

"What puzzle?"

"The whole research."

"But what does it mean? Is it a place?"

"It is what is says. Dark wood."

"But what …?"

"No buts. Dark wood is the solution."

"Oh. – You are helpful as ever."

"I answered your question. To the fullest of my knowledge. How can I help that you ask the wrong questions?"

"You promise to answer my questions, if I ask others?"

"No."

"Thought as much. So why tempt me?"

"Because it is fun."

"You are gross. It is absolutely no fun to talk to you. I can't reciprocate in your enjoyment of the situation."

"Your loss, not mine, dear girl."

"I'm not your dear girl, you hear? And when you are finished with your breakfast, I want you to leave."

"Which one?"

"What 'which one'?"

"Which breakfast? Tomorrow's or in a week's time?"

"Today's. You won't get another one from me."

"What a cruel girl you are. I see, tomorrow's breakfast will have to be my treat."

"I won't take anything from you."

"And you won't allow me to make good on the hospitality you granted me? How ungrateful of you. You really should let me, or I'll feel hopelessly indebted to you."

"Not my problem. You'll get over it quite quickly, I am sure."

Angry as she was, she still went back to her little breakfast table to get hold of her morning coffee, not allowing that obnoxious man to divert her from her essential morning dose of caffeine.

"Ah, you calmed down, little hothead."

Annoyed with him, Sophia turned her head and continued drinking her coffee, pretending to ignore him.

The ringing of her telephone fortunately interrupted the uncomfortable atmosphere in the room.

– 12 –
Unexpected Telephone Call

The call came from an unknown number and while she would usually not accept those calls with a suppressed caller identification, as they mostly were from spam-advertisements, Sophia now took it, just to get away from her guest.

The voice coming over the landline she knew well, Prof. Benning. He did not wait for her greeting, but gave her instructions immediately. "Search your mails for 'dark wood' and follow the directives there. Don't call me back on this number or answer the mail. I'll get in contact when it's safe."

He hung up, leaving her stunned and utterly surprised. Prof. Benning also knew about 'dark wood', whatever its actual meaning was.

Prof. Lynford observed her every move, but did not question her about the telephone call. Had he heard the voice anyway, she wondered. Leaning back on her couch where she had slept, he sipped his coffee, seemingly relaxed and unmoved by all the events around him, not showing the least bit of emotion that all that had happened was because of him.

Sophia immediately sat down in front of her computer and searched her mails for the word 'dark wood', as Prof. Benning had instructed. She found, that all her new e-mails had already been opened and read. Prof. Lynford! What an inquisitive man, wanting to know everything about her, but revealing nothing about himself. But she would no longer put up with his bad behavior. He had to leave, even if she died from curiosity about what was really going on.

She found the one mail Prof. Benning referred to easily

enough. It was disguised as a spam mail, starting with the usual advertisement for a sex-enhancing drug. Scrolling through the long rows of text, she found the message Prof. Benning had intended for her.

'Project Darkwood', it started. Naming diverse companies and politically as well as economically important persons, before ending in an instruction to meet with him on a certain location as soon as she had read this message. Their meeting point was a place deep in the forest, where her professor usually went jogging.

What should she do with the mail, she wondered. Printing it out together with the sender protocol and completely deleting it from her computer, for her seemed to be the wisest choice.

At least she was glad that the mail seemed to have been untouched by her snoopy guest. It must have come in directly before she had opened it, from the timestamp the mail had.

Putting the mail into an envelope together with some other papers regarding the project, she addressed it and put a postage stamp on it. She would send the news home to her parents, where she still received part of her mail anyway. Addressing the letter to herself, her parents would keep the letter till she came home next.

She also wrote a short message to Mr. Arnestone, which she would put into his mailbox at the apartment complex, to let him know that she was well.

Picking up her iPad and rucksack, where she had put her notebook and the information she had gotten from Prof. Benning, she went to the door, picking up her jacket and car keys, waiting.

"Are you leaving?" Prof. Lynford inquired.

"No, you are. Get ready."

"You want to leave and want me out of the house in the meanwhile. Throwing me to the wolves, you heartless creature."

"I am not. And you assured me quite believably, that your dear Michael was such a caring protector. So you'll do well without my further help. Now go!"

"And if I don't?" But Prof. Lynford already went to put his cup back into the sink in the kitchen. Having nothing to wear except the wrinkled shirt and trousers from the day before, which she had put into the washing machine and the dryer over night, he stood next to her in mere minutes, waiting for her to open the door.

After a rain shower during the night had noticeably cooled the air outside, Sophia went back to her wardrobe and pulled out one of her large hoodies. She hated jogging, but her sport-fanatic sister had bought that one for her to convince her to do more for her health. Sophia had never worn the large dark jacket, but though tightly, it might fit the large man.

Holding it out to him, he looked at her with raised eyebrows.

"For you." She pushed the jacket at him.

"The good Samaritan through and through, it seems."

Turning her face away, she did not comment on that, but he took the hoody and put it on. While it hung wide and slack on her, it fit him tightly, but at least would keep him warm for the moment. After the night's rain, it was still grey and quite cold outside after the heatwave of the last weeks. Even such an annoying man she could not throw out without adequate protection against the elements.

She drew a relieved breath, when he followed her out without further protests, watching her lock her door. He was out, finally. She had feared he would make much more trouble for her and was glad that it had gone so smoothly.

He even lead the way to the lift, as if knowing his way around her apartment complex quite well. That raised her suspicions immediately. He had been completely knocked out, when they had brought him up here. She hit the button for the ground floor for him and the sub-level, where her car stood, mostly unused during her semester periods and only used for driving the long way home to her parents, which was unreachable through public transportation.

But Prof. Lynford refused to step out of the elevator on the ground floor, instead pressing the button for the doors to close again.

"I'm coming down with you, exiting from there."

Sophia just nodded and did not show him any more of her anger, relieved that he so easily went along. Two could play the cold and unaffected part Prof. Lynford played so well.

When she stepped out, Prof. Lynford followed her. She tried to let him pass and showed him the direction to the exit, but he did not leave her side, just stood waiting next to her.

"What are you waiting for?" she asked irritated.

"You. Just go on as you would and don't bother with me."

"Good. I won't. I wash my hands off you."

Turning around, she went to her car and unlocked it. Walking around it once, to check if everything was in order, as she so rarely used it.

Satisfied with her superficial check, she got in at the driver's side and started the car, when the passenger door suddenly opened and without asking, Prof. Lynford slipped into the seat next to her.

"What are you doing here? Get out!" Angrily, she tried to shove him out, but without effort, he caught her arms and pressed her back into her seat.

Closing in, she felt his breath on her lips, when he started to talk. "Admit it, you would miss me, if I obeyed you."

Lowering his lips, he gently touched hers.

Sophia felt angry enough to burst and a suppressed scream escaped her lips, her body fighting against the effect he had on her, trembling with desire, only heightened by her boiling fury.

He deepened his kiss and to her annoyance, her body went weak, her lips enjoying his teasing exploration, burning for more. When he felt her capitulation, his lips drew back.

When she came back to her senses, anger bubbled out of her in harsh words. "You are insufferable. I'm not your toy to play around with. You told me you didn't want my help."

"But now that I have it, why should I give it up?"

Sophia stared open mouthed at him due to his surprising complete turn-around.

"You angered Michael's friends by abducting me. They won't so easily accept me back to hide me again now."

"They hid you?"

"Yes, among other things. Till you stormed in and made their efforts useless."

"And binding you to the bed and abusing you was just a nice treat of your dear friend Michael's protection?" Sophia could not hide the disbelief in her voice.

"They didn't trust Michael and didn't leave him alone with me to help me escape. He tried to co-operate with them, to convince them of his loyalty."

"And why should I believe a word you say now, when nothing you said to me before made any sense or gave me any hint of real information?"

"Perhaps, because your apartment is bugged?"

"What!" It took Sophia a moment to take in that piece of information. "How do you know that?"

"Michael swiped it. – And the hook in your computer was not all too hard to find and eliminate."

Sophia took a relieved sigh, before her worries rose up again.

"But why spy on me? I am just a fresh graduate, not even managing to get a research topic through to continue with my graduate studies. What sense would it make to put expensive surveillance equipment in my apartment? – Assuming, that for even a tiny moment, I believe a word you say," she added stubbornly.

Merton, Prof. Lynford, smiled knowingly, which only served to rouse her hackles the more.

'Arrogant oaf, thinking he can toy with me, with selecting the information he feeds me,' she thought, but he interrupted her.

"Drive. We should best leave right away."

"Why? Considering they – whoever 'they' are – have bugged my apartment, why should they have left out my car?"

"Because they didn't know you had one. Michael seemed convinced you didn't have one, as they told him you always walked during semester. Or was he wrong?"

"No. Just maintaining the car all semester, when everything can easily be reached on foot in town, is just an expense I can easily spare."

"A real spendthrift you are. Pretending that for once a woman should have a sense of money."

"Stop!" Sophia was not willing to endure his mockery a moment longer. "Either you are silent or you leave the car on the spot. I won't take any more of your hostility against me. You know nothing about me and you are the last person who has a right to judge me."

She looked at him for a moment, but he for once did as she said and kept his mouth shut, pressing his lips firmly together to make the fact clear that he did not intend to talk any more.

Watching him dubiously, not believing that he would follow her order so easily, she recognized the mirth in his eyes.

'That bastard! He found the situation amusing.'

Fuming, Sophia turned away from him and started the car. What options did she really have? With his earlier attack on her, he had shown her that he could easily subdue her any time he wanted. And what would hinder him from knocking her out and leaving her or taking her with him in the back of her own car? At least, when driving herself, she would still have some control and he would have a much harder time harming her.

Sophia put the car into gear and left the garage. When she was at the front of the building, she stopped for a moment and left her message for Mr. Arnstone.

Prof. Lynford was bent down in his seat the whole time hiding his presence and only came up, when they were well away from the garage and the apartment complex.

He did not ask where she was going or indicated where he wanted to be dropped off, so Sophia went on with her own agenda, heading for the post office in town, to mail the thick letter to herself.

Near the jogging trail, where she knew her professor liked to hike and run occasionally, because he had a large picture of one of the sights of the trail in his office, which they had discussed one time, she parked her car in one of the farthest parking lots from the path.

If they were followed or Prof. Benning's mail discovered,

Sophia wanted to see who was coming after her. Having no weapons and firmly being against the private possession of guns, she would not change her mind now. It would just result in her being shot anyway, she consoled herself.

Waiting in the car till she was sure no vehicle had followed her, Prof. Lynford remained entirely silent next to her, as if he wanted her to forget his presence. Aware of his occasional glances, she was the first who broke the long silence between them.

"What is it you want? Why are you still here?"

"Here? I have no idea where we are. And wanting? How would you take it, if I started with 'you'?"

"What – with me?" Not understanding his meaning, she turned away from glancing into the car's mirrors to observe their surrounding area and directly looked at him.

"I want you, as you want me, by the way. Don't try to deny it."

"I don't …" Sophia tried to object, but his last words overrode her protest.

"Why are we here? Does Prof. Benning know you are not following his instructions?"

"What?" Sophia blustered. "You know? How?"

"Did you think I would not find his message? Be glad I deactivated the hook on your computer before it came in or we would have company right now. – So, what are you waiting for? Prof. Benning is waiting for you, surely to tell you what an exceedingly bad guy I am."

"And what will you do in the meanwhile?"

"Wait for you patiently, as a good boyfriend should."

"You are not my …" She could not say the word, she was too embarrassed about his nonchalant suggestion.

"But you would like me to be."

"No! You are presumptuous, annoying, arrogant, … – Who would want that in a boyfriend?"

"You." He smiled and surprised her by planting a kiss right on her mouth, making any further protest from her impossible.

As soon as he felt no protest coming from her, he deepened their kiss. His lips exploring hers, his tongue teasing the seam of her closed mouth, intruding, as soon as she let out a sensual moan.

His hands went to discover her body, holding her neck, stroking her softly, his other hand following her body down, stroking the side of her breast, feeling her racing heartbeat all through her clothes, her gasps caught between his lips.

'Yes,' he thought. 'The girl could well be seduced and keeping her on her toes with uncertainty certainly worked in his favor. She fell into his arms like a ripe fruit. Perfect.'

When he lifted his head, she blinked her eyes, slowly coming back to reality.

"Why did you do that?"

"To seal our relationship," he stated matter of factly.

"Do you think, I would help you more, if I were emotionally bound to you? – Just so you know, that is not necessary. As I told you, my offer of help stands. I don't think you did the things they imprisoned you for. So, seducing me won't help your cause with me. It rather makes me wonder whatever it is you want to hide."

His eyes opened wide, indicating his surprise about her directness.

He certainly had underestimated this young girl. No wonder Prof. Benning wanted her in his team, when she kept a clear head even while her body reacted so unrestrainedly to him.

Sophia interrupted his thoughts: "Now, what is it to be?

Do you trust me enough to let me out of your sight to talk to Prof. Benning? After all, you have my car hostage."

"You could leave with Prof. Benning."

"And what would I gain from that? He fears he is being followed and does not want to lead them to me. Going with him would only bring me directly into the center of all the accumulated intrigues around you and your laboratory."

"You trust him not to harm you?"

"Yes."

"Then go. Be careful."

She smiled at him suddenly, the first uncensored sign of pure joy enlightening her whole face, taking his breath away.

"What was that about?" he asked uncertain about her suddenly unguarded and open friendliness.

"You really behave like a boyfriend should. Worrying about me like one."

Now he felt a smile break out on his own face. Winking at her he bent to her, giving her a soft peck on her cheek. "Go now. Don't let Prof. Benning wait. I'll keep an eye on the street for you."

"Thank you."

– 13 –
Meeting with Prof. Benning

Leaving the car, her heart was still not back at a normal rhythm. Prof. Lynford – Merton – she for the first time used his first name in her mind. Flirting was far out of her limited experience with men. Her heart leaping almost out of her breast, when he had directed his smile at her. How should a sensible girl defend herself against such a full-force attack, Sophia wondered. Her heart was certainly not up to resisting him. The only thought keeping her grounded was, that she did not think that he would be interested in her, if things around them were any different and he did not urgently need her help. Though he still tried to deny that fact, arrogant man that he was.

That thought brought her out of her dreamy haze instantly. When she came across Prof. Benning after a bend on the path, she was back to her crisp and effective self the professor was used to.

Prof. Benning must have kept an eye out for her, as he approached her, confident that she was alone.

"Good morning, Prof. Benning."

"No time for pleasantries. They are following my every step and I had a hard time getting them not to follow me onto my jogging route any longer. – Took me almost two months to get them bored enough to leave me alone here. But I mustn't deviate from my normal times. So, hurry along."

"Who … – Why … – What?" Sophia stammered, unable to form all the questions which stormed her head at once at the professor's cryptic words.

"They. I have no idea from what secret service they are or if they are even locals. But enough of them contacted me as soon as I stepped foot in Lynford's laboratory, informing me that all information should exclusively go through them. If there was just one organization, o.k., but 20? How do they think that should even work? Fools, all of them."

"But why? What is going on?"

"I thought you had taken time to have a look through the material I gave you last night."

"Yes. But from the report, the whole thing is just a theory, not really working yet. And even if it could, what would be the practical use of this transmission interference. All data cables and devices are secured, use secure code and even wireless transfers use their own security transmission identifiers. What would be the use of a data interference, after an iris photo has been taken?"

"That is the beauty of the concept. The photo already exists and as such could be reproduced, copied at will, whenever it is necessary for secure access."

"Oh!" Finally, Sophia began to understand the implications of the idea, where exactly the access to data was intended to work and why the secret services and the mafia were so interested in it. At its weakest point, the least secure instance, the taking of the photo of the iris or the placing of the real iris in front of the security system or whatever means had been chosen to secure an access-point, the process of data-reproduction would obtain the essential information to gain unlimited access, wherever and whenever required. Not, as Sophia had first believed, would the storage of data or its transfer be the points under attack. Those were highly secured by encryption algorithms by now. But it was the presence of the iris or whatever security method used which would itself be reproducible at any time, with a technique so fantastic, that she still could not fully wrap her mind around the idea that it might possibly work. Sophia tried to formulate the idea in her head, murmuring her thoughts aloud: "Being able to manipulate and create a reproduction of the access information to areas of the highest security, would make all those security facilities invalid at once and worldwide at that."

"Exactly," Prof. Benning confirmed, out of breath from the previous part of his run.

"No wonder 20 organizations want that knowledge. And those surely are only the first which have heard about the impending discovery. The rest will follow."

"I worry more about those who haven't contacted me yet. Though even from the 20, half haven't even bothered to identify themselves."

"But how can I help you?" Sophia asked. "From the material you gave me, I didn't even see the full potential that the research could possibly succeed to such an extent."

"No wonder. The material was carefully manipulated to give no hint about a possibility that the theory might work in practice. Instead, it tried to prove everything as false."

"Yes. But some of the results were so obviously wrong, that I immediately detected it. Whoever did this, was not very immersed in the topic."

"My thoughts exactly." Prof. Benning confirmed. "So why bother with that data presentation at all? That is, what I now want to find out and that is where I need your help."

"But wouldn't Prof. Lynford be able to help you much better with this?"

"I can't reach him. He is no longer in prison where he should be. Whoever has him, will surely torture him to get the information they want. And besides, I doubt he would be willing to help me, after ..."

Loud steps came closer along the path they were on and Prof. Benning immediately jumped off the trail and went behind a large tree trunk.

"Go on, as if you are taking a stroll, Sophia."

Sophia tried to appear unfazed by the behavior of her professor, but seeing her sedate professor with his greying hair jump with fear, for the first time made her aware of the real danger they were all in.

Her steps slowed to a leisurely stroll, though her breathing certainly would have given her away. Trying to regulate her intake of air only made her gasp, when two men, all clad in black like security guards, with jet-black weapon holsters strapped to their sides, came into view. Fortunately, the path was very winding here, so they could not have seen Prof. Benning hide, but with those bulky men around, she trembled in fear.

"Have you seen a man, greying hair, around 40?" The bulkier of the two men asked without preamble, when coming close to her. They both looked so similar and nondescript, that Sophia would have a hard time identifying them. They were ideal for their post, to hide and mingle, without being recognized. Their hair was cropped so short that she could not even tell exactly which color it was. Their emotionless stare from their dark, hooded eyes boring into her unblinking, not giving her much chance but to answer, was eerie.

"I just came here. So far, besides you, I haven't met anyone. But I came out her for peace anyway."

"You sure?" The bulky one questioned her statement.

"I'm certain. I just came in from the lot over there. I haven't had much time to have seen anyone yet." Sophia motioned to the closest parking area, where a few cars stood, just not hers.

"He must have gone further up," the second, skinnier one stated.

"Are you his bodyguards? Should I tell him where you are searching for him, should I come across a man of your description?"

They both looked at her hard, before the second one answered sternly, as if she was an unruly child for even suggesting such a thing: "No. We'll find him. Don't bother yourself."

They turned around and left without further greeting or even a 'thank you'.

Prof. Benning had obviously not been right about losing his escort after two months. They had just adjusted their methods for him to no longer be aware of their presence. They did not have any intention of leaving him out of their sight for even one minute.

When she approached the area where she had left Prof. Benning, going back the way she had come, he whispered from behind the tree where he hid himself.

"Where is your car?"

"We can't go there," Sophia tried to distract him, well aware that Prof. Lynford was waiting there for her.

"We must. You must drive me up to my car, or they will suspect that I have gone on a detour. Lead the way. I will stay out of the clearing. And don't speak. They might still be near."

Reluctantly, Sophia went ahead, going down the winding path to her car, still waiting in the furthest spot of the last parking area for the jogging and hiking routes.

Using her automatic door opener from her key repeatedly, she tried to alert Prof. Lynford inside of her approach and that something was going on. She could not see him sitting in the car, when she came closer. Was he still inside or had he left the car? What should she do, if he had? Sophia calculated her options. She could drive Prof. Benning to where he wanted to go and then come back for Prof. Lynford, if she could get him out of the car undetected.

But the options were taken from her, when Prof. Lynford and not Prof. Benning stepped out of the woods close to the door on the passenger side of the car and got in.

Opening the driver's door, she bent in. "Did you hear?"

"Yes. Very interesting."

Now, Prof. Benning also appeared, but stopped short, when he saw Prof. Lynford sitting in the car.

"How did he get here?" he asked accusingly, the disappointment about her supposed betrayal heavy in his voice.

"That is a rather long story. But I think you should better get into the car and both hide your presence in there, before the two thugs or others come back and see you."

"Well, why didn't you say anything?"

"I wanted to, but we got interrupted."

"Do you trust him?"

Sophia swallowed hard at that question from Prof. Benning. How could she set her trust in the annoying man in her car, keeping all kinds of information from her and trying to play her at will?

But Prof. Lynford opened his car door again, leaning out to Prof. Benning.

"Get in, you fool, or you will put us all in more danger than you already have."

Prof Benning did not hesitate any longer, but got into the back seat, drawing a blanket she was sure she had left in the trunk of her car, over his head.

"What are you doing here, Lynford?"

"I could ask the same question, but that would not lead us anywhere. Who were those two following you today?"

"I don't know. I have never seen them before."

"So new guys. Brilliant."

"I don't know."

"Even better."

"What?" Prof. Benning's voice came like a squeak from the back seat, when Sophia, after having a look around to ascertain no other cars were around close, got behind the wheel.

"Irony, my dear friend. Irony was never your strong point, was it?" Prof. Lynford was back at his most biting cynicism.

"Stop it! We have no time to argue here. We need to work together to get out of this alive." Sophia did not know where she took the courage to cut off both the leading professors in her area, but she felt their childish bickering and fight for superiority, men so excelled in, really had no place and more importantly no time here. "We have much bigger problems than 'irony' right now."

"Yes, who impregnated my wife."

"She wasn't your wife when …"

"STOP! Right now! Or I throw you both out of my car and you can see how far you get on your own."

The following silence was deafening. Sophia could not believe that those two haughty men really had followed her command, though she had shouted it out in anger so unlike her, but she could not say that she had much patience left for their annoying aversion towards each other. And all of that over a woman Prof. Lynford should be glad to have gotten rid of, from what she already knew about his background story.

At least now, she could compose herself enough to start her car, without the two men costing her the last nerve.

"Prof. Benning, now you have the source you wanted, and you, Prof. Lynford, have a scapegoat, to distract from yourself, while you continue your rehabilitation of your own good name. So why fight unnecessarily and use the precious little time we have? Better get to formulate a plan and I would suggest quite quickly. If I drive the direct route to the parking lot of the opposite end of the trail, we have no more than a quarter of an hour."

For a moment, both men still remained quiet, before both almost simultaneously asked: "Do you trust him?" "You trust that man?"

"Yes and yes. And as we have the same goal, you should, too."

"We have?" Prof. Lynford questioned her statement first.

"Yes, we do. To survive. And with the deathly weapons the two guys in the forest had, that is not overly likely, if you keep fighting each other."

"Jenny is Vanessa's daughter. But that was long before she even met you." Prof. Benning interfered hectically.

"Does Jenny know who her mother is? Vanessa never mentioned having a daughter."

"No. Vanessa gave her up after birth and never asked about her. They never met afterwards."

"That's not a topic for now!" Sophia interrupted. Were those two men dense or totally wrapped up in their jealousy? "How do you intend to proceed to handle the secret agents following your every step?"

"That is exactly what this is all about," Prof. Benning's sad voice was heartbreaking. "They control her every step at the private school she is in. If they find me getting out of line, they threaten to harm her."

"Oh. I am sorry." Sophia was really shocked to hear that. She knew how much Prof. Benning cared for his young daughter Jenny and how worried he was about her safety. "I'd thought you had sent her to Switzerland and she would be safe there."

"No. They have her under as close surveillance there as they have me here."

For the first time back in the car, Prof. Lynford spoke in a less than snide tone. "So that is why you betrayed me and took over the laboratory."

"I had no choice. They threatened to kill her."

All business, devoid of any emotion, Prof. Lynford continued: "Who gave you that report you handed over to Sophia last night?"

"You saw that?"

"Yes. Who gave it to you?"

"Dr. Ranston. He worked on it with a few of his colleagues. That is what irritates me so much about it. Being at the center of research, they should have gotten the basic facts right, but they didn't."

Dr. Ranston with both Dr. Alfredson and Mr. Farraday were Prof. Lynford's key research team, not only working on the state funded research, but also being part of his privately built and financed tag-team for his own research. The encrypted information in the report was their message intended for him and him alone. Now the appearance of their key-word in the errors of the report finally made sense.

"I need that report again."

Sophia stopped the car at the side of the street and took hold of her backpack she had stuffed and placed at the feet of the back seat behind her and took the folder out, before continuing the drive.

"Is it safe to carry it around with you?" Prof. Benning wondered. "It's the only copy we have and it took me enough stealth to get this one out already."

"I copied it." Sophia admitted. "But the second one is safe for the moment."

"Where is it?" Both men almost jumped down her throat at her calm words.

"If something should happen to me, I hope you will say your condolences to my parents."

Looking at each other, the two professors slowly comprehended where the copy would be soon.

"But is this safe?" Prof. Lynford was still not convinced by her methods. "Your parents will be the first they contact, if they find out you are involved. And as the two men in the woods have already seen your face, that is a possibility we have to consider."

"The snail mail delivery will take a few days. So that gives us at least two or three days to get out of this, before the letter will arrive anyway. And I very much hope you will have made an effective plan to get us out of this accumulated mess till then."

"Entrusting your secrets to snail mail, Sophia? In what film did you see that nonsense?" Prof. Lynford grumbled, but Prof. Benning came to her defense.

"At least, as unregistered mail, they won't have a way to track down her delivery and the material is safe till then. And as long as they don't connect you with me, your plan could work. They already know I didn't accept you for your graduate research next semester."

"What? No! I thought you liked the work I had done. I need to get in. I can't afford to wait. I can't pay for an entire semester without being able to begin my research work."

"I know, Sophia. I just had to distract them to get them to leave you alone. It was hard enough to find a reason to see you last night, without giving anything away. They believe I declined your latest topic offer yesterday."

A bit angry with her professor for making her openly appear a failure, a thought began to rise in her.

"But how can you know what they think?" Sophia burst out with those words, unable to hold her suspicion back, angry with herself about her lack of restraint.

Prof. Lynford snidely threw in: "Have you still not worked it out yet? He is working for them. How could you lead him back to me without thinking about my safety, and your own?"

"Of course I am working for them. They'll kill my daughter if I don't."

"Who are they? I thought 20 different groups contacted you. Who of them blackmails you with your daughter?"

"It's irrelevant, who they are," Prof. Lynford interrupted. "It's important that none of them with an interest in the research gets hold of the solution. – And for that I need access to my laboratory."

"You can't even come close to it. There's no way in for you."

"So, Benning, you would let me in, if you could?"

"Name it what it is you need from it and I'll try to get it out to you."

Silence followed this offer of Prof. Benning.

"Oh, crap," Sophia swore, guessing at what the problem between the two men now was, when the silence between them stretched.

"Just tell him. Prof. Benning won't try to research your secrets on his own. He is much too aware that he will be expendable for 'them', as you were, as soon as they thought they had found an alternative to you in Prof. Benning, when you refused to cooperate. – Was it not what had happened? If we want to survive, we have to work together. No secret agendas, no leaving anyone hanging. Is that clear?"

At first, neither of them answered.

Prof. Benning was the first to give in. "I promise I won't try anything. Tell me what you need and I'll try to get it to you."

"I'll only accept your offer, if you promise that no word of this will reach my ex-wife."

"But she is trying to help," Prof. Benning argued.

"Yes, help me into an early grave and to line her own pockets at the same time."

"You have her all wrong. Your fierce divorce is clouding your judgement of her."

"How you can still see her in a rosy light, when she left you alone with your daughter, is beyond me. And the divorce was not fierce. She had already gotten all she wanted, access to my private office, by getting the house in town. She just had assumed, the files there would also give her full hold over my discoveries and inventions. But that is where she was wrong. She had already handed over earlier results from me to you, so she could see if you could continue the research I had started, and with some it had worked out, like with the 'high voltage access decliner'."

When Prof. Benning wanted to interrupt, he continued.

"I don't begrudge you the success you had with publishing my research as your results. But you need to see that Vanessa is not the selfless woman you think her to be."

"But I've known her all my life. She isn't like that."

"And did she ever do anything solely out of the goodness of her heart?"

"She is …"

"No! One word leaks out to her and we will all be dead. Keep your mouth shut about us ever meeting and our plans, or I am out of here, leaving you alone in your self-created mess."

"It is all your fault. You wanted to sell the research."

"No! Stop this, Prof. Benning, Prof. Lynford. Your accusations only cost us time we don't have here. We are almost at your parking lot. We need to come to a solution."

"I agree," Prof. Lynford fell in with her. "But Vanessa will not be part of it."

Sophia supported him: "I don't trust Vanessa, your ex-wife, either. Her accusations against you, which brought you into prison, were more than lunacy. I can't even comprehend why the court took them at face value without checking them. Accusing you of trying to sell off your secret inventions to enemies of your country and when she tried to hinder you, that you would attempt to hurt and murder her."

"What was that? Vanessa told me, you tried to harm her, when you found out about us and our child together. Out of jealousy, she said."

"You never read the court report about my case?"

"No. Vanessa told me all about it. I … – I trusted her." Prof. Benning's voice cracked. Sophia could hear him swallow his tears.

"Prof. Lynford did not know about your daughter with her. – At least I think he didn't, till I told him last night."

"But how did you know, Sophia? I never told anyone who Jenny's mother was."

"I found out rather by accident when researching Vanessa and finding ancestry data one of your uncles must have collected."

"Ah, yes. Uncle Edward's latest hobby."

"I don't want to rush you, but we are almost at the parking lot. I already turned to take a round circuit, but your guards should not see my car cruising in this area for too long, or they will get suspicious."

Both men were sitting low in the seats not to be seen from the outside.

"I will need my diary and calendar from the laboratory. Also copy the address book from my computer onto a stick."

"That's all?"

"Yes, that's it."

"No research papers?"

"No."

"That should not be too difficult. They are all focused on your research reports, guarding them like state treasures."

"When and where?" Sophia pressed on. "Though with your tight escort, a personal meeting might be too dangerous."

"I don't know. I can hardly leave the campus and even here on my daily jogging tour, they are observing me again."

"What about the café off campus, where we met yesterday?"

"Out of the question. They will just follow you for sure then."

"We won't be there at the same time. You go in for lunch tomorrow and leave the packet behind the large plant between the bathrooms in the back. I will only come in when you have already left and retrieve the package."

"Agreed. That might work. Till then I should have everything together. But if the men following me today, have already reported your description, it is too dangerous for you to go back home for now. It would be too dangerous, if they could identify you."

"And with an escaped prisoner in tow, I can't well go anywhere else. That whole thing is really starting to become a bloody mess now."

Prof. Lynford, who had strangely kept quiet during their discussion of the details, harshly ended her outburst.

"We'll sleep in the car for tonight. And tomorrow, it is better you don't know. We won't need your apartment any longer."

"But if I need to contact you two?" Prof. Benning was worried about leaving the innocent girl alone with his fellow professor Merton Lynford, whom he had already thought capable of harming a woman, his beloved Vanessa. Leaving Sophia alone with such a man, though he protested to be innocent, still did not sit well with him. "I have a cottage near the coast you could …"

"No. Out of the question. When Sophia's absence is discovered, they will first search your properties, Benning."

"But I need to know she is safe with you."

"I see." Prof. Lynford really did see, what Prof. Benning worried about and for once, it was the first point in the man's favor. Long standing animosity between them aside, he gave in.

"You can contact us here via the website you gave her yesterday." Both Sophia and Prof. Benning gasped in surprise by their method of contact being discovered so easily, but Prof. Lynford continued unerringly. "Leave a message there, if you want to reach out to us, we'll check. But be careful to only access this site from a secure computer via a proxy server. We'll do the same."

"I will. Thank you. – How will I know she is …"

"She will come to no harm through my hands."

Prof. Benning hesitantly accepted this ambiguous assurance. Both men shook hands, as if they were old friends, not enemies. Bent down and lying low in her car, it still was a gesture sealing their new founded pact.

Sophia turned into the parking lot, searching for a hidden spot behind dense bushes, to let Prof. Benning exit from the car out of sight of possible observers. She also got out, not looking back at the professor, who had already hidden behind the bushes and made his way to the closest hiking path. Her way to explain her presence to potential onlookers, who she was sure must be there somewhere, waiting for the professor's return, lead her to the bathroom particular to this parking area. When she came back to the car, Prof. Lynford was waiting for her impatiently.

"What if I have to go as well?"

"That is quite unfortunate. You'll have to wait a while longer, till we are away from here. It would not do, if they saw your face."

"Stop talking, just hurry."

Sophia smiled inwardly. It amused her that the haughty professor had normal urges like every other human being as well. He acted so arrogantly most of the time, as if nothing earthly would concern him.

"What's so funny?" he questioned her, having caught her amusement.

"You," she simply threw back at him.

"You enjoy my discomfort?"

"No! – That's not what it is. I'm sorry. It was just the first 'normal' thing you said in my presence. I'm really sorry. I admit it was not that funny."

"God's mercy. A girl who thinks she's funny. How have I

deserved this?"

They kept silent for the journey out of the hiking area around the hills surrounding the town. After a sharp bend in the road, Sophia found an unmaintained path into the woods, where she stopped the car, letting the man go to do his business, before continuing the drive in unbroken silence.

Sophia mused about how different the man she had so idolized from afar was from the angry, aloof man sitting next to her. Her admiration for his ingenious inventions had blinded her from seeing the real man with all his emotional baggage, it seemed. In the beginning, she had been so over the moon, when the opportunity arose to get a research topic where the revered Prof. Lynford would be the logical choice of a second corrector. Even back then, she had wondered about the less than enthusiastic response from Prof. Benning. Had he known about the man and worried about her? Today, it had seemed that he had only reluctantly left her behind alone with Prof. Lynford. Somehow, that endeared her professor the more to her. She could not believe that he was wittingly in league with criminals and now, his efforts to help them being fugitives from almost anyone, confirmed to her, that her professor was eventually trustworthy and not trying to sell them out.

The only nagging doubt she still had about him was his relationship to the shifty ex-Mrs. Lynford, Vanessa, the mother of his child, a fact he had not even tried to hide or negate.

As she had seen him with Vanessa lately, his relationship with the woman seemed far from over. And her involvement and lies about her husband were more than dubious. The only question was, why had she so easily gotten through with all her obvious lies. Not the court, not the judges, not the police had even once put up any resistance against her and her so obvious framing of her husband. Why? What interests did they all have in the matter? Sophia did not believe in coincidences. There must be something she had overlooked so far; and Prof. Lynford was certainly no help in the matter for her to resolve the riddles surrounding him like a heavy cloak.

– 14 –
Back in Town

When they were at the outskirts of town, Prof. Lynford interrupted her thoughts.

"Where are you right now?"

Sophia looked around her. "About ten minutes from the town center."

"Not we. Where were you with your thoughts?"

She answered his question like he always did, with one of her own. "Why has your wife sold you out?"

But with him her strategy of open defiance could not work. He was a too hardened and experienced man to easily give in to her inexperienced tactic.

"Have you any idea to whom the building opposite your apartment complex belongs?"

"The W&B Holding. They renovated the whole building last year and had a big plate with their name outside."

The direction of his question and the sudden topic change had surprised her too much, to keep up her intended method of answering his every question with a return-question, till he gave her real answers.

"W&B, you say. And do you know what W&B stands for?"

"Walker & Bendrix, or something like that. It's a big holding, with many properties all over town and throughout the country."

"Well, well. Just not Bendrix, but Benning."

"Like Prof. Benning?"

"Yes, exactly. He is part of the family who owns the estates, but also who funded and finances the university he teaches at."

"What? But Camsted is an independent university."

"Yes. Something they propagate and heavily advertise, but, nonetheless, it's not true."

Sophia needed to think for a moment about all the implications this information had on their situation, driving on. Though, if not going back to her apartment, she had no idea where best to go instead. Finally, she turned into the parking lot of a main shopping center, open around the clock. Here she thought, their stationary car would draw no unnecessary attention and they would at least have access to food and sanitary commodities. She was so engrossed in her planning, that she did not even consider for a moment to consult with Prof. Lynford about what to do. They sat silently in the car for a while and he did not question her decision.

"Do you think Prof. Benning was involved in your breakout from prison?"

"He certainly was involved in my imprisonment. My freedom rather is the result that he and his accomplices have not yet found what they wanted."

"But why did he offer us the use of his house, if he didn't really want to help us, as you imply?"

"Oh, he wants to. Very much so. He is pressured for my research results, but can't repeat what I proposed possible."

"But with full access to your test laboratory, he should."

"Yes, he should, if he had access to all of them, but he hasn't."

Stunned, Sophia murmured reverently, as if to herself: "That is quite clever. To hide an entire laboratory, when the interest in the research results is so high."

He looked at her almost astonished, before turning away and uttering: "Thank you."

"But what I don't understand is, why the interest was so high, when a positive result was so very unlikely. How could you, or possibly anyone else, know that you would succeed with your unusual approach to hack into retina scanners and general data reading devices? It had already been tried out so many times and had always failed. How could you expect to get a different result now?"

"We didn't."

"Yes, I know. Of course not. Research always has an open outcome, with newly arranged components. But how did you know you would succeed and even prepare with a further hidden laboratory, when success was so very unlikely? Why did you even try it under those premises?"

"Success was not the goal of this whole endeavor. And now, I would appreciate if you could get us something to eat."

Throwing that topic change at her, he really expected her to meekly do as he wished?

"You can't lead me on like that. I won't bring you anything, if you don't explain yourself. And I wouldn't advise you to go out yourself. Your escape was certainly covered in the news channels by now. With all the surveillance cameras around, you are rather depending on me, if you want to eat."

"Not above blackmail, Miss Clever-Pants?"

"Oh, come on. Just tell me. We are sitting in the same boat, or better car, right now. You can trust me."

"Can I?"

"You still doubt that?"

"After you delivered me to my enemy right away the first chance you got, was that intended to instill trust in me?"

"Well, what else should I have done? He insisted on coming back with me to the car to drive him up to his own, after the two thugs found me on the hiking-path. I expected you to be outside or hidden and I would have come back for you. It was you yourself, who stormed to the car, revealing your presence to him. If you remember, I unlocked and locked the car repeatedly with my remote key, trying to forewarn you."

"Wondered why you did that," he murmured.

"We need to improve our silent communication skills, it seems. And if you could come to the realization that indeed I want to help you and don't want to send you back to prison without being able to prove your innocence, and sometimes could give me some information, that all would work out much better."

"You really do believe in communication."

"No, not really, but sometimes it has its advantages. Especially, if you could let me know what is really going on here."

"So that you can leave a hidden message for Prof. Benning at the drop-point in the restaurant? No way."

"But afterwards, when I have got the materials you requested, can you tell me something then? Honestly, I don't want to betray you. But if you don't explain anything to me, you might find that I accidentally blurt out something to the wrong person, just because I don't know any better."

"You won't get any chance for that, don't worry."

"What does that mean now? Now I really worry."

"Take it one step at a time. First things first, how about our next meal? I don't know about you, but I am hungry."

"Oh, you. But please, before I go, promise me to explain things to me, after I have brought back the information from Prof. Benning to you."

"What do you want to know?" He still did not give in one iota and was not willing to promise her anything, she was well aware of that.

"Who your 'we' is and who are the enemies in this game of cat-and-mouse. Can you at least tell me that?"

"Yes, after you come back from the café tomorrow. Now go."

Resigned, Sophia grabbed her purse from her rucksack and left the car, leaving the car keys behind with him, to show him her trust, though she knew that would not change his mind about her.

Lunch was taken in silence. Sophia had moved the car to the parking-lot of a park, finding it wise not to remain at the shopping mall with all its surveillance cameras overly long.

At least, she had bought them enough food and water to last them for a few days, even without a fridge.

After not sleeping most of last night, Sophia was exhausted and yawned repeatedly.

With a kind voice Sophia was not used to from him and which caused her to look at him to ascertain it really was him who spoke, he recommended: "Go, lie down in the back for a while. I'll take the first shift, while you can catch up and get some sleep."

Tired as she was, Sophia for once did not get into a long argument with the man, but instead took his advice, scrambled into the backseat and covered herself with the sheet Prof. Benning had used to hide beneath. She was asleep almost the instance her head sank down onto her arm.

– 15 –
Deep in Hiding

Merton, Prof. Lynford, watched her for a while.

What a strange girl she was. With her big brown eyes she was the picture of innocence, but in seconds could get all fired up, if he said something she did not like. And from him, she did not like almost any word that came out of his mouth. But what a joy it was to observe the fierce glimmer in her eyes. The innocence became a fiery beauty in an instance.

What he found strange was, that he could not detect even a hint of flirting in her behavior. She was as true as her piercing words, all prickly, but with an underlying naïvety which drew him to her. Her response to his kisses had been unrefined, but the fire was irrefutable. His body burned from the memory alone.

He could not remember his wife – ex-wife, he reminded himself – ever having had such an effect on him. Her seduction of him had been worldly, knowledgeable, a femme-fatal at her best, and he had fallen hard. Her teasing and withdrawal drawing him in. He, who always had easy success with women, now had to fight to win over the woman he wanted. The new experience had overwhelmed him. He had proposed with a big gesture and she had coldheartedly thrown his efforts back at him, accusing him of wanting to buy her. He had to try harder to win her, Vanessa had openly told him so, leaving the first-class restaurant, he had exclusively reserved for them to propose to her.

She had finally accepted his third proposal, when he had dedicated one of his research works to her. Now, he suspected he knew why. His research being the sole thing she had been interested in him.

With Sophia, he had to admit, he was at a complete loss. Though being the student of a rivaling professor, she could well profit from a connection to him. But from what he knew so far, she had 'rescued' him, when she had not even known who he was. Still he could not find a hidden motive, except utter kindness. But genuine kindness was the one thing he did not believe in to exist. People in this era and time were many things, but not selfless and kind.

Her naïve trust in her supervising professor was commendable, but still, he certainly could not agree with it. Prof. Benning had his own motives in all of this and though his rival now seemed to operate against his own family's interests, his ulterior motives would always be to look out for his family and to protect his cousin, lover and the mother of his child, Vanessa.

And Vanessa ultimately could not be trusted. He had to find this out the hard way. All the government protection he thought he had, had come to naught. It had not protected him from going to prison for something he had not done, or openly losing his good name in public, and more importantly, in the scholarly world he lived and breathed in. His reputation, all his research was drawn into question now. Even his CIA contacts, pulling him into their game of spooks, had left him to rot in a prison cell, though they must have known the truth about his innocence right from the beginning.

How should he now, after all this, trust a mere little girl, who knew nothing of what was going on, or the real world in general, seeing all and everything through her idealistic, soft brown eyes?

When Sophia stirred in her seat, it was almost eight in the evening.

"Why did you let me sleep for so long?"

"You needed the rest," was his curt and swift reply. "You have to watch now."

"What should I be looking out for?"

"Any suspicious cars, anything unusual."

"Shouldn't we swap parking spaces again?"

"No, not for now. Nobody came here just looking around. We should be safe here overnight. Just keep your head down and make it appear as if the car is empty."

Moving to her driver's seat, she pulled a dark shawl, she at one time had forgotten in her car, over her head, just leaving her eyes uncovered, to hide her skin, should some passing headlights hit the interior of the car.

Prof. Lynford moved to the back, taking over her place. His deep breaths almost immediately showed her that he was asleep. Only then Sophia took a deep, relieved breath. What was it about this man, that kept her so on her toes at all times? His every word could raise her anger. Sophia could not tell why she even cared so much. Normally only people she cared for could raise her into heated arguments. Did she care for Prof. Lynford? She knew she admired his research, but could her scientific interest have grown to more than mere adoration of his scientific prowess?

How on earth could she have developed feelings for an arrogant, self-centered hypocrite like the man sleeping in the back of her car? But the kisses, her first real kiss, still burned through her body, whenever she brought up the memory of it in her mind. Her breath caught just from remembering the touch of his lips on hers, the soft stroking of his tongue.

Wistfully, she sighed.

"You take your job of watching our surrounding seriously?"

The calm voice from the back made her jump in her seat.

"You half scared me to death. How could you!"

"What – or better – who was it, you were thinking about? Your absent boyfriend?"

Sophia kept silent, not wanting to give him even a hint of whom she really had been thinking about.

"Not in a fighting spirit, it seems," he mocked her, his voice coming closer. His breath touched her cheek and she started to shiver uncontrollably, especially, when she felt his hand on her neck, stroking her softly and pulling her shawl and hair away to open the way for his exploring lips.

"S… st… stop this," she whispered, her weak voice not even convincing to her own ears.

"You don't want me to stop."

"Please."

"Please what, my sweet thing? More? Readily." His hand turned her face. The shawl she had draped around her falling uselessly into her lap. Her lips now exposed to the fiery exploration of his lips, her mind forgetting all further thought of protest, willingly opening for him, though her inexperience making her slow in answering his demanding kisses. His arms came around her, as if trying to pull her to him to the back seat. But that finally brought her back to her senses and cleared her mind.

"What are you doing?"

"Isn't that obvious? Passing the time in an enjoyable way."

"Oh."

"Is that all you have to say about it?"

"Well. What should I say? You can pass the time on your own.

I don't want to take part in your entertainment."

"You would rather lie to yourself and pretend there is no attraction between us? It would be to our mutual enjoyment, I assure you."

"I don't want your empty enjoyment."

"Is love empty to you?"

"Not love, but what you propose is not love."

"What is it then?"

"A quick sating of an urge, which would mean nothing to you."

"But it would to you? Why do you protest against it? I felt the reactions of your body. You want it as much as I do."

"Not that way. Not with a cynical man who is just bored and for a moment wants to sate his lust. I am not a tool for you to get that."

"You have higher goals then?" His voice was angry and cutting. "Like my ex. All for the money and prestige. No heart involved."

"Would your heart be involved, if you slept with me?"

"Would yours?" he countered, throwing the question back at her, but not answering hers, as usual.

Sophia did not want to answer, so she kept silent. To give herself to a man for her first time, she wanted to be madly in love, but also wanted to give her virginity to someone to whom that present would mean something. Not just for a sating of his lust and to pass the time, as in her opinion it would be for Prof. Lynford. He would use her, boast about it and his prowess and then throw her away as having no further use to him. No, she would not demean herself to become his means to get revenge on all women, after his wife had betrayed and hurt him so much.

Now, she began to see it more clearly. That was it, why he was so obnoxious to her. He wanted to show his strength and independence, but also his power over her. She would not give in, not even her admiration for his work could make her fall for him.

Was there not a saying that knowing was half the way to preventing something? Knowing his reasoning for trying to seduce her surely would prevent her from falling for it, wouldn't it?

If only it was so easy, to tell her body not to react to him and not to go up in flames each time he touched her.

Strangely, he had not tried to press the answer to his last question from her, but had fallen silent as well.

She handed him the bag with food and water and they ate without speaking. Afterwards, he went back to sleep, but only a few hours later took over the night watch, which passed without disturbance.

In the morning, a car cruised the parking lot repeatedly, checking out their car, but the man who got out must have thought it abandoned, as they were well hidden under dark blankets in the foot areas of the seats. He left after trying to look into the interior of the car. Sophia was glad that her car, though old, had tinted windows, helping enormously in shielding them from the view of the man outside. Before he left them alone, he shouted back to a second man that the vehicle was abandoned.

Whoever was checking on them, must have found out about Sophia's rarely used car.

"Who were the men? You got a good look at them. Did you recognize them?" Sophia could not help but ask Prof. Lynford, when she struggled up from her hidden position under the steering-wheel. He had been the one to detect the suspicious car and had pushed her to the floor before she could have a closer look.

"No," was his monosyllabic reply.

"Fine, you don't want to talk to me. I get it. At least, let me take over the front seat again and I'll drive us to the town center."

"They'll be waiting there for you. It will be better for you, if you go through the park and get to the café on foot."

That would almost take her two hours to get all the way around the green belt of town to the other side.

"So, if I need your help, you are far away. Convenient for you. Do you even intend to be here when I come back? Or was this all just an elaborate plan to get Prof. Benning distracted and off your back for a while?"

"Don't be ridiculous," he snapped at her, but Sophia had the strange impression, that her perception was not so far off the truth.

"You have no idea what you are talking about. They won't expect you to stroll through the park. Get on your way. We need those documents. And afterwards, you can get the information you blackmailed me into telling you. So, get on your way." And she did just that, glad to leave the grumpy man, who so dominated her emotions, behind in the car.

– 16 –
Marty's Café

Only far into her journey, she recognized that she had left all the water bottles behind in the car with him. In the heat of this new day, she could well have used some of it, but did not want to interrupt her journey to buy something on her way.

Behind the restaurant, she waited for a while, sitting on a park bench and watching the surroundings. Some of the cars she had seen following Prof. Benning at her first meeting here, were there again. Strange men, sticking out from the student body, usually seen in this area of town, like a sore thumb, were patrolling the surrounding area. Nobody stood out to her as a recognizable face she had seen before, though.

From her vantage point behind a bush, she managed to remain hidden from them, but they made the moment clear to her, when Prof. Benning left the café. They followed him at once and the area at this time in the year during semester holidays became almost abandoned.

Waiting for a further half hour, to be certain that nobody had stayed behind, she left her hiding spot and entered the café. Greeted by the owner she knew quite well from seeing repeatedly, who was a nice, talkative woman, though only to people she liked, Sophia ordered a big glass of water and her usual cappuccino.

Before she left, she went into the back to the bathrooms, where she found a large brown parcel, well wrapped and sealed with large stripes of duct-tape. Putting it beneath her jacket and t-shirt, she went back out and left Marty's Café after waving her good bye to Mrs. Arnold, the owner.

Her way back was more arduous than anticipated. Men in black were patrolling the park now. As their outfits aroused all her suspicions and they did not even try to hide their weapons under their tight dark jackets, Sophia soon departed from the park and made her long way back to the car through the dark back alleys of town. Though she normally would have avoided those filthy and narrow streets, today they were exactly what she was looking for.

With a sigh of relief, she slipped into the front seat of her car, which still stood at its place exactly as she had left it, after she had checked the surroundings for potential observers.

"I am back." She turned to the back seat, not finding Prof. Lynford in the front, but expecting him inside, as the car had been unlocked. But the man showing his face under the seat-colored blanket on the back seat was not Prof. Lynford. She tried to scream, but a firm hand clapped over her already opened mouth.

"Quiet," Prof. Lynford's voice hushed close to her ear. "Turn around and drive," he ordered loosening his tight hold over her mouth.

"What's going on?"

"Later. Now drive us out of here."

"But he … – What is he doing here?"

"Helping us and now go."

"Where?"

"I'll direct you."

Sophia could not help but tremble with fear. Almost not being able to get the key into the ignition, she fumbled around.

"Today, if you please," Prof. Lynford urged on. Michael, the man sitting in the back next to him, not uttering a word.

But having tried to avoid this man so determinedly and now

finding herself so close to one of the abductors of Prof. Lynford, the one bent over him in her video, made her crazy with fear.

Help them? Certainly he would. Her to an early gave, for sure. After a few attempts, she managed to turn on the car and backed out of their parking lot, getting into the traffic through town and out to the highway to the coast.

Prof. Lynford never for once interfered with her choice of route, neither giving her any direction. He let her drive on for almost an hour, before he ordered her to turn around and take the highway back to where they came from. Michael meanwhile was snoring from the back seat, not bothering with their route at all.

Whispering, Sophia now found the courage to try again. "What is he doing here?"

"Helping. – Next exit, then left."

Sophia followed his orders, which made her repeatedly change lanes and turn into obscure side streets at the last minute. Still, she was too curious to let those haphazard driving maneuvers distract her.

"Why didn't you bring him over right away?"

"I had to be sure I could trust you."

"And now you do?"

"No, I don't. But now, you no longer will be able to contact anyone with your information."

"But I helped you, left my home for you, …"

"I don't trust a student willing to sleep with her professor to get into a graduate program. So, don't even try to pry into my plans. You won't like the outcome."

"I didn't sleep … – Oh, you arrogant prick! You don't know the first thing about me."

"Look where you are driving," he growled back between clenched teeth.

Their angry voices awakened Michael, who scrambled up from his sleeping position on the back seat.

"What's the matter? Danger?"

"No. Everything is all right. Don't worry. We are on schedule. No cars are following us any longer. Our last couple of turns got them by surprise. No further sighting of either the spooks or the mobsters. Francesco and Andrew lost us at the last turn half an hour ago."

Sophia had not detected anyone tailing them, but now it explained their strange route, she so far had not been able to make sense of.

"Good. Then we can finally go to our hiding place and lay low for a few days. I am so tired I could sleep for a week." Michael yawned audibly. "Get off the highway at the next exit and turn right there."

Sophia, still frightened by the presence of the bulky man Michael, said nothing in reply, but followed his orders, while checking and memorizing the route they were taking.

– 17 –
Out by the Sea

The directions lead them to a secluded area of the coast, rough and scarcely populated. There was quite some distance in between settlements, while they were driving along a bumpy coastal road, which had been mostly made redundant by the highway further inland. Abandoning the main roads, they followed a gravel path, which lead out to a rocky cliff with a solitary house, cutting far out into the sea. The building, looking more like a battlement, standing there for centuries to fight the sea and storms, than a lighthouse, which it for some time must have been, though now the tower built right next to the stone-house looked abandoned and decrepit.

Michael retrieved the key from a hidden spot above one side-window and then let Sophia into the house, following her and checking the rooms. The inside of the old house greeted them with a well-aired smell and was clean and friendly. Food was stocked in abundance in the kitchen and the fridge was filled to the brim.

"Patty really outdid himself. Good boy," Michael muttered, checking their supplies first thing when he entered.

Waving a hand at Sophia, he ordered: "Get to work, woman. I am hungry."

At first wanting to resist his sexist order, she thought twice about it, when she felt him appreciatively taking in her body from head to toe. At least while cooking, he could not attempt anything and the kitchen appliances should provide her with a sharp knife to protect herself from him, should he dare to try and come close to her, she thought with some relief.

Merton, Prof. Lynford, had stayed outside, not coming into the house with them, as he had wanted to immediately check their surrounding before they settled in.

He must be overly tired by now himself, having taken most of the watch during the night. Sophia wondered how he even managed to still stay upright, but he had not shown any sign of tiredness, except some occasional yawning he could not suppress. After a healthy meal, he surely would not be much of a protection against Michael, if he even wanted to try and stop his friend, should he attempt anything with her. Sophia was not convinced that the professor would help her or just willingly hand her over. Had that been the reason why they had taken her along after bringing the information from Prof. Benning back to the car and had not left her behind in town? Did he want to use her as a kind of payment for Michael?

Sophia trembled in fear at the thought and a while later, when Prof. Lynford came into the house, his look switching between Michael and her did nothing to lay her worries to rest. He clearly expected something to happen between them, she just had no idea about the direction his thoughts took.

Having finished preparing a hearty meal, after they had missed lunch and it being almost nightfall now, she decked the table in the living room directly adjoining the open kitchen area.

Michael and Prof. Lynford had exchanged words she could not overhear, because of the sizzling of the steaks, but she had the impression the men had intentionally wanted to exclude her.

Serving the meal together with some beer she had found in the fridge, she drew back to eat alone in the kitchen, leaving the men alone in their hushed conversation.

Not caring for being excluded from the further planning, Sophia took up her rucksack, which though not containing much, at least held her bare necessities.

Prof. Lynford must have had an eye on her, because he immediately stopped her, when she tried to leave the main living area, enclosing almost the entire ground floor of the house.

"You can sleep in the left room right after the staircase. It has an enclosed bathroom. Good night, Sophia."

"Good night," she replied and hastened out of the room.

Since Michael had turned up, she felt strangely abandoned by the professor. How could that be possible, she wondered. She had no right or not even the slightest reason to expect anything from the man, but now, as he had a new help, he had no longer any need for her and the connection she had thought existed between them, seemed to be gone. Had it only been in her imagination, that he had slowly started to trust her, to see her as a valuable associate, even with all their bickering and heated arguments?

Now, with Michael around, he obviously no longer wanted her help. She had been relegated to kitchen help for him. She had intentionally left the dishes unattended. Sophia had cleaned up the cooking utensils, but had even left her own plate in the sink.

After the exhausting night before, she slipped into the bed, wearing a spare t-shirt from her rucksack after only a superficial wash; and finding a new toothbrush in the adjoining bathroom, she used it gladly.

The bed, a strong wooden frame, was comforting with its large and fully stuffed feather pillows and covers. She fell asleep almost the moment her head sank down into their softness.

In the morning, a teasing sun-beam woke her. She had no idea what time it was, disoriented by the foreign surroundings.

It took her a while to get the events of the last days together, leading her here.

With a sigh, she jumped out of bed, ready to take the shower she had omitted last evening. Stripping off her night t-shirt, she checked her clothes she had worn yesterday, which she fortunately had quickly rinsed in the sink with the hand-wash and hung up in the bathroom the evening before. They had dried enough so that she would be able to wear them today.

Putting them onto her bed, she went back to take the shower she so craved after sleeping in her clothes the night before.

Naked beneath the warm water, enjoying the soothing stream, she jumped, when suddenly two hands came around her wet form to hold her against a large body. A scream formed in her throat, but was suppressed by a large hand, pressing her head back against the rough shoulder of a man. Struggling, her feet found no purchase in the slippery shower stall. Her hands rose to punch the man behind her in the face, but he caught them easily. Taking his hand from her mouth, he brought her hands to her front, binding them with one of his own, pressing her against the full length of his own naked body.

"Calm down, my little dovey. You'll enjoy it, I promise." The voice of Michael did nothing to calm her, renewing her efforts, though her kicks and struggles felt useless against the bulky mass of this large man. He even had the audacity to laugh at her useless attempts to fight him off.

"Stop, or I'll scream."

"As much as that would help you, little dove. We are alone out here, all the house to us, to enjoy ourselves in the meanwhile. But do as you please."

"No! Stop!"

"You don't want me to. I can give you more pleasure than that stuffy dick Professor Benning."

"No!" Struggling, Sophia felt his second hand wander down her stomach between her kicking legs, slipping in between them and touching and exploring her female core. Her winding and wriggling body only driving him on the more and she felt his hard dick press into her back with urgent pushes, while his fingers continued their exploration of her sex. The hot water enabling his progress, he tried to slip a finger into her, but her tight body resisted his entry. Trying again, she answered his attempt with an agonizing moan.

"What's the matter with you? You are so very tight. You can't be a virgin, can you. Not even my fiancée was as tight …"

Slowly, realization hit him. "You are a virgin!"

With a loud crash, the bathroom door was thrown open.

Prof. Lynford stood in the doorway. "What is going on here? What is the talk about a virgin?"

Sophia, completely shocked that now two men were watching her naked in the shower and overcome by the relief of her rescue, broke out in tears. To her utter mortification, Michael took her now unresisting body up in his arms and stepping out of the shower, wrapped a large bath-towel around her, embracing her in it and pressing her to him in a comforting hug.

"Hush, my little dovey. I won't harm you. You have nothing to fear from me. Michael does not harm little innocent girls, deary. Hush now." He spoke of himself in the third person, as if talking of someone else. And the behavioral change seemed that two Michaels existed. He carried her out to her bed and sat down with her in his arms, letting her cry into his shoulder, all wrapped and bundled up in a big bathing towel, unable to move, his hand on her neck, preventing her from lifting her head.

Merton stood to the side open mouthed and watched the strange pair. The girl ineffectively pushed against the broad chest of Michael in a halfhearted effort to free herself, being engulfed in the wide, comforting hug of this tower of a man, who tried to be gentle to the girl in his arms and calm her down, after being the cause of her tears.

"What happened here?" Merton's voice was rough from suppressed anger, though he had a rather good idea what had happened, from the shouts he had heard outside. Fortunately, he had come back from his check earlier than anticipated. Though his own jealousy about the girl surprised him and his efforts to suppress this unreasonable emotion rising up inside him, made him unable to act and step in between Sophia and Michael. What cause did he have to be jealous, seeing Sophia in the arms of another man? She was just a woman. What had he expected? But he could not help but feel betrayed by seeing her cry into Michael's shoulder while he gently stroked her towel covered back, when he wanted to be the one to give her such comfort. Where had that mad idea sprung from? Had his hostile divorce from his wife now driven him to complete lunacy?

But the sniffling sounds from her almost broke his heart, an organ he only shortly before would have insisted he no longer possessed.

Finally, Sophia managed to struggle her way out of the hold of Michael's arms, rolling into a tight, protective ball on her bed, among the clothes she had spread out before taking the shower.

Helplessly, Michael looked down at her. Turning to him in his search for reassurance. "I didn't want to hurt her, I really didn't. I thought she would like a bit of action during the wait."

"What was it you said about her being a virgin back in the shower? Did you molest her?"

"The little deary is still untouched. Much tighter than my Hannah ever was. I really didn't want to hurt her."

Merton, throwing an angry glance at Michael, who cringed under his gaze, approached her on the bed, but was stopped by her words.

"Go away. Leave me alone!"

Prof. Lynford lead Michael out of the room, assuring him at the door that she would be all right again in a while.

But he could not leave her alone himself. Going back to her, he took her clothes off the bed and folded them neatly on a chair. Then pulling up the bed covers, when she did not again protest his presence in the room, he wrapped her into the covers, sinking down on the bed next to her, enfolding her with the bulky covers protectively in his arms, laying down beside her with all his clothes still on.

"Everything is all right now. Michael will not try to force you again. You do not have to worry about him."

His words seemed to soothe her after a while and slowly her tears and sighs abated.

When he thought that she had already fallen asleep, she asked in a tiny voice, quite unlike the vivacious young woman he had seen so far: "Did you promise me to him as payment?"

"What?" Sitting up in bed, he looked down at her big brown eyes, which were still red rimmed from her tears.

"Is that why you took me along?"

"What gave you that idea?"

"You immediately cut me out of your plans as soon as we arrived here. What else did you bring me here for?"

"Perhaps to keep you quiet. Besides, I did not cut you out, you were never in."

He saw the disappointment on her features.

"I thought you started to trust me and you had promised to tell me the background after I came back with your material. But as soon as we arrived here, I was only good for cooking. And I'm not even good with frying steaks."

He smiled down at her annoyed face and could not resist bending down to give her a kiss on her still stubbornly upturned nose. But she struggled against him and tried to throw him out of her bed.

"Hush, my girl. I am not here to harm you."

"Is this why you took me with you? To use me yourself?"

"No, and besides, it would be hard to 'use' you through those voluminous bed covers."

They were indeed fluffy, thick things filled with goose down and bulkily engulfed Sophia, who together with her wrapping, was held by Merton.

"I am here to give you comfort and show you that a man's touch need not be hurtful."

"Ah, a lesson then. So, no Bond-girl role for me."

Laughing out loud at her comment, which showed him that her usual spunkiness, if not fully, at least partially had returned. She would be all right and overcome her shock about Michael's assault soon and without lasting harm done, he was convinced. To take her mind from the events, he continued her joke, to further distract her.

"Though the Bond-girls are all experienced femme-fatals or at least know what they want, not studious Miss Innocents."

Did he only imagine the sadness in her voice, when she replied?

"I know I am not your type. You don't need to make that any more clear to me."

"Come on, little girl. Who could resist a studious Miss Nightingale, coming to one's rescue? I certainly could not wish for more."

When she did not reply, he felt her body relax in his arms and saw the exhaustion on her face.

Stroking some hair out of her face gently, he looked down into her innocent eyes, no longer seeing them as an elaborate scheme to beguile him, but as the eyes of a truly innocent young woman without ulterior motives, frightened and wary of the surroundings she found herself in.

Michael in a way had done him a favor in finding that out about her. He doubted she would have told him that fact herself, or if she had done, he would most likely not have believed her, thinking her to be the loyal lover of Prof. Benning.

But her being a virgin explained so much about her, which he previously had not understood. Her idealism, her trust in him, her guileless behavior. And though he knew he did not deserve it, her wholehearted adoration for him based on his research, which he previously had just seen as a way for her to try and manipulate him into doing whatever she wanted.

He had put her on one level with his wife, who had been far from innocent, but rather the driving force behind this mess they all found themselves in, though his ex had always carefully maintained an innocent façade of being a victim.

He just had to bring out in the open the true motives of his wife and why she had given up on their marriage and the easy opportunities to milk him dry of his further inventions. Why had she stopped and killed off her main source of profits, when he was far from discovering her true character and had been a willing victim in all her schemes?

Sophia felt him tense through all her bulky armor and saw his determined look.

"What is it? What are you worried about?"

"Nothing. – Everything. My ex-wife is somehow behind all this and I am no closer to discovering her true motives in all this than at the beginning."

"Aha. Wouldn't Prof. Benning know? He after all did try to help us, though he still seems to care for her."

"Did he truly help us?"

"Well, yes, of course. What other motive could he have? He gave you all the material you requested and more."

"And more? What more? Show me."

Sophia had not shown him the whole content of the package Prof. Benning had left hidden in the café. She had held back the second part addressed to her. Documents Prof. Lynford had not requested and so she had kept them for herself to have a look at them when she was alone. She had intended to show Prof. Lynford when he told her more about the true background of the situation they were in, but the presence of Michael had disrupted that plan. She had not even had a chance to get a closer look at the papers herself, yet.

But when Sophia wanted to get out of the bed to get to her backpack, she became aware of her nakedness and abruptly drew the covers up to her neck, wincing under his gaze. Tears once again began to well up in her eyes and Merton, sitting up, did not dare to draw her into his arms, conscious of her fragile emotional state and not wanting to frighten her the more.

"What is it, my dear?" he gently asked.

"You saw me without clothes, as did Michael."

"Yes, and a really pretty sight it was." He tried to make light of it.

Sophia blushed ferociously and hid her face in the covers.

Moving closer to her, he put an arm around her shoulders and whispered into her ear: "Did he hurt you? Did he rape you?"

Taking in a wobbly, reassuring breath, Sophia lifted her face from the sheets and shook her head. "No, he didn't get that far. Thanks to you."

"I'm not sure it helps, but I think Michael did stop as soon as he recognized your true resistance, even without me coming in. He is not such a bad guy, you know. Just sometimes perhaps a bit rough."

Sophia threw a doubtful glance in his direction.

"He really is sorry for having frightened and hurt you so. He isn't someone who would want to cause you any harm. Prison was not the right environment for him to hone his social graces. He was there for too long, it seems. And his former fiancée, the woman he had before prison, did not help matters."

"He had a fiancée? But I thought he was into men."

Merton laughed humorlessly at her comment.

"No. That was out of necessity and it is the only currency well understood by all prison inmates, as well as the mob bosses. Even Francesco and Andrew, the two thugs keeping watch over us, respected this relationship, when they did nothing else."

"But he is … – He is the one I rescued you from. How can you stay so calm now that he has found you?"

"He didn't find me. I called him."

"You can't be serious. He harmed you."

"He's not the one I need rescuing from. He only did what

needed to be done to convince our guards."

"Really? So you are into it then?" Remembering their heated kisses, she could not believe what he told her. Admittedly, she was not experienced in those things, but his kiss had not merely been to silence her. It had been more, she was certain. He had made her body crave and burn. It could not have been just one-sided, could it?

"If it buys me the protection we need, yes." He answered after a while, thoughtfully.

"Why him?"

"He was the one who protected me in prison from being the punching-bag and fuck-toy for our fellow inmates, when everyone else thought they had gotten what they wanted from me and left me there to rot."

"Why was he in prison?"

"For a murder he did not commit."

"Are you sure?"

"Yes, absolutely. He is a good guy who couldn't harm a fly. Don't let his rough exterior and strength fool you."

"And you are a couple then?"

"No. Only out of necessity. They had already locked him up for more than ten years. And it is the usual currency for protection in prison. The big guys feared him for his strength, as you can imagine."

"But if he can't harm a fly. Would that not contradict his usefulness as protector?"

"He can if adequately provoked, and he, right at the beginning of his imprisonment, sent a mafia guy holding some power in prison into hospital. Afterwards, they left him alone. But parole was out of the question for him as a consequence."

"What was he accused of?"

"Of killing his own father."

"Why?"

"He did not kill him, but his brother did."

"Are you sure of it?"

"Yes, absolutely. When we first met in prison, I helped him figure out who really did it and framed him for the crime."

"But how? You were in prison with him."

"By following the line of who wins most from his departure. His recollection of the events helped a great deal, leading me to the real culprits. – He first thought, his fiancée preferred his older brother, till she suddenly changed track and when he finally had the courage to ask her himself, she immediately accepted his proposal. – But, you see, his first impression was correct. She had only changed her behavior towards him, after his father had announced that he would give their car-repair company to him, as his older brother had gone to college and had never shown any interest in it, while Michael worked and learned everything to be known about the business and loved the car-repair work."

"Oh, I begin to understand. They wanted to get him out of the way to get the business-fortune. It was a very successful car-repair company, was it not?"

"Yes, unfortunately so for Michael."

"Poor man. He never saw it coming, did he?"

"No, he loved his father. Seeing him dead on the floor in front of him, surrounded by the cars he had loved so much. – He even started crying when retelling the events to me. So, yes, I believe him."

Sophia tried to speak, but a yawn interrupted her words.

"Sleep now. We have time later. You are exhausted now."

And indeed, she was. Sophia had not been aware how much

her emotional upheaval had exhausted her, but she almost immediately fell asleep, when he arranged her comfortably in his arms, wrapped in the warm covers.

– 18 –
Information at the Sea

When she awoke more than an hour later, Merton was no longer next to her in bed, though she could still feel his warmth.

Searching the room, she found him sitting in an armchair by the only window in the room, the additional package from Prof. Benning still untouched and wrapped on the little table. He must have taken it out of her rucksack, but so far was only filing through the material he had requested.

Pulling up the sheets, to cover herself, Sophia sat up in bed.

"What are you doing, Merton?"

Using his first name still felt strange to her, but sleeping in one bed with him, though nothing sexual had happened between them, made calling him 'Prof. Lynford' now even more strange to her.

He looked up at her and smiled.

"You slept soundly. Do you feel better now?"

The care in his voice made her forget any discomfort or shyness in his company and she immediately relaxed and smiled back at him. "Yes, thank you."

But she instantly realized, that he once again had successfully distracted her from her initial question.

"What are you reading?"

"The papers Prof. Benning gave you, of course. I want to find out what he meant to tell you with them, but so far I've had no luck. But I also didn't really expect to. He meant them for you, so the message must be in a form only you would be able to understand. I just didn't want to leave you here alone, so I took my chance with the material."

"Can I have a look at it?"

"Later. We have time. We'll stay here and wait for at least two days, if nobody manages to find out our whereabouts, that is."

"Why wait? All the secret services and criminals of the world are after you and your discovery and you want to sit the problem out?"

"Yes. It's our only option. Let them get nervous and try to figure out who made the deal with us in the meanwhile. That'll make our work much easier then. Besides, Michael is back from his check of the surroundings."

"How do you know?"

"The smell. It's definitely not my doing."

Wafts of homemade pancakes teased her nose. Carefully hiding in the big cover sheet of the bed, she jumped out and went to the bathroom, taking her neatly folded clothes from the chair.

When she came down into the kitchen alone, not having seen Prof. Lynford on her way down, Michael stood behind the historic hearth, waving a spatula and preparing delicious looking pancakes.

"You can cook?" Sophia could not help but ask. After all, he had so haughtily ordered her to cook last night. But the image she had of him as a gruff and bulky car-mechanic just did not sit well with these wonderful smelling delicacies.

Looking at her in surprise, not having heard her entry over the sizzling of the two pans on the stove, Michael kept silent, just staring at her.

Only when Prof. Lynford entered behind her, did he shake off his rigidity.

"No signs of them so far. We must have lost them for now,"

was his swift report.

"Thank you for taking over my tour."

"No problem, boss. The little one all right again?" Michael asked as if Sophia was not in the room with them.

She had the feeling Merton indeed was right about Michael. He treaded from one foot to the other nervously and seemed to be too shy to address her directly. But Sophia, still wondering how such a bulk of a man could feel nervous and shy in the presence of a woman that was not even half his size, spoke up for herself.

"I'm fine, Michael. You did no permanent harm to me. You just frightened me very much."

"I'm really sorry, little one. I didn't think you'd mind. Really sorry." He mumbled his last words, scrunching up his nose at the smell coming from behind him and hastily turning around to rescue a very dark pancake from one of the pans, while explaining: "Worked in the kitchen back in prison. Inmates liked my pancake special."

He prepared a couple of perfect pancakes on a plate, together with fresh fruit and syrup and set it in front of her on the table. Seeing him nervously looking at her, she gave him a reassuring smile and thanked him, but he only left her side, when she tried them and could not help but release a contented moan upon the melting taste of deliciousness in her mouth.

Only moments later, Michael came over with full plates for both Merton and himself and they joined her in silence, to do the delicacies justice.

"No wonder they wanted to keep you in prison forever and rejected your appeal. You should make a career as cook." The lighthearted and relaxed teasing of Merton was new to Sophia. She had only seen him tense, if not angry and a bit distant.

But now, he gave the impression of someone enjoying his breakfast with his family and loved ones. The idea brought color into her cheeks, thinking about the intimate way he had held her on the bed, naked under the bedsheets.

Merton, seeing her strange reaction, intensely bored his gaze into her, watching her with her bent head and rosy cheeks, which normally were so pale from all her time spent in the lab. Michael, observing both of them and finding that his own reply had gone unnoticed over the silent exchange between the two, finally broke the tension by standing up and taking her empty late.

"Want some more?"

"Yes, please. They are just too delicious to resist."

Michael had the impression, from the way Merton followed the girl's every move, that for him the pancakes were not the only delicacy in this kitchen.

Would do him good to finally forget his bitch of a wife, he thought. And if that slip of a girly did it for him, he would do his best to put a bit of meat on her bones. The boss needed a bit of innocent enjoyment in his life. Loading her plate, he brought it back to her and then, with the announcement of doing the dishes later, left them to make a new tour to check their surroundings.

Uncomfortable with leaving all the work to Michael, who had already cooked for them, Sophia started with the wash-up, while Merton brought her notebook and Prof. Benning's papers down to the large kitchen table.

"Is it safe to go online here?" Sophia was worried about their safety, reading about all the various ways security services and hackers had to break into the privacy of people.

"We will only use a secure line and access via proxy servers.

That should be safe enough for now."

The last words became more and more a murmur, when Prof. Lynford sank into a state of concentration and clicked and entered information on the keys, till finally, he blurted out: "We are in. Prof. Benning wrote us a message."

Distracted from the dishes, she was immediately at his side, dish towel still in hand.

"What is it? What did he write?"

"He asks for a meeting, in person. – Out of the question!" Merton agitatedly answered the request for himself.

"Why does he want to meet? He knows we can't show our faces now. Why would he risk that? The news he has must really be ground breaking, if he would take that risk."

"Or he wants to lure us out right into a trap, making us believe exactly that."

"He could have easily done that yesterday, but he did not."

"Perhaps because he was followed by more than one party."

"Of course he is. If it has anything to do with hacking into the securest security systems, I can imagine the whole world is after your technique to do so."

"And that's it, why he didn't do it yesterday. All his followers would have tried to get their claws on us simultaneously, potentially killing us. That might not have given those who paid him a chance."

"No! Prof. Benning would not sell me out."

Burning jealousy rose in Merton's throat, that it threatened to choke him. Sophia loving Benning, the undeserving 'crétin'? No way. He had to make her see what an undeserving man her professor was.

"You can meet him, if you want. But if you go, you won't come back here."

"No. You're right. It's much too risky. We wouldn't even make it into town safely. Let me write back to him, to see what he wants. Is he online now?"

"No, but he was only minutes ago and promises to check regularly, as it's so urgent."

Taking the chair next to him, Sophia sat down on the rough wooden table, trying to look onto the computer screen from the side.

Merton pushed the notebook over to her.

"You just need to write. Don't publish your comment. It will stay there for Benning to find."

"All right." Silently reading Prof. Benning's message, she saw that no hint whatsoever was given about what had made him so nervous that he contacted them directly after their exchange yesterday and checked back almost every hour, even during the night, from the activity timestamps she could access in the account.

Searching for a hidden message or meaning, Sophia came up with nothing, except that Prof. Benning wanted to warn them of something.

Irritated, she took the papers Prof. Benning had packed together for her. But her irritation only grew. The papers he sent had nothing, absolutely nothing to do with the current research or Merton's discovery.

They were news reports about crimes, some going back years, fourteen years, to be exact, when his parents were murdered, but the culprits never found. Shortly after, his cousin Vanessa's parents had died in a suspicious car accident as well. Both incidents were supposed to have been instigated by warring crime syndicates.

A report about a crime family and all their members killed at a wedding with one large bomb detonating, disguised as a gas leak.

A copy of a birth certificate, Sophia found to be of the daughter of Prof. Benning. His daughter was born only months before all those killings. No hint about who had taken over the lead of the surviving Benning crime syndicate, or rather the official cover for it, the successful pharmaceutical company operating world-wide, having diverse other business interests as well, like weapons, oil, drugs, human trafficking, prostitution, gaming, as one crime report about the death of Prof. Benning's grandfather, the former head of the crime syndicate and sole leader, hinted at.

"I think I know what he wants to tell you, or rather what he wants to talk with you about. I think he wants to know from you at least if you could imagine his idea to be a viable possibility," Sophia broke out with alarm in her voice.

"What? Seeing all the killing in his family and you still think he is innocent and out of the goodness of his heart wants to warn us from his mafia connections? He took over the lead of one of the largest criminal conglomerates in the country and had to eliminate all who stood in his way to the top."

"No. You must be wrong. He would never do that. He couldn't have."

Seeing red at her naïvely loyal defense of her professor, if not her lover, as he had first thought, made him jump up in anger.

"You with your romantic female notions can't see straight."

Michael came back in at just that moment, hearing their angry voices.

"All clear outside, but that doesn't seem the case in here."

"He doesn't want to see that with caring for a little child, his daughter, he wouldn't have had time to build up his power in a crime syndicate, while at the same time building up his reputation as a scientist. That just does not make sense. A child needs time and care. It can't be him wanting to trap us for his criminal gains now. Why would he send us those articles now?"

Sophia complained to Michael, when Merton so clearly refused to listen to all her arguments.

"She is just too much in love with him to see that he is working together with his cousin Vanessa." Merton also directed his argument at Michael, who looked between the two, not taking sides, but looking at them with amusement, clearly enjoying himself.

"You do agree, that it is his cousin, your ex-wife, who took over the crime syndicate?" Sophia tried again.

Only now, looking back at his marriage with Vanessa, suddenly so many small things made sense. Her many telephone calls with her family. Never introducing him to any of them.

Slowly, as if a veil was taken from his eyes, he saw clearly, what she had really been up to all this time he had thought her a loving wife to him.

"Oh, my god. You must be right. Vanessa must be the main instigator, having wanted to gain access to my inventions and get an advantage with required technology. Only when she had thought she had everything she ever wanted, sole access to all the most securely kept secrets of the world, did she quickly prepare to get rid of me, and that quite effectively, even with the help of the CIA. But she had been too hasty, falling into the trap I had set up for my security, safeguarding the discovery. – Yes, that it was Vanessa all along, is quite possible, even very likely. But that does not mean Prof. Benning is not involved. On the contrary, he would try to do everything for the mother of his child."

"And what, if he, till now, did not know about the extent of it? Of why Vanessa had really given up their child?"

"Naïve girl." Merton spoke the words as if they were a condemnation.

"Better naïve than a cynic," Sophia countered snidely.

"Better safe than sorry."

"I didn't say we should go and meet him, just ask him what he wants to warn us about."

"That sounds like a good idea, doesn't it," Michael now intervened. "With your techy skills, he won't find us and you can find out what he wants."

"Go on. Ask him," Merton finally conceded.

Sophia, who had been about to rush out in anger and storm up to her room, sat down again and began to write.

"*Dear Prof. Benning,*

I have just seen the material you sent me. Is what you want to warn us about personal and about your family? Is that why you sent the articles? Is it about Vanessa? Is she the leader now?"

"Is that how you want to lure him out? You almost tell him what to answer you."

Prof. Lynford was still angry with her. Why that so easily made her angry herself, was quite a mystery to her. Why did this man affect her so? Was it, because she had felt so protected in his arms earlier this morning? Or was it, because she cared about his opinion of her? But why it was so important to her that he thought well of her, she could not say.

"What should I write then?"

"Leave out your suggestions and ask him what he wants. We can't meet and that's final."

Sophia deleted her writing and started again.

"… *I received your material well and had a look through it. We can't meet right now, as we are safely in hiding. Coming out would jeopardize that and put you and us in danger. What is it you want to warn us about?*

If you use a secure access point and go via a proxy server, you can leave us a secure message here and tell us."

She had just saved her message in the backend, when a new message turned up:

"*Vanessa must have taken over the 'syndicate'. She is out for blood, as Lynford betrayed her in keeping information from her. Her connections are everywhere. Be careful, trust nobody. Not even I am sure when I am manipulated by her. She wants this information and does not care how she gets it.*

I am not certain if it really is possible, but be careful to get the information into the right hands, not her emissaries. Be very careful and God's protection may keep you safe,

Your mentor."

He did not sign it with his name, but the signature told her more than anything that it was really him, Prof. Benning, who had written this message.

Merton stood directly behind her, but he did not say a word.

Michael first broke the silence. "What is it? Did he answer?"

"Yes. He warned us about Vanessa. No, actually about anyone involved, even the CIA."

"Your favorite guys at the moment anyway," Michael commented in a joking tone.

"Why is that?" Sophia turned around towards Merton to see his reaction.

"They left me to rot in prison," Merton spoke with a hint of emotion.

"But why should they have any say in your prison time? You were accused of trying to murder your wife out of jealousy." That much she now had learned from all the articles she had found about the criminal Prof. L.

"And my constant CIA watchdog conveniently saw nothing. And for whatever reason, they kept silent about me having a solid alibi against all her accusations."

"They could have proved your innocence?"

"Yes, without a doubt."

"Why didn't they …?"

"Like my dear wife, they already thought they had all the information they needed in the laboratory under the new supervision of Benning. And with me in prison, I was kept out of the way, no longer able to intervene with their own intended use of my findings. As a further bonus, they could press me to further work for them to cut a deal to get me out of prison, or just to better my conditions. They just didn't realize that the mafia would figure out before them that vital information was missing from the research notes. The syndicate offered me a deal including the release of Michael, before they even got close to figuring that out."

"So my rescuing you from those criminals who held you prisoner was not so inconvenient as you made it out to be?"

"You told the little dovey that her rescue was useless? Your ex really smashed your brain in, boss. Where would you be without the girly? Where would we both be? Right in this Vanessa-woman's clutches. I at least am grateful this little girly was caring enough to rescue you."

"She rescued me from you, to be exact."

"Only because she believed what we played for them."

"It looked extremely realistic," Sophia interrupted their

dialogue.

Bright red color spread over Michael's cheeks, who averted his face from her in shame, stammering: "Well, we ..., pretending ..., fellow inmates ..., rough ..."

"It was a necessary smokescreen. Don't worry, Michael. It's all right. It's none of her business anyway."

Shocked by the professor's abrupt dismissal of her, Sophia turned back to the computer to hide her emotions. Looking at Prof. Benning's message, Sophia tried to ignore both men, though it did not work that easily. Her head kept roaming around the question, why Merton was suddenly so angry with her. Was it solely because she did not believe that Prof. Benning wanted to do her harm?

Looking at the screen, she tried to blink back tears. She was annoyed with herself for being so pathetic to still have feelings of hero-worship for Merton, when by now she should know better that he was a cynical man. But this morning his genuine care for her had lulled her in.

When her vision cleared, she found a new comment by Prof. Benning with the header "*To Sophia*".

Making certain that both men were still occupied in their discussion, she opened the comment starting with "*delete after reading*".

Her eyes flew over the text Prof. Benning meant just for her to see:

"*Get away from them as soon as possible. Prof. L. is betraying the country and selling out his inventions. An attack is imminent. Location has been discovered. V. knows and made comment that the problem of her ex will be solved for her tonight. Get out of there and come back to town, immediately!!!*"

Sophia sat frozen in front of the screen. What to do? Could she leave, leave both men behind to die? But what about the invention? Did the secret service no longer want the information? Did they rather want to extinguish it than let it fall into the wrong hands? Was it that, why they so callously planned to kill now? Or had it been their plan all along, for leaving Merton in prison to die there? Nobody would care for a further inmate killed in a prison riot or brawl.

But one thing became clear to Sophia in that moment, her heart aching at the mere thought of harm befalling Merton in any way. She could not leave him here to die.

Interrupting the two men in the middle of their discussion she had not paid the least attention to, she stood up from the table and turned the notebook around to show it to Merton.

"We have to leave."

Her words abruptly brought the attention of both men to her. Merton and Michael both stepped closer and read the message on screen. Merton drew up an eyebrow in irony, as if not sure about what to think of her showing him this message.

"What information did you delete?"

"None. That is it. We have to leave this house. It's no longer safe."

"Says your dear professor."

"He might be right. He is worried. Better to be safe than sorry, to use your own words. We should go somewhere else quickly."

"And do you have any idea where we would find such a convenient and safe hiding place just at the spur of the moment?"

Prof. Lynford opposed her suggestion, while Michael without hesitation had turned to the kitchen cupboards and fridge and had started to pull out food and containers, to pack into a large clap-box he had pulled out from under the kitchen sink.

"Don't tease her, boss. We have no time to lose."

Merton quickly shut down the computer and packed it with Prof. Benning's notes into the computer bag.

"So we are leaving then, aren't we?" Sophia stood uncertainly next to the table, not knowing if she was welcome in whatever Merton prepared to do. Their happy and relaxed time from just this morning seemed so far away now.

"Pick up your rucksack, but don't leave the house."

Not having much to pack, she went up to the room where she had slept last night and picked up her bag, stuffing her jacket into it, then coming downstairs to find the two men waiting for her, ready to leave.

Taking her car keys, she expected them to head for the door, but Merton stopped her, holding her back by her arm.

"You can leave the keys here. You won't need them where we're going."

"Astonished, Sophia reluctantly dropped the keys to her old, reliable car on the table in the entrance hallway.

"But I have my handbag and purse still in my car."

"You won't need them. Leave them." Merton's instructions were curt and clipped.

Then, he lead the way to a stairway in the back of the house, leading to a roughly hewn cellar of some kind. The steps were uneven and seemed very old. The electric lighting obviously had been an afterthought and the rare light-bulbs did not help much in discovering the way into the complete darkness of the cliff-stone abyss.

The path felt musty and slippery and Sophia tried to stay as close as possible to the stone wall on one side of the stairway. The smell of saltwater intensified, so Sophia slowly understood where they were headed, when neither of her companions cared to enlighten her about their plans.

At the bottom of the seemingly endless stairway, the stonewalls opened up to a larger cave with a small opening to the sea, where a boat waited for them.

– 19 –
Distraction

The cave had such a small entrance, that Sophia was certain it could only be accessed through low tide.

"What would you have done at high tide?" Sophia could not help but ask, neither addressing Prof. Lynford nor Michael specifically, as they had not spoken to her through their entire descent.

"Waited," Merton answered monosyllabically. "Get in."

The boat was new and sparkly, and though she had not much knowledge about boats, she appreciated the length and slim form. It should be fast from what her un-discerning eye could make out.

Michael heaved his heavy bags and boxes on board and then helped Merton to stow away his things, when they heard voices from outside the cave.

"I'll go and distract them …" Michael began.

"You need to lead the way through the cliffs. I won't be able to make it out in time, looking for obstacles and maneuvering it at this low tide."

"I'll go," Sophia threw her rucksack on board and did not wait for a reply, but jumped from the wooden jetty down into the sand, leading in a thin stripe out through a bright blue hole in the cave.

"What is she doing? Hold her …" Merton pushed Michael with an urgent whisper, but the voices of two men approaching the entrance of the cave made him fall silent immediately.

Sophia rushed towards the light, blinking her eyes, to adjust them to the bright sun outside, trying to reach the last turn around the cave entrance, before the approaching men did.

When she came out, a long but narrow coastline opened up in front of her. The sand stripe continued for miles, but was empty as far as she could see. Still, she could hear the voices of the two men quite close.

Silently trying to find her way up the rough cliff, she determined the men must have found a hiding place somewhere above the cave entrance between the large boulders of cliff-stone, observing the house from a safe distance.

Prof. Benning was right after all. Their hiding place had been discovered.

Grateful for her comfortable shoes, which did not make a sound on the rough stone, she climbed further up, trying to circle around the supposed hiding place of the two men.

When she was certain she must be in the men's line-of-view to the house, she came out into the open, climbing over a large rocky peak.

Her plan was based on the hope, that the two men would want to stop her from getting information from Prof. Lynford ahead of them. Perceiving her as a potential rival for the research results, they hopefully would want to know for which rivaling organization she worked for and would not see a direct advantage in killing her immediately.

But when shots hit the stone next to her only moments later, she was quickly disabused of such optimistic hopes. One could not have everything one wanted, she thought, still not fully believing the reality of the danger she was in, but hurriedly scrambled down from her elevated position to hide from their view.

At least, they were no sharp-shooters, but only had pistols, firing in a wide range around her or where they presumed her to be. Fortunately, she was well hidden behind the solid cliff-stone for now, but she heard them approaching. So, they had taken interest in her, not just wanted to frighten her off. Her attempt to lure them away from the cave entrance and Merton could still work.

Sophia heard them coming from different sides. They tried to trap her behind the boulder. But she had chosen her position with intent. The path to the forest, which covered the whole area behind the house, began behind her, well hidden by the large stone-wall, shielding her from the view of her attackers.

Running with all the speed she could muster, thoughts of her sports lessons at school came up in her mind. She should have listened to her teacher better, as she had never managed to learn the right running technique.

Quite out of breath, she reached the first trees, but the two men had come up to her former hiding place and their wild shots spurred her to draw the last ounce of energy from her body. Surging through the trees, she tried to get as deep into the forest as possible, to find a place to hide and throw off her pursuers.

With relief, she finally heard the engine of a motorboat. Michael and Prof. Lynford must have managed to escape. She therefore changed her route to get closer to the house, to reach her car, but was cut off by sounds of cracking twigs coming from that direction towards her. Hurriedly she sank into a heap of leaves next to the path, which must have accumulated because of an overhanging boulder.

"She must be here somewhere," she heard a man's voice coming from the direction of the house.

"Who is she?" one of her pursuers from behind her asked. "Why did we have to shoot at her. She is surely just a girl on vacation."

"There are no school vacations right now. And didn't you see? She is the girl from the restaurant," the first man returned impatiently.

"No way. That girl in the restaurant was Prof. Benning's doctoral candidate. What would she be doing here?" the second man following her from the cliffs intervened.

But a new voice interfered, cutting the others off. – Could that be? Could that possibly really be Prof. Benning's new assistant, Dr. Stewart?

Sophia had always tried to avoid him, as he had so intensely stared at her, not moving a single muscle in his whole body. That had made her feel distinctly uncomfortable in his presence. But now being in league with the men shooting at her made him immediately plummet further in her esteem.

"We need to catch her, whatever she's doing here. She must be one of the syndicate, sent to spy on Prof. Benning," Dr. Stewart instructed the others with an authoritative voice. Like an afterthought, he added: "I never liked her anyway. Uptight bitch. Always so high and mighty and never deviating from work. That alone should have made me suspicious of her. But Prof. Benning trusted her and kept her in the dark about what was going on with all the work he gave her, so I thought, she was safe. But see what my putting a tracker into her purse brought up. It lead us directly to the hiding place of this Lynford-convict. See what an innocent bystander she is now. – Whitchurch, Stockton, bring her in, dead or alive. I don't care."

The tightly spoken order, not much above a whisper, came

from directly next to her.

Sophia trembled in her hiding place between bushes and the lush vegetation of high grass and rambling weeds, which beneath the boulder had caught the straying leaves and built her cover. She hoped, jumping from the path directly into the middle of the underbrush, where she sank in quite deeply, would hide all her tracks from her pursuers and not show where she was by leaving bent grass and broken twigs. Crouching down into the dirt, she made her body as small as possible.

She could only hear the steps of two men close to her, but the deep vegetation and mound of old grass she had drawn over her, hid them from her view. Praying that her cover worked both ways, she tried to remain as motionless as possible.

With sticks, they poked into the undergrowth, one move almost hitting her, but then slipping over the side of her neck further down to the bottom of the hole she was sitting in, leaving an ache behind. She heard the stick twisting and turning around, but drawing back, it did not come close to her again, the overhanging boulder forming this hole protecting her back.

"Nothing in here," the second of her pursuers from the cliff spoke up only feet away from her. "Where could she have run to?"

"Not to the house. That's for sure. Markham had that covered."

"Stewart's right. A little troublesome bitch she is. We didn't even know she was here. Who else might be around? Tony reported a speedboat checking out the coast just moments ago. None of our guys, though. Who might they have been? Her accomplices or just some more of the hyenas circling around this self-proclaimed inventor-god? Much too arrogant for my liking. Did him well to sit in prison for a while. Should have remained there to rot, as intended."

"Markham and Tony were glad to be rid of their surveillance duty over this dratted professor, that is for sure," the second of her followers fell in with the babbling of the first man, as if not caring the least if she could overhear them. They clearly did not fear her getting any information that was not intended for her, or rather seemed certain she would not be able to tell anyway. Sophia shuddered at that thought.

"No sign of her. She seems to have dissolved into thin air. Must have used the boulders in the area to throw us off her track. But it doesn't matter. When the air-strike hits, her goal will no longer be available anyway. Might even take her with it, as she seems to have escaped in the direction of the house. So, either Markham or the detonation will get her."

The steps of the two men receded, but Sophia did not dare to move for a long while after.

From what the men had spoken of, she presumed they were with a secret service agency, if not the CIA itself. Merton had been right. They had wanted to get rid of him by letting him go to prison.

'Nice gesture, guys,' she thought. And trying to eliminate her only made it clear that they wanted a full cover up and no longer the invention itself. What a comforting thought that was.

But not being able to reach the house or her car, while Michael and Merton hopefully had successfully escaped in the meanwhile, she had no idea where else she could go.

The speedboat the men had spoken of, must have been Merton's long, sleek vessel. Though she had always thought speedboats had no masts like the boat she had seen in the cave. Could she reach them and would Merton even care to rescue her from the predicament she found herself in? At breakfast, all her hero-worship for him had come back with full force. He could be so very charming when he wanted to. But normally, he was just blunt and as annoying as possible towards her.

Had he been jealous that she had defended Prof. Benning? As soon as she had mentioned her professor's name, all the relaxed atmosphere they had shared during breakfast had gone out of the room with a puff. But being jealous would mean that he had to care for her, at least a little. And that he certainly did not do.

Though the memory of him holding her in his arms this morning, made silent tears trickle down her cheeks. She had felt so safe and protected then. And now, she was alone and cold and all wet in this watery dump, a hole of leaves and old grass beneath a large stone in a forest far from town.

Should she try to reach Prof. Benning? But without a mobile phone or computer and something to eat, her only option was to go on foot. She would need days to come anywhere close to town and the roaming agents would pick her up long before that.

After what must have been about a quarter of an hour gone by without hearing any more of the two men from the cliff, or the man they had called Markham and Dr. Stewart, she slowly untangled herself from the old grass and wet leaves and with aching bones carefully made her way back to the hidden cave down below. On her way, she used every protection she could get, hiding behind stones and bushes.

At least, the cave would give her protection against the

elements and an eventual air-strike – if what she had heard really could be believed. Who had ever heard of a secret service having access to missiles or anything like that? It also threatened to rain again any moment now, as if her descent on the slippery stone was not dangerous enough as it was.

– 20 –
Tension at Sea

Hurting and exhausted, Sophia came around the last bend to enter the cave and what she saw totally threw her. In her relief and happiness, she sank to the soft sandy ground onto her knees. Looking into the cave, she saw the long boat still in its original place, with a sail set up, waiting at the jetty.

"What …?" She stammered, but her voice must have carried, as Merton jumped onto the wooden plank and came running to her. Sinking into the sand next to her, he took her into his arms, not bothered by her muddy and wet state, tightly drawing her to him, his hands wildly roaming her body, as if to make certain that she was still in one piece.

"Stupid girl," he murmured into her dirt encrusted hair. "How could you do that to me?"

"What did I do to you?" Sophia asked, not understanding what he meant.

"As if you don't know. You cost me years of my life with what you did. Running into danger like that."

"But they would have killed you, if they had found you."

He did not seem surprised by that revelation, but continued unerringly: "That's no reason to put yourself in danger, ever. You must promise me never to do something so stupid ever again. – Promise me."

Taking her up into his arms, he carried her to the boat.

When he tried to bring her on board, she began to struggle. "No. I am much too dirty for that."

Irritated, he looked her up and down.

"There is a shower on board."

But Sophia just jumped from the jetty, with clothes and all. The coldness of the clear water shocked her, but it took away all the leaves in her hair and the dirt all over. It felt wonderful to get rid of all the mud, that not even the icy water could dampen her joy.

Splashing and swimming back to the jetty, she tried to get up, but it was so high that Merton needed to help her on.

Laughter in his eyes, when he studied her, standing wet like a soaked mouse next to him, made him appear younger and carefree, like she had never seen him before.

"Come now, we need to get on our way," he urged her on, helping her not to slip on the wooden planks of the ship.

In the surprisingly comfortable cabin, he offered her a large blanket and was about to leave her to let her have a shower and get changed, when she held him back:

"Where is Michael?"

"He went out with the motor boat, to distract them from you. We'll meet him again later."

"And you took the risk to stay behind? To wait for me?"

"What else was there to do, when a girl goes crazy?"

But his tender smile, something she was not used to, took the sting away from his words.

"Now go, change, before you catch a cold. You'll find a shirt and things in the cupboard behind you."

Leaving her alone, only moments later she felt the boat move, no motor, but he seemed to have pushed it away from the jetty in the direction of the cave's exit.

While still in the shower, she felt, when outside the cave the sails drew wind and the boat took up speed.

Coming out of the shower, she felt warm again and wearing comfortable clothes, a much too large button-down shirt and sailing pants, which fortunately had a string to pull together and bind around her waist to hold them in place. She went on to wash her own soiled clothes, not knowing when she would ever see her own wardrobe again.

Merton found her still splashing in the small bathroom stall of the cabin, when he came down about twenty minutes later. Hesitating at the sound of water, he came in, when he saw her fully clothed, standing in the doorway to the shower.

"Everything all right with you? He asked, watching her.

"Yes, I just wanted to be prepared in case I need my clothes again."

"Ah, all right. Are you hungry? You've been away for almost two hours."

Sophia had lost all sense of time during her flight, but now she was ravenous.

Before she had a chance to answer, a loud detonation some distance away from their boat brought them up on deck. The bright sun clouded by plumes of dark smoke coming from the top of the cliff where they had been just hours ago.

What they saw was an image of destruction. A large globe of fire and dark smoke hid the top of the mountain where once the cozy old house had been.

"The air-strike. They really did it." Sophia could not help but stammer.

"They? Who?" Merton asked inquisitively.

"The CIA, at least I think."

"What makes you think that was the CIA? You don't know any of them. Did you talk with your pursuers? Are you one of them?"

"No! – How can you even think such a thing? I would never …"

"I used to trust people I would never have thought could betray me, but they did without even blinking an eye. – Now, tell me the truth. How do you know they were CIA?"

"I don't really 'know'. I just presumed, because one voice I thought I recognized was that of Prof. Benning's assistant Dr. Stewart. The one who re-formulated all my topic proposals, till you refused to take them on."

"Mangling your research ideas proves his involvement with the CIA for you? I personally never heard of Dr. Stewart."

"No. It's not just that, but all together. His influential position with Prof. Benning, his being involved everywhere, his appearance here, his announcing an air-strike, his knowledge of your whereabouts, his commanding of Markham and Tony, as if they were all in the right to eliminate you, as they already had intended for you in prison."

"He said that?"

"Not he alone, but the two men who shot at me, who knew Dr. Stewart and followed his orders. They no longer seemed to be interested in getting the results of your research, but rather to prevent you from distributing it to the highest bidder. But you would never …"

The roaring of a distant motor interrupted their discussion, but though trying, they could not find the source of it. Only after a while, a helicopter emerging from land, landed on the now already far distant cliff-top, where still small lines of smoke rose up into the sky.

Their boat moved unhindered and though they met with fishing boats and later on some cruise ships, their comparatively small boat did not draw much attention.

When dusk settled, they were already far out at sea and out of sight of any further ships or boats.

The question she had begun to ask before they had been interrupted, had not been brought up again. Sophia feared what his answer may be. But as Merton had taken over the helm, Sophia had gone down to the minuscule kitchen, preparing a light meal for them. She was just bringing up her results, when once again the sounds of a motor could be heard, this time clearly approaching in a direct line to them.

Sophia, not knowing what best to do now that they were the target of the approaching motorboat, jumped up, but Merton reached out and drew her into his embrace, still holding the helm steady.

"Hush, it's all right. Everything is as planned."

When Sophia only shuddered in fear, she felt his embrace tighten.

"But …," she began, but her protest was stopped by warm, soothing lips, stroking hers.

Forgetting her initial thoughts, she opened to the gentle caress of his lips on hers and her hands moved up to embrace his neck. The warmth of his body in the frisky air of the sea gave her a peace like she had never felt possible, blotting out every other thought from her mind. It completely eluded her, that the approaching motorboat had reached their vessel, till the voice of Michael spoke almost next to her.

"Obviously, I don't need to ask how you have been during my absence."

Jumping away from Merton like she had been burnt, Sophia slammed into the helm right in her back, the professor's arms trying to keep her steady, but she pushed them away.

"Everything as planned?" Merton asked Michael, seeming quite unaffected by their kiss.

"Patty will surely lynch me, as soon as he hears about the

house."

"Don't worry, Michael. He'll get enough from the money to rebuild it twofold."

"Money? What money?" Sophia's worst nightmares were confirmed. All her fears about the motives of Prof. Lynford came crashing onto her, weighing her down, so that she could hardly take a breath.

"The money from the sales, of course," Michael confirmed, smiling smugly, while Merton watched her carefully.

"What sales?" Her voice quivered wearily.

"The sales of the research results." Merton calmly answered her, as if he patiently had to explain things to a slow child.

How could she have been so mistaken in Prof. Lynford? She had thought him to fight for the good. Had she placed him so much on a pedestal that she had not been able to see the truth? Making her help a man who was about to betray his country to get the most profit out of his research, not caring for the lives he crushed on his way?

"No! You can't do that. You can't sell your research. It will be devastating. You can't do that!"

"I can and I will."

She felt Michael's watchful eyes on her, while she glared at Prof. Lynford.

"Please don't."

"You can't change my mind. Things are already set in motion."

"No! Please. You can't mean to do that. It will destroy everything. The results are completely incalculable. You must stop your plans."

"That's no longer possible, I fear."

"Please!"

"No. You have no idea what you are asking."

"Then explain it to me," Sophia begged, trying to get him to rethink selling the knowledge to the highest bidder, giving them a technology that would enable them to break into the most secure vaults with ease.

"It will be a catastrophe, whomever you sell it to. Who is it you have chosen?"

Merton looked at her coldly. From his gaze, she would never have guessed that he had held her in his arms so comfortingly just moments ago.

"That depends." His voice matched the icy coldness of his eyes, when he saw her picking up her notebook computer which he had used back in the house, ready to throw it overboard.

"On what?" she challenged.

"Just tell her, boss. You're playing with her," Michael tried to intervene.

"She must learn that it's none of her business to whom the technology goes. She can't prevent it. Even with such childish antics."

"She won't do anything hasty. I'll take care of her."

"You what? You want to ..." Sophia was speechless, that Michael, approaching her with thick rope, wanted to bind her to prevent her from interfering with their plans.

While Sophia tried to evade Michael, Merton easily grabbed her from behind, preventing her from throwing her computer overboard. She had held it tightly, still clinging to the hope that Merton could not possibly be so callous as to sell his invention to the highest bidder, whoever that may be.

Michael easily and efficiently bound her and took her below deck like a sack over his shoulder. There, he bound her to a chair, which was screwed to the cabin floor. Sophia in her emotional upheaval, began to cry silently, but Michael sensed her distress, looking at her with sad eyes, unsure what to say.

"I thought Merton would be better," Sophia sobbed. "I hoped you both would do the right thing with his invention. But all you want is money. How could I not have seen that?"

Michael's sad face, without words, begged for her understanding. Kneeling in front of her, he came to her eye level.

"It's not as bad as that. Everything will be all right. You'll see, little girly. He's not a bad man. He's just a little bit hardened, you see, after what his wife did to him and all."

"He made me risk my life for him, just to sell his technology to dangerous criminals. No knowledge will be safe any longer, if it gets into the wrong hands."

"You'll see, everything will work out. Don't lose your trust in him …"

But Merton's voice from up on deck interrupted them.

"Come up here, Michael. Leave her alone. She can simmer alone in her idealistic daydreams."

"It is night and thinking about you gives me nightmares," Sophia petulantly shouted back up, but the only reaction she got, was the sound of male chuckling.

He did not even take her protest seriously, but found her amusing. Good that she was bound to the chair, or she would be tempted to kill him with her bare hands.

Patting her knee gently, Michael left her and went up to Merton, where she heard their murmuring voices, but could not make out any words.

After a while, she heard the motorboat again, but this time, it seemed to pull their sailing boat along, as she felt the swift movement in the hull.

Being left alone and unable to do anything at all, Sophia's fantasy ran wild with possibilities, and as her fantasy never lacked fodder, the possibilities she came up with were quite various. By the time steps approached a while later, her heart-rate had accelerated to a frantic speed in fear of what might happen.

It was Merton himself, who came into the small kitchen-combined-living-room area on board the boat, where Michael had restrained her.

Stopping at the entrance, a smile broke out on his face, when he saw her bound form.

Angrily, Sophia hissed at him in response: "You traitor, you betrayer, ..." But adequate words for his heinous treachery failed her.

Her accusations did not seem to faze him, though he at least started to defend his actions.

"Come on, Sophia. In time you will see that we have no other choice. Or would you rather have Michael's friend remain without recompense for his completely flattened house?"

"But the CIA surely ..."

"No. They don't. Or do you truly think they will pay him to rebuild his house? Even admitting to what they have done is rather unlikely. Dream on, if you really think that will happen."

"They can't just ..."

"They can and they did. Just to get rid of us and an inconvenient problem."

"And how does it help to bind me here?" Sophia mustered all her bravery, but strangely, she did not fear that Prof. Lynford would really do her harm. Though from the sound of the discussion between Michael and him, she had had the impression that Merton had insisted on keeping her restrained and in the dark about their plans.

"It helps to let me do my work without your interference." Prof. Lynford drew out her notebook, plugged it in and began to work as if she were not there.

"You can't just ignore me. What's going on?"

"I can and there's no need for you to know."

"Please. I can't just sit here and not know. I thought you to be brilliant. How can you do something that will most likely harm so many people? People who have done nothing to you, who are innocent bystanders in your fight against those who tried to harm and kill you."

"What do you think I am about to do?" Merton asked without showing a sign of emotion, not leaving her out of sight for even a second.

Sophia felt as if being pinned like a butterfly to a board under his watchful scrutiny. "You'll sell your discovery to the people who pay you the most for it."

"And who do you think they might be?"

"A government, a mafia organization. Whoever can pay the highest bid."

"Well, there are many who try. Offers are coming in by the minute. Therefore, it is essential that you don't hinder my work right now, at a time where it is vital to show that the airstrike did not prevent the execution of the deal."

"You've already prepared for every eventuality?"

"Yes. It was my plan all along. The intervention of the CIA just makes it necessary to confirm the go-ahead of the transactions."

"Who is it, who will get your technology?"

The smile on Merton's face was so cynical, that Sophia

shivered under its coldness.

"Whoever is ready to pay."

"What? You don't know yet?"

"I do know." Merton glanced down at his wrist watch. "The transaction will take place in exactly two hours at midnight.

"We've reached international waters by now and by then, we will be in place to hand you over."

"What? You want to leave me with the criminals you sell your technology to?"

"If you see the CIA that way, yes."

"You'll sell to the CIA, though they tried to kill you?"

"It will be the safest place for you."

"But … – Where will you and Michael go?"

"I doubt the CIA will see our presence in their midst favorably."

– 21 –
Preparations at Sea

Sophia creased her brows. Something was going on which she did not grasp at all. She was missing some essential parts of his plan, but what?

Merton used her silence, to tap onto the keys of her notebook forcefully, not the least disturbed by her quietness.

If he sold to the CIA, shouldn't they be happy and welcome him back, if not gladly, at least reluctantly? But why would they be a dangerous place for Michael and the inventor of the technology the CIA was so determined to get a hold of, that they were prepared to kill for it or to destroy it in its entirety to prevent it from getting into the wrong hands?

They already held all his research and had access to his laboratory. So why would they be unhappy, if they even could get a hold of the inventor himself, solving all the remaining riddles they had not been able to solve on their own?

"You are selling it to more parties than the CIA!" Sophia blurted out, too shocked at her own thought to keep it to herself.

After the silence before, Merton jumped in surprise at the way she shouted out her realization.

"Took you a while to figure that part out, my dear," he conceded, as if he had never had a doubt she would finally work the essence of his plan out.

"That's too dangerous. You can't do that. How could that possibly work? To whom will you sell?" Questions stumbled out of her unhindered.

"Whoever is willing to pay. And to say the least, there are quite a few who are, all around the world, as the money is flowing in from all sources right now."

"And you are collecting? And do you intend to deliver as well, to all of them?"

"Of course. I stand by my word."

"Oh my. God help me. You can't be sane."

"It's not that bad. You'll see. Only two more hours to go. The CIA will collect you."

"And if I don't want to go with them?"

"You shouldn't. Or they will see you as my accomplice. You should rather not want that."

"Why?"

"Can't you imagine? The world will want to hunt us down, when the information no longer has the value they thought it to have."

"But you said it does work as intended. You have the proof, don't you?" Sophia no longer sounded so confident and Merton observed the quickly changing emotions her face so easily revealed, seeing her doubt and disappointment in him.

The change from her opposition to trust and back to her fighting his plans bothered him more than he had anticipated. The urge to let her loose, take her into his arms and comfort her, like he had held her just this morning, surprised him. Feeling responsible for her and wanting to see her approval of his plans, made him more vulnerable than he wanted to be. He had thought he had left the manipulations behind, when he got his divorce from his wife. But Sophia put him under quite a different emotional pressure. He wanted her to condone his plans, to work with him and to smile. Images of her rushing into his arms, embracing, kissing … – He had to break off his line of thoughts forcefully. He had to hand her over to the authorities. He had to keep her safe. He could not be so selfish as to force her to risk her safety for an ideal, like he and Michael were ready to do. He could not, would not ask her to risk her future for him.

Michael had called him a fool earlier. He knew he was. Wanting a girl much too innocent and idealistic for her own good. How could he want a fate for her to always be a fugitive, to look for assassins wherever they went. He could not do that to her.

It just surprised him, how hard it was for him to stick to that decision.

Her next words made his steadfastness waver even more.

"Please, don't send me away. Let me stay with you and Michael, please. I do trust you. I am convinced you could not betray your ideals. However you plan to do this, I know it's for the best for everyone. Please let me stay." Sophia did not know if her words were completely true, but what she did know was, that she could not bear the thought of being separated from him.

How did that happen, that this haughty and imperious man suddenly meant so much to her? She had thought that by now she had been able to overcome her infatuation with him, which had been solely based on his ingenious inventions. So why did this man suddenly mean so much to her, that she rather argued with him than was apart from him?

It took Merton some effort not to give in to her plea but to reestablish his hardened façade. "You know no such thing, little Miss Innocence. What do you think your role would be in the relationship between Michael and me?"

Sophia's features fell, her disappointment obvious.

Stammering, she tried again: "But Michael … – You said it was just a smokescreen, not real, not true …"

"To get you to trust us, to comply with whatever we did."

"No! Michael wouldn't. He's not like you."

"And you would want to stay with a man 'like' me?"

Approaching her, his eyes bored into her wide-open ones, disbelief in her features.

But Merton had to convince her, for her own sake. Even if seeing her that way, tears streaming down her soft cheeks, broke his own heart.

Her safety was more important than his own happiness. Knowing her to be safe would have to suffice for him, as being with him, she would be in constant danger, hunted down by every opportunist and organization of the world. Her future safety depended on staying far away from him, even if he had to fight her and convince her of his own irredeemability, to get her to stay away.

Standing close behind her, his hand wandered down her cheek to her throat and following the exposed line of her collarbone. He felt Sophia shiver under his soft caress, her bindings preventing her drawing back from him.

She held her breath, closing her eyes, but he would not allow her to cut him out of her consciousness.

Bending down to her ear, his breath touched her skin and her rushed intake of air showed him that she was as aware as he of the electrically charged tension between them.

"You want me, my girl. Don't deny that. Would you rather have me make you my toy, whenever I am not occupied with Michael?"

"I'm not … – I don't …"

"Nice try, my sweet, but your body shows me differently."

His one hand moved down from the top of her breasts into

her cleavage, grabbing her naked breast beneath her bra, which she had put back on still damp, not to feel so naked under the borrowed shirt.

When she gasped and tried to scream, his other hand took hold of her neck and turned her head towards him, to give him full access to her opened mouth, of which he took merciless advantage.

His lips on hers were far from gentle, demanding her submission, taking complete control of her, giving her no choice but to give in to him.

Only after long moments of dominating her unresisting mouth, did his kiss soften and his tongue gently stroke her lips, teasing a response from her, which she hesitantly, but full-heartedly gave.

Her lips left burning imprints on his, when he finally drew back, staring down at her with unblinking eyes.

Her first attempt to speak was just a croak, so she cleared her throat and tried again: "Why did you do that, if you love Michael?"

"To show you that I could easily use you as my little sex-toy, if you indeed want to stay with us."

"I don't believe you. What use would you have for me, if Michael is who you desire?"

"What is it you don't believe? Me wanting to fuck you as well as him? Well, we could start right now."

"You can't mean that."

"Should I show you?" Merton began to loosen the bindings on her arms behind her back, fastening her to the chair. As soon as her arms were loose, he drew her up into his arms, not waiting for her feet to be released. He pulled up her shirt, freely exploring her naked upper body beneath her clothes.

At first, Sophia did not protest. Only when his callous treatment of her broke through the fuzziness in her brain, which still lingered from his devastating kiss, did she try to ward him off, his hands much too experienced for her to evade him easily. His deep throated laughter showing her that he treated her protests rather as a funny interlude than an effective distraction from his plans. His hands roaming over her, touching, stimulating and though she was now fighting him in earnest, strangely arousing.

"Have you changed your mind about her?" the loud voice of Michael interrupted them.

They had both not realized that in the meanwhile the boat had stopped, the motorboat no longer pulling them along, and Michael had come back on board.

Merton immediately let go of her and stepped back, to evade further temptation.

"No," he answered harshly.

"Well, you still have time," Michael returned with a smirk.

Sophia looked between the two, now, after what Merton had just told her, once again re-evaluating the relationship between the two men.

"There's no place for her with us. You know that." Merton's voice was gruff, as the two men left the cabin. Though Sophia could still hear their voices from up on deck this time.

"Oh, that's the card you are playing with her again. Don't you think she deserves a bit more from you, for running right into danger to save your hide? The little deary loves you and almost killed herself for you."

"And that was the first and last time she should get a chance to do something as stupid as that."

"You want to push her away, because you fear you could return her feelings. You fear you could love her back."

"She has no reason to love me and she shouldn't. It is better for her if she forgets all about this."

"You really want to send her away just like that?"

"It's for the best. – Are we in position, yet?"

"Not completely. Everything is right up to plan. We will be at the time of the exchange."

"Good. Keep her here. I need to check the last details."

When Prof. Lynford came back into the cabin, he did not pay her the least attention, but fully engrossed himself in what had formerly been her notebook. This helped her disguise the fact that she had managed to free herself from her foot-bindings.

Sophia was so angry with him about being completely ignored and her wishes not taken into account at all, that she jumped up, took hold of her notebook, to effectively stop Merton from executing his plans. But her escape was cut short, when instead of running up the steps to the deck, she rammed full speed into the bulky form of Michael.

How could that be? She had just heard his steps go to the other end of the boat. But though she held tight, the computer was wrestled from her hands and Michael easily held her securely around her waist.

"No!" Sophia wailed desperately. "Please, don't give it back to him. It's mine."

"It's for the best, deary." Michael held out the computer to Merton, far out of her reach and all her efforts to get it back were in vain.

"Please, Michael. Don't let him do this. It will hurt so many people."

"No, deary. You have it all wrong. It's the only way to prevent people from getting hurt. – Merton, you should tell her. Surely she'd understand."

"It's better for her if she doesn't know anything. Otherwise they will try to make her a pawn in their twisted games. She must stay out of it. I made certain they did understand that she was an innocent bystander. Otherwise they would lynch her during the release."

"Release?" Sophia did not understand anything any longer. What had the CIA to 'release'?

But neither Michael nor Merton answered her.

Sophia's mind spun around in circles, but she did not get any more chance to ask questions, when Prof. Lynford ordered Michael to bind and gag her this time.

Glaring at him, Sophia wished her eyes were lasers to burn right through him and cut him into pieces.

But Michael just pulled out a dark grey hanky from his pocket, which smelled a bit like grease and motor oil, and shoved it into her mouth, to bind the ends tightly in her neck. Her long hair caught in his knot and she winced, when he tore her hair out.

Michael patted her on her head like a little puppy, when he was finished. This time at least, he had not bound her to the chair.

"Don't worry, little girly. It's for the best. You can trust him. He knows what he's doing, and he cares for you too much to put you into harm's way."

Sophia fervently shook her head 'no'. How should she trust a man who bound and gagged her and was about to betray her ideals? Well, to be exact, to sell knowledge to your own country's secret service by a lot of people's standards would not be seen as betraying one's ideals, but Sophia was convinced they would use this sensitive knowledge to harm others without remorse. Selling those men who had tried to kill them this sensitive information was just not right.

Having the information on how to break into secure vaults would mean they would use it, giving them an unjust advantage against those unsuspecting of such machinations, throwing over the fragile balance of power in the world.

Sophia did not believe in a world where only money and greed ruled everything. She would try to protect those not able to do it themselves with her last breath if necessary. But all her efforts to loosen her newly fastened ropes were useless against the expert nautical knots Michael had bound her with. He had pushed her onto the small bunk in the cabin, sitting down next to her. To prevent her from jumping up and crawling away, she presumed.

Prof. Lynford once again was engrossed in the notebook without paying her struggles the least attention. Michael left her alone from time to time, checking their position, while Merton clicked and tipped away on the notebook for almost an hour, before turning away from the screen.

"All is in place now, Michael. We can proceed. The clock is ticking."

"Are you certain you want to hand her over with it?"

"There's no other way. And right now, I have my doubts she would even want to stay with me."

"You frightened the little deary away. She could come with us …"

"No!" Prof. Lynford's voice sounded rough from suppressed emotion.

Sophia could not tell what it was. Was he angry with her, that she did not agree with him and could not sanction his greedy deal with the men who had shot at her? What did he expect?

That she fell into the role as his plaything, as he had so vividly drawn for her? But handing her over to those men she did not trust was no better than making a deal with them. What would they think of her, after they had tried to kill her before? Would they finish the job they had not been able to complete earlier today?

Sophia had no idea why Merton thought her to be safer with them than with him. She would still prefer to stay with him – though he thought her to have changed her mind. As much as he tried to irritate her, she still felt a deep-seated trust in him. She even tried to make excuses for his greed in selling his invention to the highest bidders. At least, she trusted him more than the authorities, though with the sleazy Dr. Stewart on the side of the CIA, that was not such a big stretch.

If given the choice, she would rather avoid having to confront the agents again, who had tried to shoot her without warning. But for the moment, a more pressing matter forced her to struggle with renewed force against her bonds. Both men fortunately had left her alone in the cabin for a check on deck and she tried with vigor, but the knots did not even budge. When Michael came back a short while later, she pushed her bound feet against him, to get his attention.

"What is it, girly?" He easily grabbed her around her waist with one arm, to pull her upright.

Annoyed with her inability to answer him, he pushed her gag down, the strong cotton fabric cutting painfully into her skin, but Sophia was much too glad to make her problem known to pay any attention to her scratches.

"I need a toilet, urgently."

"Thought as much," Michael stood up to give her space.

"Keep a good eye on her," Merton leant down from the upper

deck. "She's sure to try something."

"Why would I, when all I want is to get away from you?" Sophia shot back.

"It was so peaceful, when you were gagged," he retorted and left her and Michael alone again.

"I can't go like that," Sophia stated matter-of-factly, standing up next to the bunk on her bound legs, wobbly balancing with her hands still tightly bound by the scratchy rope.

Michael without hesitation released the tight knots as if they were nothing, where she had fought for almost an hour and had not made them budge even a tiny bit.

Giving him a cursory smile of thanks, she turned to the bathroom, where she had taken a shower before, but Michael turned her around and lead her to a tiny store-room next to the stairway on deck, a room she had not even taken note of before.

He stepped away and she was glad that he let her do her business at least with some pretense of privacy on the tightly fitted boat.

Finished and straightening up her clothes, she had no intention to let herself be meekly bound and gagged again.

Opening the door, she found Michael sitting on the bunk at the other side of the cabin.

Taking her chances, she rushed up the few steps on deck, escaping him. She immediately heard his heavy steps behind her, but did not pause, instead rushed out to determine where the professor was. Seeing him at the helm, Sophia rushed to the motorboat, fastened to the side of the sailing boat. Jumping overboard, the motorboat shook heavily, as if wanting to throw her off, but Sophia managed to settle it and find the rope with which it was bound to the main boat. She just had to try and run from the plans Prof. Lynford had made for her.

But before she could loosen the rope, the whole rope was thrown down to her.

Lifting her head up, she found Merton looking down at her with a strange mixture of emotions on his face. Not anger, like she would have expected, but rather sadness and resignation.

"Good bye, my sweet girl."

"What's going on?"

Michael appeared at his side, waving down at her. "Take care of yourself, little girly."

"That was your plan all along. You throw me out to the wolves. I rescued you. Is that the thanks for that? – They will kill me."

"No. You need to insist that you had nothing to do with all of this. And indeed, you didn't. You are a civilian accidentally caught up in these events. I made that clear to them. The CIA will find and protect you. They know where you are and will come for you. Don't try to run. It will only make them suspicious of you."

"That's it then?"

"Yes," Merton stated with a sad smile. "It has to be."

Unable to form adequate words out of the maelstrom of her mind, she gaped at the two men, slowly disappearing into the darkness with their boat.

Unmoving, Sophia was even unable to make the decision to start the motor of her little boat. What sense would it make anyway? Like Prof. Lynford had said, the CIA would find her in no time, even if she tried to escape them.

And indeed, she had to wait no more than ten minutes, before a large military vessel with a brightly lit American flag approached her in her comparatively tiny cockleshell. She had no idea what kind of war ship it was, but is towered skyscraper-like high over her.

A rescue ladder was thrown down to her and feeling out of options, Sophia climbed up the precariously swinging rungs.

– 22 –
On a War Ship

On deck, a surprising sight met Sophia's eyes.

Prof. Benning and Dr. Stewart, surrounded by officers in diverse uniforms, were waiting for her. But those she feared most, were the ominous men in dark suits standing in the background.

Behind her, she heard metallic clicking and turning around, still too surprised to speak, found the motorboat being lifted up on deck by a large pulley.

"Good to see you are well," Prof. Benning came forward from the strange assembly, but his greeting was stiff and formal, even for him. The men around him did not leave his side, but observed their interaction closely.

"Thank you, Prof. Benning. Good to see you are well, too. – What is going on here? What is this all about?"

Her general questions, pretending not to know anything about what was happening, made the tension on Prof. Benning's face lessen a tiny bit. Sophia took that as a hint that he, like Prof. Lynford, wanted her to pretend that she had no idea about the importance or the nature of the deal that was about to take place here.

Two of the dark clad men jumped into the small motorboat, now hanging over the dark grey metal deck and were searching it, only moments later coming up with a red metal box, like a little safe for cash.

They obviously had the combination, because they had the box open in mere seconds, and were holding the content, a storage device, out to Prof. Benning, who stepped away from Sophia to take it.

A marine held her back, when she tried to follow the professor. A harsh command was shouted out, which took her a moment to identify Dr. Stewart as the one who had ushered it and herself as the one who was indicated in it: "Get the traitor down and keep her locked up and out of the way. We will question her later, as soon as one of the interrogation-rooms is free again."

He seemed to hold some significant authority with the CIA, taking command of this entire ship so undisputedly. Perhaps that was why he had always appeared so misplaced in her university laboratory. His efforts to command everything and everyone around had irritated her greatly. His interference regarding her research had only made her try to oppose and evade him. At a commanding level, his personality suddenly made much more sense, though Sophia heartily pitied his subordinates.

But her still too stunned brain had not much time for further musings.

Two men at her side harshly grabbed her arms and rushed her below deck into the deep bowels of this metal box of a war ship and pushed her into a minuscule cabin. She presumed it must be close to the engine room of the ship, as it was suffocatingly hot.

The two men fortunately left her alone in the room immediately, obviously not liking the burning heat in the room either. They did not even search her, though that would not have brought up anything anyway. But still, Sophia wondered as to why.

The metal door was shut and securely locked, but as she was not bound, Sophia immediately started to inspect her surroundings.

If her future depended on the likes of Dr. Stewart, she did not trust her safety at all. She'd rather try to get out than depend on his non-existent goodwill, when he openly called her a traitor.

What grated a bit on her, was the fact that Prof. Benning had not contradicted that statement, but she pushed that diverting thought out of her mind and instead concentrated on her own rescue.

Sophia did not find hints of surveillance in the room, so she proceeded to examine the metal door locking her in more closely.

She had once read that a door's security mostly depended on the lock to deter the attention, while their weakest points were their hinges. To her relief, this door was not even a challenge for a beginner like her. The hinges were just screwed on and as she was in a kind of supply room, there should surely be something around that could be used as a screw. And indeed, a whole case of screws sat dusty and unused in the corner of one of the inbuilt shelves, covering all the walls of this tiny room, which was not much wider than the door.

Happily, Sophia tried to lift the box, but found it locked to the shelf. Well, she thought, that made sense, as this way the box could not be thrown around during heavy seas. Delving into the tool-case, there were more screws than she thought one could ever need and the problem now lay in finding one that fitted. But with that wide array, that was the least of her worries, though it took her a while to find an adequate one.

Not hesitating, but carefully listening for anyone being close to the door on the other side, she remained with her ear to the door for a while, before feeling safe that she was really alone down here in the furnace of the ship.

She began to unscrew the hardest to reach screws first, high above her head. They were rusty and she fought to get them loose, but she succeeded much more easily than she had anticipated. Leaving the last of the four screws at the top slightly inserted, to keep the door upright, she proceeded with the lower ones, which were much more difficult, as the paint on the door had been repaired and reapplied various times and whoever had done the job had generously spread the paint over the screws.

When Sophia loosened the last screw, she was out of breath, but did not wait and immediately tried to move the door. It came away from its frame without difficulties, though the bolt still kept it in place. Loosening the last screw on top, the door sank down to the floor with a loud bump.

Frightened that she might have drawn attention with that sound, Sophia froze, not moving, but listening intently, expecting to hear approaching steps, but everything remained quiet around her.

The two men who had brought her down, must have left her entirely alone, thinking her safely secured in the deepest bowels of the military ship.

Only after a long while, Sophia dared to move the door aside from its place, opening up her escape route. Though from the outside, she tried to pull it as much into its original place as possible, to hide her departure.

Her progress on board of the big ship was slow, as she always stayed to listen, if someone was coming her way. But the hot engine area was not a favorite part of the ship and she progressed unhindered, till she found another supply room with clothing, from bits of uniform to blouses, shirts, trousers and skirts.

Having no idea about military ranks or how to behave according to one, she changed her clothes to ones that seemed to belong to the kitchen crew.

Reluctant to leave her last connection to Prof. Lynford behind, she kept on the button-down shirt he had given to her, beneath the white uniform jacket and apron.

With more courage now, equipped as one of the ordinary crew, she stepped with more vigor up the next flight of stairs and explored the upper level of the immense ship, pretending that she knew what she was doing and belonged where she was.

It did not take long till her stance was tested, as a group of uniformed young men passed her in a corridor, not taking any note of her. With a relieved sigh she released the breath, which she had kept all during their passing, continuing on her way up to freedom. Though she had no idea how she would even get off such a large mountain of a vessel, much less escape it safely without being detected. But 'cross one bridge at a time', like her mother always said.

Her attention was abruptly dragged from happier thoughts back to her present predicament, when a hand from behind grabbed her arm. Holding her back and turning her around, a large uniformed man stood in front of her, with a plate covered with a silver bell in the other hand, which looked very out of place for a soldier of some kind.

"You, bring that in, girl."

It took Sophia a moment to realize that she had not been detected, but instead was meant to do a job adequate to the clothes she had so cavalierly rededicated.

Catching her breath, she responded: "Where do I need to go?"

The man pushed the plate into her hands and shoved her along the long hallway.

"The last door on the right. Hurry. The lady is waiting."

Sophia hurried to follow the man's orders and politely knocked on the indicated door, entering directly after, not waiting for a response.

But the sight made her gasp in shock, when she entered. Finding Prof. Benning sitting next to the woman she now knew was Prof. Lynford's ex-wife, Vanessa Benning, as she had never taken on the last name of her husband.

She had presumed Prof. Benning's role on board of this ship was to scrutinize the material Prof. Lynford had handed over to the CIA. What was he doing here, just sitting around?

His reaction to her appearance was not much better, but he covered his surprise with an awkward cough. At least for the woman it seemed believable, as she knocked on his back to help him.

"Finally," she arrogantly greeted Sophia. "It's high time someone came. Get on with serving."

Prof. Benning stood up, helping her to find the plates stored in a side cupboard.

Serving them the delicious smelling food, Sophia was reminded, that her last attempt at eating something had been thwarted by the discovery of Prof. Lynford's greedy motives.

Her stomach rumbled audibly and Prof. Benning looked up at her, blinking at her, giving her a sign she could not totally interpret. But at least, he had not given her away.

"Look at that girl. Standing around like a mule. Pour me some more of this delicious wine over there."

Sophia hurried to do her bidding, ready to leave the room afterwards, when Prof. Benning held her back, ordering her to serve him seconds.

Eating slowly, he seemed to wait for something, and Sophia had not long to wait to discover what it was.

"Send her away," Vanessa Benning stated, as if Sophia was not in the room with them.

"I want her to take the dishes away with her after we are finished. Let her stay."

"But you'll join me in a moment, won't you, dear?"

Mrs. Benning rushed out into the adjoining room and closed the door behind her.

Prof. Benning waited a moment longer, before he whispered: "Now we can speak. How did you get here?"

"I escaped from the prison they put me in. They forgot to leave someone behind to watch me." Sophia smiled halfheartedly.

"Good girl. Dr. Stewart is convinced you were in on it right from the beginning. I can't convince him otherwise. We need to get you out of here somehow. Do you have a place to stay at the kitchens?"

"No. I don't even know where they are. I just found the clothes and a man grabbed me outside in the corridor and pushed the plate into my hands. That is how I came to be here."

"Not good, not good at all. – We need to find a hiding place for you, till I can get you out."

But the door to the next room was pushed open and Vanessa's head appeared in the doorway.

"What do you have to discuss with this girl. Send her away. I am waiting for you, honey."

"I just asked for a good drop of whiskey, but the girl has no idea where to find some."

"Oh, darling. Just check in the cabinet next to the window."

With that, she was gone again and the door closed behind her.

"You can't stay here, as these are her rooms. But mine is across the corridor. Hide there. – Oh, and take the food with you." Prof. Benning added with a swift smile.

Opening the outer door to the corridor, he looked out, but found the hallway empty.

"It's safe. You can go now."

Hurriedly collecting all the plates and dishes, Sophia approached the door. Turning around to Prof. Benning, she nodded at him gratefully. "Thank you, Prof. Benning."

"It's all right. I just hope we get out of this whole mess safely. Somehow."

That did not sound all too enthusiastic or promising. At least, she was no longer alone in her fight for freedom, but had an ally she trusted.

Rushing over to the other cabin, Prof. Benning held the door open for her and let her in. She found a much more ascetic cabin without even a deadlight over there.

"Thank you," she murmured again, but Prof. Benning was already about to close the door behind her and just nodded in acknowledgement, lifting his hand in a warning to keep silent as well as a farewell greeting.

As sparse as the cabin was, it held all the necessities she needed. And the most pressing matter for the moment was her hunger. Fortunately, the plate was still well filled and the two eating from it had not made much of a dent into its contents.

Well sated and cleaned up for the night, Sophia searched for a lock in the door and secured it, before she exhaustedly fell asleep on the narrow cot.

– 23 –
On a Sailing Boat

Michael was cross with Merton, after Sophia had slipped away into darkness in the middle of the sea, not speaking to him, but instead avoiding the professor by going up on deck to steer the boat.

Prof. Lynford tried to not let that bother him, too much weighted down by his own feelings of loss for her. Instead, he tried to occupy himself by checking his final arrangements on Sophia's computer for one last time. His plans had been expedited by the CIA discovering them in their hiding place and he wanted to make sure everything was going smoothly.

Sophia, in her rush to leave him, had left behind all her things, not only her computer, but even her rucksack, so much had she found his presence unbearable. He knew he had to act that way, but it did not console him, now that she was gone.

In the end, she had believed the worst of him, even if it was all lies. He and Michael had never been lovers for real. Though it had proven convenient to let everyone believe it, so that they were left alone. All their pretense that Sophia had observed with her camera from the other house, had been staged, for Michael to gain the criminals' trust by pretending to be on their side, all with the goal to weaken their watchfulness over them and enable them both to flee their tight clutches. The men had guarded them both like hawks, not trusting Michael alone with him. They had not yet extracted the information from him they had been ordered to get.

Michael had planned to make them believe he wanted to join their ranks and had pretended to be on their side. The punishment sessions had been his attempt to get their trust and pretend he wanted their hostage to spill his secrets, while it had been Michael and his combined effort to get away.

Admittedly, Sophia had effectively shortened his torture and the escape process considerably, though he had been reluctant to openly admit that to her. She had been so enthusiastic to be involved and he always knew he could not let her, though it had been surprisingly hard for him to push her away.

If she had stayed, he could not have guaranteed her safety. How could he be so selfish and take her with him, when he knew she most certainly would be in constant danger with him? During her distraction on the cliffs, his heart had stopped with worry about her. He could not bear to see her in grave danger again. She deserved better than that – better than him. It had been in her best interest to let her go. Even if it hurt, it was for the best.

And finally, she had believed his lies and they had proved to be the best way to chase her away, convincing her she would be the third wheel on the cart and never would have a future with him.

He tried to convince himself, that his cravings for her were just lust, but in comparison to his only simmering feelings he had had for his ex-wife, his whole existence burned for Sophia when she was around, one glance at her could swerve his emotions and put them in a tailspin. And now he felt like sizzling ashes, still hot, but with no kindling any longer, now that she was gone. Burning and aching for a girl he had only known for no more than three days. How was that even possible?

His plans would come to fruition shortly, everything prepared and ready, but all he could think about was Sophia.

He worried how she was faring in the meanwhile and that thought brought him up on deck to Michael, who had the device to watch over the girl and receive the signals from the bug in her shirt-button.

Breaking the silence between them, he confessed: "I miss her, too."

"Told you, you should have let her come with us," Michael answered without a hint of mercy for his plight.

"You know why that was not an option."

"Yes, yes. I know. But still, she would have been much safer with us than with them."

"She would be on the run for the rest of her life with us. She is much too young for that. I just could not do that to her. In the cave, she just ran off to put herself in danger for me. I could not let that happen again. How could she even do that?"

"Isn't it obvious? The little deary is in love with you and wanted to protect you."

"But she almost killed herself."

"That's love, my friend," Michael commented smugly, but abruptly stopped and listened attentively. "Hush, I hear something!" Michael almost shouted out in anxiety, when the transmitter in his hand stuttered alive.

Their attention focused on the static, then they could clearly make out her voice and those of the men welcoming her on board. Prof. Benning's greeting and then Dr. Stewart declaring her a traitor.

"They aren't treating her well," Michael whined and was so distressed, that he let go of the helm. Merton took over and steered the boat.

When nothing more could be heard from the transmitter, after firm steps and then the finality of a locked door, they both waited with tension. Then there was something like the scuffing and scraping of cloth and hard breathing combined with scratching sounds, but no words, till a while later a loud bang interrupted the silence, followed by an "Ouch".

"They shot at her, Merton. Do something! We must turn around to help her!" Michael jumped around, making the whole boat shake in his agitation.

"I turned around miles ago, when Stewart called her a traitor and ordered her interrogation. I don't trust him to handle this right. He has broken his promise already. He should have let her go as was agreed upon. After all the information I handed over, and the assurances I gave him about her, he had more than enough to let her go free as he had promised. And Benning, that leach, did not even try to come to her defense. What a weakling." Looking up at Michael, he added: "Calm down, we will rescue the little fool, who's not even able to defend herself."

"Don't be too harsh with her, boss. The little girly has no experience with this kind of thing."

"No, you are right. She is much too trusting and innocent to stand up for herself against the CIA. And now, after all, we can test if my latest invention truly works. We should find out shortly."

He did not have to imply that their lives might depend on it. His trusted friend knew what was at stake. But Michael seemed not at all worried about that and happily took over the helm again, steering them back to the CIA meeting-point they had arranged for the transfer of the top-secret material.

– 24 –
On a Military Vessel

In the early morning hours, Sophia was rudely awakened by alarm sirens, followed by a loud knocking on her door.

"Prof. Benning, open up. There are intruders on the ship. Dr. Stewart wants to see you and Mrs. Benning immediately," an unknown voice of a man shouted directly outside her door.

Sophia, groggy from the lack of sleep, sat up in bed, frantically looking around for a place to hide in this little cabin.

To her relief, she heard Prof. Benning answering almost immediately from the room opposite to hers that they were coming. Only moments later, they left with the man. Mrs. Benning complained loudly about the inconvenience of the disturbance all the way down the hallway, so Sophia could hear where they went, as they stayed on the same floor of this large ship, till a closing door cut off Vanessa Benning's rants.

What was happening now, Sophia wondered. How could such a big military vessel go all crazy about unknown 'intruders'? She had problems even imagining a secure way off this ship and someone should have gotten on board without anyone discovering that fact long before they even got near? Impossible, the thought alone was ludicrous and hardly believable to Sophia.

Much too curious about what was going on, she hopped around, unable to go back to sleep. She had to find out what was happening and just could not stay behind in Prof. Benning's room without doing anything. She had to see for herself, what Dr. Stewart needed of Prof. Benning in such a situation, when he had not let him examine the material received from Prof. Lynford in the first place, as she had initially expected. The men in suits at first had handed the material to Prof. Benning after finding it, but Dr. Stewart seemed to have taken it at a later stage, as the professor had been with Vanessa Benning, when Sophia later had found them together in her room.

She had presumed Prof. Benning, having Dr. Stewart in his laboratory for so long, was fully co-operating with the CIA on this and would immediately check the validity of the material they had received, but Dr. Stewart and he did not seem to especially trust each other.

Was the presence of Vanessa Benning somehow responsible for that? She seemed to reside here like a queen, while Prof. Benning, the expert on the vitally essential topic, was kept on a much shorter leash.

Sophia checked her appearance in a tiny mirror in the small enclosed bathroom, hoping she could still blend in as a member of the kitchen crew and not look too bedraggled, after sleeping in most of her clothes, fearing discovery at any moment.

She took the plate from last night and then carefully looked out of the door, if anyone was close by. But the alarm seemed to have drawn all personnel on this level away. Still hesitant, she slipped out and followed in the direction she had heard the voices leave.

Running feet above her indicated, that the whole crew of the ship was still in an upheaval. But her path, except from uniformed crew-members passing her in a hurry, running up staircases leading on deck, was unhindered. Fortunately, nobody paid any attention to her.

Loud clonking sounds, like those when the motorboat she had

come with had been heaved up on deck, could be heard again and the rushing steps of the crew slowly ebbed away, replaced by a series of shouted orders she could not fully understand from her position one deck below.

Sophia came to an area on her floor which was separated from the corridor by a glass wall, with a recessed cubicle next to the entrance, where she presumed at other times a watchman would have his place, but was now empty.

Entering that area, the first thing that grabbed her attention was a gun in a holster, left there hanging over the back of a chair. The watchman really must have left in a hurry, to leave something that important unguarded.

Not having much knowledge about weapons and hating the principle of them in general, she still took the holster in her hand. The pistol with 'Walther' written on the black butt, weighed heavy in her hand, but she did not wait, instead searched for the mechanism to open the magazine and see if it was loaded. That was much more difficult than Sophia had expected from all the films about police and gangsters she had seen. They always made it appear so easy to get the ammunition out, while she took a while to even find the right switch to unblock the magazine on this high-end weapon.

Not trusting her own abilities with a gun, she removed all the cartridges and replaced the empty magazine in the pistol, afterwards placing the weapon under her apron in the seam of her trousers, while storing the bullets in her apron-pocket, not to leave a sign of her doing behind. Perhaps it could aid in her escape.

At least, she would not accidentally shoot herself this way, Sophia mused, and besides, she had no intention of shooting anyone else either. Continuing with her search of the room for something useful she could have need of on her flight, Sophia carefully listened out for anyone approaching.

Therefore, the sudden scream of a man close by made her jump in fright.

It took her a moment, to discern that the muffled sound of the scream had not come from the corridor behind her, but a monitor on the desk of the watchman whose cubicle she was searching. Checking the screens, she saw three of them turned on among the long row of dark monitors. Each of them showed an interrogation room with a man being questioned by two dark clad men in suits. Now, being closer to the monitors, Sophia could even discern a low murmuring of voices, which was coming from a headset plugged in to one of the monitors. This must have been where the sound of the scream had come from.

One of the imprisoned men, though like the other two all beaten up and his face all wet and grimy, still looked somehow familiar to her. It took her a moment, but Sophia realized that it was the one of the abductors of Prof. Lynford. The one Tom the fireman had knocked out during their rescue mission in that apartment opposite her own. Could those three men have been the team holding the professor captive and pressing Michael into proving himself to them?

Sophia was so engrossed in the thought, that she overheard the opening of a door she had not even recognized as an entrance at all. The door was the narrow backwall of the room, opposite to the corridor she had come from, and was totally covered by shelves that had disguised its purpose.

One of the dark clad interrogators came into the room and, as if she was not even there, pushed a button on a small device on the desk, speaking into it.

"Dr. Stewart, we are through with questioning for now. No intel about the head of the organization. Seems they really don't know who he is. Await further instructions."

The response of Dr. Stewart came only moments later: "That is enough for now. We will get to that through other means. Our new guests will tell us that anyway. – Get the crew to stop investigating the ship they came in. It's top secret. Benning will have a look at it later."

"Yes, Sir," came the prompt reply from the man in front of her.

Not to raise his suspicions, Sophia stayed where she was, as if she had a purpose being there, turning around utensils on the plate she carried.

No further acknowledgement came back from Dr. Stewart, but the man in the dark suit proceeded to push another button on the small device he had used for communicating and after a short identification with a code of numbers and letters announced: "To all crew, stop the search of the sailing-ship immediately. Examination of the sailing vessel will be taken over by the CIA from now on."

Only after shooting off that order, did the man turn around to her.

"Where is Brian?"

"He had to rush out just a moment ago."

"And what are you still doing here then?"

"I was waiting for breakfast orders," Sophia explained with her pre-made-up excuse for being around here.

The man did not question her any further, so she by chance must have hit a common or at least likely procedure on board of the ship.

"Bring a full 'continental' for me and Markham." He went

back into the room he had come from without further acknowledging her.

Grateful, Sophia turned around, trying to hide her trembling from the mere mention of the name of one of the men who had hunted and shot at her back at the cliff. Before she left the room, she slipped the small device the CIA agent had used to communicate into her other apron-pocket. Who knew, how she could later use that tool for her escape, especially as she had seen how the CIA agent had handled it.

The remainder of the corridor she had come along, was cordoned off from the rest of the ship, guarded by the watchman in the booth she had just raided and successfully escaped from again.

Were these the parts the CIA had commandeered on board of this ship to use for their interrogations?

An angry voice from up ahead seemed to confirm this assumption, as she immediately recognized it as that of Dr. Stewart. He shouted at someone, though no answer could be heard. Sophia approached tentatively, so engrossed in trying to understand what was spoken, that she almost fell over a delivery cart, which was only barely hip-high. Not knowing what it was for, as the two metal levels of it were empty, Sophia took hold of it and placed her plate of food on it. It made a good utensil, giving her role as a kitchen help more credence.

With more confidence, Sophia now pushed forward on her way further down the long corridor of a row of closed metal doors on both sides. At the end, Dr. Stewart's voice was the loudest and she carefully looked through a glass window into a room behind. Not finding anybody in there, Sophia grew more courageous and inspected the room, which appeared to be used for meetings. It held a large oval desk with many chairs all around. A coffee machine was set up in the corner and empty cups and plates were strewn all over a large table in the middle of the room. That must be where the contents of her hijacked serving trolley had gone.

Trusting her role to hold, Sophia stepped into the room and, while listening to the conversation in the next room, began to clear the table to appear unsuspicious, if someone should jump on her like in the last room. Her nerves could only cope with one such shock in a while and this time, she wanted to be more prepared.

– 25 –
Headquarters on Board

The voices had become more sedate now and Dr. Stewart mostly relied on Vanessa Benning to support his version of things, as far as Sophia could make out from that part of the conversation.

Prof. Benning, threw in a word here and there, but clearly had not the weight his cousin and lover had.

"That can't be true, Stewart," the professor argued against the man's suspicions of a mafia spy with international connections in their midst, whom they just had successfully detected and incarcerated.

'What? Who was that spy and head of mafia? And why did Dr. Stewart still trust Vanessa Benning, when she was the head-conspirator of everything?' Sophia had not heard the context and why Prof. Benning was so fired up about this sensational CIA success.

"You can ask her yourself, if you don't believe me," a voice interfered in the discussions, she had not thought to ever hear again.

'That rough, deep, but soothing voice. That could only be … – No, impossible. Prof. Lynford could not be on board,' she chastised herself. 'It would mean his death sentence, if he were. After all, he had sold the information the CIA wanted elsewhere. He could not possibly be such a lunatic to come here, could he?' Sophia's mind reeled. Prof. Lynford on board the ship? That would mean all she had thought, all suspicions she had, could not be true, or could they? After all, he had sent her away by making her believe the worst of him. He had sold out his country, selling his information to the highest bidder. But what of all that was true, when he now was with the people he just had betrayed?

Why did he come back, when before he could not leave the vicinity of the CIA quickly enough? He had to have a reason to so completely change his mind. Had it been his wife he came back for? But he could not have possibly known beforehand that she would be on board. The only person he could be certain would be here was her. Could he be here for her? But why then send her away in the first place?

Her mind was still spinning around all the options and possibilities, when she heard Dr. Stewart's voice coming closer to the door.

"We will see. That girl is in it up to her neck. She will break down under pressure. That will finally give us a lead, who the real head of the organization behind all this is."

The door to her room opened and he strolled through it, not taking any notice of her. Sophia kept busy putting cups and plates on her cart, not looking up at him.

Just outside the meeting-room, he shouted down the corridor: "Bring the girl up."

Running steps could be heard in answer and Dr. Stewart, expecting to be obeyed immediately, went swiftly back through the meeting room to the others.

Sophia could not help but lift her head a bit to take a look into the adjoining room, meeting the watchful eyes of Prof. Lynford, who had clearly recognized her, but kept silent about her presence. His expression remained grim, not seeming at all happy for her to be where he himself had sent her. Angry with him for manipulating her to leave him alone, she lifted her head in annoyance, but quickly stopped when Dr. Stewart turned around to close the door behind him.

It was Prof. Benning, who first protested against Dr. Stewart's assumptions: "The girl has no idea about what is going on or the importance of the discoveries. We kept her in the dark completely. You know that. It was your plan and we all agreed to follow it."

"That girl is a fool and you know that, Stewart" the voice of Prof. Lynford now threw in. "Her topic suggestions alone should have shown you that she is far away from discovering anything really important. She is just a busybody with no real inspiration or talent. Don't waste your time on her. We rather need to find the head of the organization who pushed this whole mess into action, and you know it can't be her who masterminded the organized crime's unhindered access to sensitive military information. She is just not resourceful enough for that."

'What?' Did Prof. Lynford just speak about her, Sophia wondered. That Dr. Stewart thought her to be a traitor, was hard enough to take in, but Prof. Lynford's derogatory comments hurt much deeper. Ire rose in her throat so much that even her head heated up in suppressed anger, till she willfully forced herself to calm down and her mind to think clearly again.

That could not be his honest opinion, could it? He in some tiny way had relied upon her expert evaluations on their flight or at least had expected her to appreciate the greatness of his discoveries, when she had brought back the papers from Prof. Benning. And she really should know Prof. Lynford's manipulative ways by now.

'Think clearly again, Sophia,' she called herself to reason. 'What does he want to reach? Think! He always has his own hidden agenda. What might it be?'

And with that question, his motives all of a sudden became obviously clear to her.

How could she have been so dense to take so long to decipher his intentions, when they were all so single-minded? He wanted to save her, keep her out of harm's way, like he had done on his boat. Keep her far away from all the people who could hurt her, especially himself, who was in the center of all danger, and get her to the most secure fortress the States had, a U.S. military vessel.

'But who would protect him?' she wondered. 'Stupid man.' Rushing right into the heart of danger, just to keep her safe. Sophia no longer held any doubt that the 'mysterious intruders' on this military vessel were Prof. Lynford and Michael. Miraculously appearing on a well-secured and guarded, highly-equipped and protected military ship of the U.S. Marine. What other man was arrogant enough to even attempt such a ridiculous endeavor, much less succeed in it.

Running steps could be heard from the outside and in mere moments, four uniformed marines of different ranks stormed into the meeting room, passing her without paying her any attention and knocking on the door to where Dr. Stewart held court.

"The girl is missing!" the first man, not waiting for an answer to his knock, said, bursting a few steps into the next room.

"What do you mean – missing? You locked her away!" Dr. Stewart shouted. "And you thought her not resourceful enough to be the head of the syndicate? Breaking out of her cell on a military vessel. She is the head, I tell you!"

"Nonsense," Prof. Benning could be heard.

"Well, I did not say she was entirely stupid, just not criminal-minded enough," Prof. Lynford conceded, his amusement discernible in his voice.

"Find her!" Stewart shouted at the four men. "Search the ship. She can't be far. – Do you at least know, how long she has been gone?"

"No," came a clipped response. "She was just locked in last night. That is the last report about her we have."

"Bitch. I always knew she was trouble."

The four men left, without throwing her a glance. They were too determined to leave the screaming and raging Dr. Stewart behind, to mind her.

Who in his right mind would think that she was standing right next to them, in close proximity to the one man who was searching for her? Sophia inwardly smiled, but carefully regulated her breath, to continue in her calm cleaning of the conference table, as if she had not heard what was going on.

"Now, Lynford. You came back for her, just to find that her fake innocence lulled you in, as much as it did everyone else. She does not need your help, but you most certainly do need some now, handing yourself over as a spy and traitor. Don't you want to change your statement and tell me what you really came here for? – And besides, thank you for the boat. We will find out, how your new shielding-technology works. An added bonus for all the trouble you have caused."

"Don't be too hopeful in that regard," Prof. Lynford countered coldly. "Even when you have the solution directly in front of your eyes, you won't recognize it."

Sophia froze in her movements. Was that a hidden lead? Did he want to give her away?

But fortunately for her, Dr. Stewart did not make the connection that she was right under his nose, just a few steps away from him. Instead, he tried to enrage Prof. Lynford, possibly to draw out some information from him, by teasing him with his tight relationship with Michael: "Or was it your wife you could not live without? Michael obviously is not enough entertainment for you any longer, now that you're free."

"You wouldn't understand. It is much better to have someone who cares for you than a cold stick in bed, don't you think, Vanessa?" Prof. Lynford's voice was so calm, that the cynical comment had its full effect, when he addressed the so far silent Vanessa Benning.

A spluttering and spitting sound followed and Sophia was not kept in suspense for long about what was happening.

"You leach, you murderer. How could you try to accuse me in our marriage, when you coldheartedly tried to kill me, as we both know."

"That is, what we both know as a lie, Vanessa dear." Prof. Lynford had quite evidently got to the end of his patience, as his tight voice indicated.

"What are you talking about? You know you tried to strangle me. And all for your profit with the mafia."

"But, my dear, we both know, the 'Mafia' is not who did all this. The syndicate, or organized crime we are actually talking about, is much closer than the 'Mafia'. Even now, they are listening in."

"Just because you are working for them," Vanessa accused Prof. Lynford. "You could have been brilliant, but you never got enough and always wanted more, so you started to work for them."

"And what then was the reason for you to steal my research and hand it over to Benning?"

"Vanessa never had access to your research. She could not possibly hand it over," Dr. Stewart threw in.

"Oh, how green you are, Stewart. And it was just an accident, that Benning repeatedly published exactly my research results just a hair's breadth before my final conclusions were ready to be published? – What guarantees that Benning was the only one she handed the information over to?" Prof. Lynford directed his answer towards Dr. Stewart, but it was Vanessa, his ex-wife, who made sure Stewart did not get a further word in.

"Nonsense. You are just jealous for his successful endeavors where you were stuck and failed to make something useful of your research. I had not thought you to be so mean spirited, Merton. Really, you of all people, always proclaiming to live up to such a high standard and then, not even able to admit when others are better."

"If they are, and not had been handed my results to publish as their own. I have no problem to honor the merits of others. Just tell me one thing, Vanessa. Why did you do it?"

"You accuse me, of all people? Me? The one you tried to murder?"

"I never even tried to rip a hair from your body. But you instead, had a clear goal."

"What? To have a successful husband?"

"No. You did not care about me or being my wife. All you wanted, were the access to my discoveries and the chance to exploit them. But with the 'illustrative interference' or 'project darkwood' you fell into a trap I had set up for you and did not even recognize it before it was too late."

"You and your scheming! Stewart, here you see what he is doing. He is manipulating everyone around, cheating the CIA out of their own research project."

Dr. Stewart audibly cleared his throat to speak, but he was interrupted again by Vanessa Benning.

Turning back to Prof. Lynford, she continued: "You are a liar and manipulator. If it were not for your inventions, nobody would care for you. You stole the results from the CIA. It was their work and product and you tried to betray them, not revealing what potential your results had."

"No. That's not true. The CIA got the results they paid for, even more, directly after the research-run was finished. They had the same starting basis I had," Prof. Lynford stated agitatedly. "They just could not make anything of it, but I did. And now they even have my further results in full and are still not able to make sense of them."

Dr. Stewart had not interrupted the heated argument between the ex-couple. The thought that he might have made a grave error of judgement in basing his whole CIA-investigation, to get to the head of the feared criminal syndicate ruling all over the United States with connections and economic interests worldwide, on the sole testimony of one woman, the attractive Mrs. Vanessa Benning, had made Dr. Stewart hesitate for once. But he soon dismissed his worries. The woman was believable. He had seen her injuries, inflicted by her own husband, and all because she had wanted to stop him from selling his inventions to the syndicate and other criminals worldwide. She had even provided him with proof about previous deals Prof. Lynford had already made with crime-bosses and had handed over all the details of the payment transfers, which connected the man to over ten of the most wanted criminal organizations worldwide. She would lead him to the head of this criminal organization, which had eluded the

CIA over and over again. He would succeed where all his predecessors had failed. After all, she had already lead him to the three syndicate members who had freed the professor from prison, to gain access to his final resolution.

"Lynford, the results you handed over are illogical. The things you put together can't work. My experts sit over it for hours now and none of it makes sense."

"I told you, you would not recognize the solution if it stared you in the eye," Prof. Lynford shot back at him. "It works as stated. Test it wherever you want. It might even reveal some things about your key witness, the oh so trustworthy Vanessa."

"What? Who told you it was her? Besides, I know my witness. We did all the required background checks on her."

"For example, that she has a child she kept secret from her husband? I am sure you know about that."

"What?" The tone of Dr. Stewart was enough to reveal that he had had no idea about that. "Vanessa, tell him that he is lying."

"Yes, Vanessa, explain that," Prof. Benning spoke up now, too. "Why did you tell me he was jealous about the child, when your husband had no idea about Jenny at all? Why did you try to feed me such a lie?"

"How did you get that idea? I told him about Jenny when we married."

"Jenny? Your daughter, Benning? That is your child, not Vanessa's." Dr. Stewart turned between Vanessa and Prof. Benning, not knowing any longer what was going on here, seeing his career and supposed success of his investigation go down the drain.

"Yes, my daughter, and Vanessa's. Ours, but Vanessa never cared for her."

"I was much too young at the time. You know that. I wouldn't act the same any longer, honey." Vanessa came to Prof. Benning and in an ostensible stroke of affection rubbed her hand over his chest to assuage his fury.

Calmly, as if all the accusations thrown at her had not meant anything to her, she turned around to Dr. Stewart. "The one you should be looking for, is the bitch my husband …"

"Ex-husband," Prof. Lynford loudly interrupted.

"… ex-husband …" Vanessa Benning corrected, but continued otherwise unfazed. "… is sleeping with. That girl has access to all the plans. She was the one trying to break into the laboratory, after her access was withdrawn, and she was the one who singlehandedly came to the rescue of my ex, knowing exactly where he was being held and how to trick even seasoned criminals from the mafia …"

"The syndicate," Prof. Lynford fell in.

"Yes, yes. Whoever. The criminals in this whole scheme." Vanessa played the poor victim of criminal conspiracies brilliantly, blinking back the rising tears from her eyes and innocently looking up at Dr. Stewart, who completely fell for her theatrics. Her next words took him down hook, line and sinker.

"And I have to defend myself, proclaiming my innocence, when this super-woman just appears, gets in wherever she wants, sleeps her way up and then is at the center of everything just by mere chance, as my ex-husband insists, while all and everything around goes completely haywire." She put an ironic emphasis on the word 'ex-husband', before she continued in an acidic voice: "Get her and you have the head of the mafia, I tell you."

"Syndicate," now even Dr. Stewart corrected her. "The mafia is mostly under control, but this syndicate completely went under the radar for much too long, taking over all the major holdings all over the U.S., effectively killing off all the rivaling families, making their deaths appear accidents and growing to enormous international proportions without us even noticing the appearance of a new threat. Now, they are even trying to take political control over the country, by putting their puppets into offices and making their demands known. We have no idea who their leader or what his background is. In the mafia, a sense of 'family' rules, everyone knows everyone. Not easy to break into, but easy to get hold of the names, once one of their members breaks. But in this organization, none of the members we caught so far had had the least idea who their leader even was. No chance to find the head, when even his own men don't know who he is. So what help could just one more of his emissaries be?"

"She turns up wherever there is information to be had. Are you certain, she is not already in your labs stealing the results from your team on board?" Vanessa Benning did not give up trying to convince Dr. Stewart of her brilliant idea, making Sophia the main culprit in her invented fable.

"That is just ludicrous," Prof. Lynford growled. "Stewart, not even you can honestly fall for this shit."

"But it's the truth," Vanessa insisted. "Don't listen to him. He is just in league with her and came here to rescue his little lover, when his plot with the bomb did not work and destroy his material."

"What bomb?" both professors asked simultaneously.

"Don't pretend you don't know, Merton. The one you planted in the box together with the material you handed over."

"There was no bomb," Prof. Lynford objected.

"Then I have been right all along. You can no longer deny it.

It was her who planted it." Vanessa gleefully smiled at her astonished audience.

Dr. Stewart was the first to comment: "It must have been her. She was always at the right places and had access to the box on board of that sailing boat. – I was right, to keep an eye out for this nosy Miss Know-It-All and to put a tracker into her purse."

"You did what? Have you completely gone crazy now?" Prof. Benning shouted angrily at Stewart, so untypical to his usually calm and sedate behavior. "Did you plant one in mine, too?"

"Ahm, yes, of course, somewhere. It's really of no importance. Truly, just a precaution. Nothing serious," Stewart stammered.

"Of no importance, when you break our agreement? Spying on our own people." Prof. Benning was beyond angry now.

"Our own? Nonsense! You must see that I was right. She lead us directly to the hiding place of Lynford." Dr. Stewart saw his whole strategy confirmed and his momentary insecurity about his main witness Vanessa resolved without a doubt by the new revelations.

Prof. Lynford glared angrily at him. He obviously did not share his conviction. "And what did you use the information about my location for? To blow up an entire historic building? – How did you even get a hold of a missile for this airstrike? I never knew the CIA had access to one, much less the power to command an airstrike."

Prof. Benning, who had already been brought on board the ship by the time of the hit, had no idea what had been going on back on land. The information about an airstrike was news to him. "You tried to kill them all, wiping them out with a blast? Have you completely lost your marbles, Stewart?

We need them, urgently. – We need them both to get to the core of the invention. Without them, it is of no worth at all. I repeatedly told you so. And forget about Sophia being the head of mafia. That is just pure nonsense."

"Syndicate, they call it," now Vanessa was the one to correct him.

"It was the only sensible way to go." Dr. Stewart defended his action. "It would have solved all our problems at once. A clean cut, so to speak."

"By getting rid of the technology and the people who could replicate it all? They were not supposed to survive your clean cut, I presume. Have you any idea, what you have done? Have you had a look online lately? I presume not, or you would think differently about your 'clean cut'-nonsense. The information is all over the net, available all around the world."

– 26 –
Sophia in Hiding

Prof. Benning must have been checking the web, Sophia thought, still listening in on them from the other room, though she in the meanwhile had found a halfway secure hiding-spot beneath the large conference table, in case someone suddenly came in and still found her there. She had hidden the cart out of sight behind the door from the corridor. 'That must have been why Prof. Benning had been ready when he had been called to come to Dr. Stewart so early in the morning. But still, why had the professor not warned the CIA of the fact of the information-leak before now?' Sophia was at a loss about that and turned her attention back to the conversation in the next room.

Dr. Stewart was stunned by the revelation as well and barely stuttered the words while trying to form a clear sentence. "What? No! We paid you! It is ours. No!"

"It is open-source material now," Prof. Benning said smugly, clearly not too unhappy about the information leakage, while Prof. Lynford remained surprisingly silent, not commenting or confirming any of it.

Sophia held her breath. 'Prof. Lynford had put the information on the web for free? Truly?' She could hardly believe it. That had been what she had asked him to do right at the beginning, but he had rudely cut her off. And now, he had sold the information to the CIA and who knew who else and then published it for free, to even out the playing field for all and everyone worldwide. But how could he willingly hand himself over into the clutches of the CIA, when such a revelation was imminent? This man was certifiably crazy, totally and utterly and without a doubt. Sophia trembled in fear for him. She knew how much Dr. Stewart must hate Prof. Lynford now, his whole career at risk by what was going on. He would not let Prof. Lynford go unscathed. He desperately needed to show off some kind of strength and success. Whatever could still be salvaged from the current mess he would, to confirm his own worth in the investigation about the head of the unknown entity of the 'syndicate', especially now that his main efforts about the 'dark wood'-technology had been such a blunder.

With Vanessa Benning out to further smear Prof. Lynford's name, the professor would be held indefinitely, before they would risk him to invent anything meaningful ever again. And his ex-wife did not seem to lessen in her efforts to discredit him with her farfetched theories, trying to convince everyone who listened to her: "You see I was right. He is working for the criminals, handing over all the material for free, which he sold to you for such a steep price. Perhaps he and the girl together are the head of the organization. That would explain her coming to his rescue so readily."

"Keep it for a moment," Dr. Stewart interrupted impatiently. "I need to check some facts."

Not waiting, he headed out of the adjoining room. Sophia was glad that she was kneeling beneath the conference table and well out of his sight and anyone's in the other room.

– 27 –
Reasonable Doubt

Dr. Stewart, as before, only stepped out of the door and shouted his orders down the corridor.

"Carson, Harold. To me, with updates. Stanley, to me as well." The man called Stanley was the first to arrive, to receive further instructions to check in with their headquarters. He was to clear everything which mentioned 'dark wood' and anything relating to their key project, on the web. He left with a swift "Aye, Sir."

The other two men arrived shortly after.

Dr. Stewart immediately questioned them: "Did you get results?"

But both men vehemently stated the failure of all their efforts. Enraged, Dr. Stewart drew the two men into the room where Vanessa and the two professors were waiting for him. "Your files are worthless," he shouted at Prof. Lynford, but the professor did not react to that or wait for permission, instead addressed the two men directly: "Did you get 'dark wood' to work?"

"Yes," the men answered almost simultaneously.

"But you just told me …" Dr. Stewart spluttered.

"I handed over what you requested," Prof. Lynford interrupted.

Dr. Stewart now turned to the two men and almost screamed: "Explain!"

"The technology he handed over does work. Just the results are – hmm, how to say it – unclear."

"More like an overload," the second man added.

"Too much to get to anything meaningful."

Female laughter started quietly, but quickly rose in volume, till it was a full blown out cackling. Vanessa Benning was gasping for breath in between her bouts of laughter.

"He tricked you as well. He really dared to trick you, the CIA!"

"Fine work, Lynford," Prof. Benning commented, unable to entirely hide his admiration and cover it up as irony, which only further enraged the already boiling Dr. Stewart.

"Get back to it!" Dr. Stewart shouted at his men. "I want better results the next time I call you in."

"There is nothing to be done. The technology does what he told, just doesn't direct the focus on things in particular. There's no way to get anything meaningful from it, beyond the rush of an information overload or taking up of an atmospheric scatter. We're sorry, Sir, but that's all there can be done about it."

"Bring in the headquarters. They should put all the available experts on the task. We need to crack it. All the world is searching for the solution by now and we need to be first."

"It is futile, Sir. This technology can't work in a way to get to anything useful."

"Don't tell me that it's futile. Get the information to the headquarters. I want results in an hour."

When the two men had left, not taking note of Sophia still hidden beneath the table in the next room, Dr. Stewart turned around to Prof. Lynford, trying to ignore the still hysterically snickering Vanessa Benning.

"You knew that all along. You so willingly sold the information to me, because you knew it would not reveal anything."

Prof. Lynford appeared calm, when he answered: "You asked for the access and I gave it to you. I did whatever you requested."

"Then hand over the information to direct the device."

But Prof. Benning fell in with sarcasm dripping from his voice: "How fortunate now, that they didn't die in your airstrike, Stewart. As they are conveniently still alive, they can provide you with the answers you need." He was still not over the fact that his CIA contact had tried to kill an expert together with innocent bystanders, just to keep the information about 'dark wood' hidden and buried.

"You have all the required ingredients already," Prof. Lynford stated. "There is nothing more I could potentially give you in that regard. But I have something you need much more urgently right now. – I can lead you to the head of the syndicate, the one person, who started this whole war of technological supremacy and tried to get hold of 'dark wood' in the first place."

"Who is it?" Dr. Stewart was immediately interested, but Vanessa Benning spoke over him.

"See, he is in league with them, as I told you. He has access to their leader and knows who he is, if he is not the head of them himself."

"Not so fast," Prof. Lynford stopped them all. "I want something in return for my information. I help you and you let Sophia go. And this time, you will keep your promise, because otherwise, I will also reveal the information I have about you."

"You can't have anything on me. Impossible. You are just bluffing. – Show me what you think is worth the girl's life." His words sounded brave, though the sweat appearing on his forehead and neck indicated, that Prof. Lynford's threat was not an empty one.

"Benning, hand me over the rucksack you so desperately seem to cling to. I brought it on board and it is mine."

"No, it is Sophia's."

Sophia in the next room wondered, why her otherwise so formal professor spoke of her just using her first name. He never did that, except in the company of Prof. Lynford, it seemed. But then it dawned on her, that he might be jealous of Prof. Lynford, who was using her first name so easily. Prof. Benning might want to proclaim his own hold on her. 'Men,' she thought irritated.

Prof. Lynford did not let himself be distracted by Prof. Benning's protest, but continued: "Sophia handed the backpack over to me and showed me its contents. She intentionally left it behind on board my boat when she went, so now it's mine to do with as I please."

"Get over your little quarrels over that slut, you big boys," Vanessa Benning chastised them, her voice sounding like that of a well-meaning mother, now that her laughing bout had ceased, but her piercing words were far from such a role.

When Prof. Lynford held the backpack, Dr. Stewart argued: "What holds me back from just taking the information from you now? You hold no position any longer to make any demands, Lynford. You are in CIA-custody. Whatever you have here is confiscated."

"Did you not just reveal, that your team can't make sense of my technology, even holding the full information in their hands? And besides, did you find out how my boat works, or did your team by now find anything remotely different on it, to even know what to examine to get to the core of the hiding-mechanism, which let me get on board here unnoticed? No, of course not. What makes you believe, you could make more sense of the notes here in this backpack?"

"Just tell me. What is the solution? I promise, the girl can go."

"… with me. That's part of the deal. She leaves with me and Michael. No hindrances, no planted spy-devices, not anything underhanded. And rest assured, I will know."

"You didn't with her purse."

"Just because I did the sweep while she was out with it. All the other devices I did find."

"Others?" Now clearly Dr. Stewart was at a loss. "There were no others. Even that one was just a mere precaution. We didn't suspect her. Not at all. It was pure chance when her whereabouts raised our suspicion."

"Someone else must have clearly suspected her much earlier than you then. Now you see that she is not as harmless as you make her out to be." Vanessa was back at her most cutting insinuations. "I told you all along she must be in league with the criminals."

"And what about you, my dear ex-wife?" Prof. Lynford spoke with a voice dripping of sweetness he obviously did not mean.

"You spread lies and rumors and are always in the center of things. How convenient for you, to play the innocent victim, get all the sympathies and stir up a storm, just to harvest the results you thought ready for the picking. What a pity that you did not get what you wanted."

"You murderer and cheat. You are the one lying to everyone. Telling things work, just to get attention, while nothing you start really works out. Just like in bed. Beautiful package, but emotionally distant."

Vanessa Benning must have physically attacked Prof. Lynford while uttering this tirade, because Sophia could hear a struggle from the other room.

"Who are you to talk? You were no ounce better, Vanessa. Never giving our marriage a chance, not even at the beginning."

Stunned, Sophia listened to the argument for vital technology becoming a marriage-war or rather a post-divorce war. She did not understand Prof. Lynford. How could he emotionally still depend so much on his former wife. He should much rather hate her after she had gotten him into prison. In Sophia's opinion, he should be jumping with joy to be rid of her. But as a woman, she most likely just did not understand the conqueror's mentality men had, accumulating possessions instead of feelings. In that regard, he must think of his marriage as a personal failure and loss as well as a sign of weakness, in a life that was otherwise overly blessed with success. One smear on his personal record, one possession lost.

Sophia was strangely disappointed in him. She had unreasonably hoped their own connection had developed into something stronger and could eventually help him over his issues with his former wife, at least a tiny bit. That he was still so hung up on Vanessa, deeply cut into her and she had to admit, she was fiercely jealous. She wanted to be the most important woman in his life. That was why his sending her away had hurt so much and now, seeing him so fixated on his ex-wife, cut into her deeply, more than she wanted to admit even to herself.

With her thoughts buzzing in her head, she must have overheard some of the discussions in the other room, because Prof. Lynford's next comment threw her out of her musings.

"Your sole reason for marrying me was to get my inventions – and now I can prove it. It was never love which lead you to me, but you singled me out after you read about the research deal with the military I had just received. The timeline fits exactly. When we first met, you already had a clear agenda of what you wanted from me and our marriage. Unfortunately for you, you did not get everything you wanted. And when you realized that, you tried to get me out of the way. You thought, in prison I would no longer be able to prevent your free access to the laboratory."

"You murdering liar," Vanessa Benning screeched. "Pretending that you are the saint in all of this. You tried to throttle me. You are the one who tries to profit the most from inventions that are not so hard to make in the first place, if Bernard could so easily replicate them. He is the one who should receive the merits, he's the essential one, bringing them to fruition. But no – everyone flocks around you as the brilliant one."

"Of course, his work was essential to you. Benning solved the unfinished research papers you could get a hold of and provided you with the methods to give your gang of criminals an advantage over the others."

"You have no idea what you are talking about. Bernard is congenial, while you can't finish what you are doing. Your lab's not even getting the research for the military right. It's all just piecework and erroneous statistics."

"Good way to hide the real inventions from a snoopy enemy of the state, isn't it, dear Vanessa? And besides, how do you even know that the new statistics of my lab contained errors? Did the good Dr. Stewart share his progress so intimately with you?"

"You are the criminal, dear husband. You were the one who sold state secrets to our enemies. And now the CIA has caught on to you. You'll spend the rest of your life in prison." Vanessa shouted over him, trying to hide her blunder.

Prof. Lynford did not seem the least bit bothered by her hysterical insinuation and calmly answered: "We'll see. There is no use for the CIA to lock me up, when your gang-members need my research and cut me out."

"You liar! You cheat! You traitor!" Vanessa screeched, aware that she had revealed too much already, but Dr. Stewart so far had remained silent and not given any hint that he had become aware of her admission. The lab-results had been 'top secret' and besides interrogating her as his main witness, Dr. Stewart had not shared any information with her at all.

– 28 –
Painful Realizations

Dr. Stewart slowly threw off the fog around his mind and became aware of his surroundings again. He had been evaluating all options in his head about how to cope with the current developments, now that his main witness proved more than untrustworthy. He still could not believe that it had been Vanessa all along. She had somehow gotten access to his most securely kept information, the new report of Prof. Lynford's laboratory, and had even found out about its faults. Only the criminal head behind all this could have known about the existence of this highly guarded material.

Angry with himself for falling for the intriguing woman's 'honey-trap', he snapped at Prof. Lynford: "Show me what you have as proof for your theories."

Prof. Lynford, opening the backpack, revealed the genealogical family-tree Sophia had drawn from the internet and the printouts from the ancestry website her father had a membership to.

Gesturing to the family-tree, he began to explain: "Here, see. These are the family connections of the former crime-lord Arthur Benning. Fourteen years ago, twenty people died in short order, either of sudden and unexpected health issues or by accidents. Coincidence? – Potentially, but for the high number and their close connection to the crime-lord and the short period of just one year for all their deaths to take place in. All those who died, were part of the inner family-circle and had a right of succession in the 'family-business' because of their close relation to the crime-boss. Only few survived, beside his right-hand-man Robert and the two present grandchildren of the crime-lord."

"Robert Benning was injured, hardly able to move most of his life. We ruled him out as the lead or even a significant influence in the crime organization long ago." Dr. Stewart waved the suggestion off as unimportant and farfetched, not wanting to give the suspicion awakened by Prof. Lynford any credence.

Prof. Lynford continued unerringly: "The sole survivors beside the present relatives were Edward Mathers and his wife and two children. Mathers had married the much younger sister of Arthur Benning some years before the family extinction. – My theory is, that this is due to the fact that his sister had married against Arthur Benning's wishes and she and her husband had never been welcome in the inner circle of 'family-business' in the first place. This seems to have saved their lives. – Do you see now, where I am getting at, Stewart? – Arthur Benning left nothing to chance. He cleared the way for his successor, killing off everyone who could counter the claim of his chosen successor. – That leaves us with only two options, now that Robert Benning, or 'Uncle Bob', as his right-hand-man was called, died of old age a few years ago."

The nickname and his role he had for the crime-boss was among the information Sophia had received from Prof. Benning in his last messages and it now allowed Prof. Lynford to connect all the loose ends about the crime-family they – he corrected himself in his mind – Sophia singlehandedly had found and accumulated.

He had not had contact to Vanessa's family during their marriage, as she had always told him that they were not close and she did not care to see them. She had not even invited anyone from her side to their wedding. Before Sophia had dug into the family-tree, he had been completely unaware of her connections to Prof. Benning or the criminal significance of her relatives. Vanessa had repeatedly assured him, that she was not related to the professor with the same family name. Her insistence in keeping her name, when it always reminded him of his rival, had annoyed him no end, but he had given in to her wishes, fool that he had been.

As silence met his words and Prof. Benning did not interfere or correct him, he continued: "Uncle Bob was one of the few in this family who was allowed to die of a natural cause. – And that is only the number of deaths in the family. The executed members of other crime organizations dying at that same time are not even added to the headcount here."

"What do you mean?" Vanessa Benning vehemently interrupted. "You can't seriously accuse me, a mere woman, or Bernard, my study-obsessed cousin, of having killed all those people in our family. All the deaths have been declared natural; none had raised suspicion at the time. You yourself must see how ludicrous your implications are. – Your material proves nothing. Just that our family was exceedingly unlucky in that year – or targeted by those who also decimated the other families, if you want to accuse someone." She still tried to insist on her innocence, though all assembled in the room looked at her with a mix of astonishment and revulsion.

"With the one exception, that the other families were extinguished, while yours still had strategically essential survivors," Prof. Lynford countered, putting one newspaper article after the other, which Sophia had accumulated in her internet research, on the table between himself and Dr. Stewart.

– 29 –
The Turn

Dr. Stewart's victorious scream interrupted Vanessa Benning's heartfelt confession. He jumped at Prof. Lynford and forcefully took Sophia's backpack from his grasp. The professor had kept it in his hand to reveal document after document from it, to support his statements. Now the only thing remaining was the research-report Sophia had received from Prof. Benning.

"You had the secret files all along and now want to cast suspicion on your former wife to distract from your own guilt. – Perhaps you yourself gave the information to her, to make her appear guilty. It was you behind all this, now trying to put all the blame on the woman you wanted dead." Dr. Stewart summarized all the revelations in one grand swipe.

Prof. Lynford and Prof. Benning were too stunned by this crooked interpretation of what had been revealed just moments ago, to immediately be able to contradict Dr. Stewart's new version of things.

Prof. Benning was the first to get back his voice and stuttered, still not being able to fully comprehend this new turn of events: "You can't be serious, Stewart. I myself gave the material to Sophia and she handed it over to Lynford."

"So, you finally confess that you are part of the conspiracy. Had my doubts about you all along, Benning," Dr. Stewart shot back.

Prof. Benning shook his head in annoyance over the hard-headedness of Dr. Stewart, lost for words and not fully believing yet, how the man could misinterpret all the facts so fundamentally.

"You are a fool, Stewart, if you believe she will let you get out of this alive," Prof. Lynford now also tried to convince Dr. Stewart of the error of his doings. "Trusting Vanessa means trusting the devil himself."

Sophia in the other room blinked her eyes in astonishment. How could things go so wrong? Just moments before, she had thought everything was about to be finally resolved and cleared up. She had believed Dr. Stewart would be content to catch the head of the syndicate after all his efforts and everything would be solved in mere minutes. But no, he had to be his annoying self through and through and direct his CIA power against the only innocent parties in this mess, Sophia thought with annoyance. To her, it rather seemed that Dr. Stewart himself was part of this criminal scheme, something she would have never suspected before.

Sophia racked her brain. She had to do something to set things right. She could not let Dr. Stewart win, not like that, supporting a criminal and trying to harm her … – What was that? – Did she really just think of Prof. Lynford as 'hers'? No way, but still, she could not let Dr. Stewart harm him or Prof. Benning.

Sophia did not fully trust the protection of her pilfered weapon, but she left her hiding place under the conference-table and pulled the Walther out of her waistband.

Not really impressed by herself holding the unloaded weapon, she looked around for further ways to distract and cause some kind of havoc. To get Prof. Lynford and Prof. Benning out of the incompetent clutches of Dr. Stewart, she had to use all advantages she could possibly get.

Her eyes fell on a heating stove, supposedly for a tea-can, with two unused candles and a lighter next to it on a sideboard. It must have been prepared for the meal she had cleared away already, but not been necessary, as another stove next to it was used and the candle tins in it empty.

Placing the stove onto the conference table, approximately in the middle of the room, she then lit the candles and put them in their places, positioning the cartridges from the emptied pistol on top of the stove, which fortunately had a slightly hollowed-out center, so that the ammunition could not roll away immediately.

Sophia prayed, the candles would provide enough heat to make the cartridges explode, but she would have to get out of this room soon, not to be in the way of the exploding bullets, if they actually did get hot enough. They would fly around wildly and to not accidentally hit someone passing in the corridor outside, Sophia silently closed the door to the hallway.

The voices from the neighboring room were still arguing fiercely, though she could not clearly understand them, because they all shouted over each other. Vanessa Benning was the only one not participating in this heated debate, so she had trouble evaluating her position in the other room.

As a further backup, she did not know the value of, she switched on the device for the speaker system on board the ship as she had seen the other CIA agent do and clipped it onto her apron.

Sophia was still worried, but now, as she had cut off her retreat with the hopefully soon exploding cartridges, with a mask of bravado, stormed into the next room, the gun held tight in her outstretched hand.

Almost instantly, she became aware of the stupidity of her

action.

She only saw the three men in her line of view. Vanessa Benning was nowhere in her sight, though Sophia did not dare to look around and search for her, fearing that Dr. Stewart, at whom she aimed her pistol, would reach for his own weapon at his side, if she took her attention away from him even for just a moment.

"Release them. Let Prof. Benning and Prof. Lynford go," Sophia demanded with a strong voice. "You well know they both have nothing to do with the syndicate-machinations."

Dr. Stewart seemed unperturbed by her pointing a gun at him and turned his attention to her, as if they were having a relaxed conversation over a cup of coffee: "So you admit, you are the real culprit, Sophia, if you can say that about the professors with so much certainty?"

"Of course not. The idea alone is ludicrous. Before coming on board of this ship, I did not even know anything about a 'Syndicate', much less belong to one."

"Don't play stupid, girl. You are its head and have lured your two professors into helping you. Evading detection on board of this ship for hours makes it clear how harmless a bystander you are."

"Nonsense," both professors threw in, but it was Prof. Benning who went on: "She is much too young for it. She must have been in fifth grade at best, when the new head took over. Think, Stewart. Not even you can make up something so stupid."

"And wielding a weapon so aptly should make me believe that she is innocent? Far from it, Benning. She is in league with both you and Lynford and her handing over your lab-reports to Lynford proves it."

Dr. Stewart nodded in Sophia's direction and she was not kept in suspense for long what he meant by it.

Vanessa Benning must have been hidden from her view behind the door and now tried to wrestle the gun from her hand with expertise. This woman was not a mere bystander, but an experienced fighter, that much was clear from her handling a supposedly loaded gun in enemy hand.

But though Sophia tried to hold onto the weapon, the vicious turn of the gun in her hand nearly tore the fingers from her hand and she could not help but let go with a pained gasp.

Prof. Lynford tried to come to her aid, but Vanessa Benning already lifted the gun and pointed it at him. "Go back, Merton, or it will be a pleasure for me to put a hole into you, and don't ever think I have the scruples you had," she declared with a victorious glare at him, still holding Sophia in front of her own body with a tight grip around her wrists. When Sophia tried to struggle against the vice-like hold, keeping her pressed to the front of the woman she hated, Vanessa continued in a falsely seductive voice: "Keep still, or I will shoot your lover, my dear. You have no chance to win now, or he will die."

"Vanessa, that's it. Kill them. We can't have witnesses or both of us will go down for this. Nobody may know what happened here today. Shoot her and then the others. We can't let them tell anyone what they know." Dr. Stewart gave the order as if he had just requested a meal in a restaurant. Even for such an order, Sophia would have expected more emotion than he showed.

Sophia kicked out with her legs in a wild attack, putting the weight of her upper body on the arm Vanessa still held her with. She saw a glimpse of disbelieving shock and pain on Merton's face, when Vanessa Benning put the gun to Sophia's head, following Dr. Stewart's suggestion. Prof. Lynford tried to jump at her, but was too far away to reach her in time to prevent a shot. But anguish distorted his features when he realized that Sophia did not cease her struggles even with the gun held to her temple. Sophia pushed back her head in a sudden move and the woman behind her cried out in pain, but Sophia did not relent. She could not allow the woman pause to regain her balance to find out the gun in her hand was not loaded, or Dr. Stewart would replace it with his own. Though so far, he had made no attempt to come to the aid of Vanessa Benning with his own gun, which still was secured in the holster under his left arm. He seemed to want a clear record for the bullet report of a later investigation of the events here, which was for once in Sophia's favor.

A salve of gunshots could be heard from the next room. Sophia, who was the only one who knew what it meant, thanked the God Almighty for the timely rescue. She had already given up hope that her bullet trick would work at all, taking its time. But now, in short order four shots had exploded and had paralyzed all present.

'Four. Oh my!' Sophia counted the shots in her head, repeating the rhythm of the sounds in her mind again to count anew. But there had definitely only been four shots. Where was the fifth bullet she had put onto the stove?

Dr. Stewart, irritated by the unexpected attack so close to his interrogation room, now drew his own gun and took position at the door, carefully opening it a tiny bit, but all remained silent in the next room.

Looking around with more confidence, he stepped out, finding bullet holes in odd places, one directly in the ceiling of the room, the others in the wall to the hallway and the closed door leading out into the corridor, but otherwise, the room was empty of any potential attacker.

"All clear," he shouted back and went on out to the corridor, putting back the pistol into his holster.

– 30 –
Binding Arguments

Prof. Lynford, who had hesitated to approach Sophia before in fear she would immediately be shot, now took the opportunity of this distraction and came to her rescue. Wrestling with Vanessa for the gun, which she still held to Sophia's head, he was easily able to avert the direction of the gun and finally force it from her grasp without a shot being fired, as Vanessa had been too preoccupied to keep her balance while holding onto the frantically bucking Sophia.

Prof. Benning, observing Prof. Lynford's struggles, joined in from behind by pulling Vanesa's arms back and restraining them at her side, though a crunching sound made all of them look down to the floor, where the parts of a technical device now lay strewn and smashed.

That was the unglamorous end of one of Sophia's haphazard rescue-plans. Hopefully, the crew of the ship had been able to hear some of the discussion going on in here and make sense of that small part the now destroyed device had transmitted. Sophia had her doubts that it had been enough to convince anyone, but Dr. Stewart's order to kill certainly must seem suspicious in whatever context one looked at it.

Glad to be free, Sophia turned around to her professors and smiled thankfully at them, much too breathless from her fighting with Vanessa to thank them with words. But that did not prevent her from glaring back at the hissing woman, who still tried to reach out to get hold of her.

"Calm down," Prof. Benning shook Vanessa, but that only enraged her the more and made her turn her anger against him.

"You traitor. Can't you see what they are trying to do? Turn you against me, your own flesh and blood, the mother of your child."

"Vanessa, stop this. Your lies no longer work with me. Your game is up."

"Not for long. Stewart is on my side, have you already forgotten?"

"No. He wanted me killed. Is that your way to show me how much you care about me?" He held on tightly so as not to let the still fiercely struggling Vanessa out of his hold.

"Help me get her restrained," Prof. Benning wheezed from the effort.

Sophia and Prof. Lynford had stood aside and observed their wrestling with astonished fascination, but his words made them come to his aid instantly.

Sophia was immediately rewarded for her effort, when one flying fist of Vanessa slipped from Prof. Benning's hold and landed with full force on her left cheekbone. The punch made her stumble back with pain and so she watched the two professors from the sideline binding Vanessa to one of the chairs in the room. Though she still held her painfully throbbing cheek, a smile escaped her, when she saw what Prof. Lynford used as a rope. Loosening his tie, which he now wore with the suit he must have had on board his boat, he used it to tie Vanessa's wrists together and then gestured to Benning to hand over his own tie to bind her legs to the solid, metal, tubular chair, using his belt to give the bonds further strength. Prof. Benning, having enough of Vanessa's screeching, threatened to gag her with his handkerchief, when she was already securely bound to the chair and that finally brought some quiet into the room.

"Tell me …," Prof. Benning now addressed the no longer beautiful woman in the chair, whose otherwise magnificent features were marred by anger-lines. "Was it Dr. Stewart's idea to send those men to Jenny?"

"Stewart? No. With all his pomp, he's a simple one. Wouldn't see the benefit in speeding up things."

"It was you then?"

Her cunning smile was all the answer Prof. Benning needed.

"Have you no feelings for your own daughter at all?" He could not believe the cold heart of this woman he for so long had thought to be in love with. Threatening his dear, innocent little baby-girl. His heart stopped at the thought alone and he shuddered that he for so long had been used as a cover by this woman, thinking her in need of his protection.

Looking up, he saw the sorrow on Sophia's face, recognizing that she was aware of the turmoil going on inside him and sensing his pain. Sophia was a dear and compassionate girl and he had not been wrong to set his trust in her. At least that thought was small consolation for his grave error in judgement regarding his cousin Vanessa, the woman he had loved since he could think.

Prof. Lynford stepped towards him and gave him an encouraging pat on his shoulder.

"Thank you, Benning. Well done," he said, taking the tension out of their former relationship and defusing the current situation.

Prof. Benning gave him a swift nod, acknowledging his praise and accepting the peace-offering it was.

"Where is Stewart?" Prof. Benning became suddenly aware, that the man had not come back into the room after exploring the source of the shots, which had been fired so close to them. "Gone, most likely. Trying to escape undetected, would be my guess," Prof. Lynford snidely commented and tried to approach the door into the next room, but was hindered by Sophia.

"No, let me go first. The last bullet has not exploded."

"What bullets?" three voices asked almost simultaneously.

"The ones I put on the stove."

The irritated look on all the faces around her made Sophia stop in her awkward explanations. Her efforts admittedly were not very helpful.

"Oh, just let me go first. I'll try and find out what happened to the last bullet, and then you can follow."

"And leave me behind alone?" Vanessa screeched again.

"It's better I don't keep you company right now, Vanessa, or I would be hard pressed not to kill you. Threatening my little girl …" Prof. Benning growled at her like an angry dog.

Sophia did not spare one thought for the woman staying behind, bound to the chair, instead cautiously entered the adjoining room, where she had hidden beneath the conference table.

The candles were still burning in the stove, but there was no sight of the fifth bullet. The holes in the wall, door and ceiling confirmed, that one shot was missing.

Crawling around, she looked on the floor, as the cartridge was not on the table.

At that moment, her backside up in the air, trying to get a look under the chairs, Prof. Lynford came out, taking in the view greeting him.

"What a sight for sore eyes," he cheerfully commented.

"Oh, you!" Sophia scolded and tried to get up, but bumped

her head soundly against the chair she had just looked under.

"Are you, by chance, searching for this?" Prof. Lynford bent down and then held the last, still intact cartridge up between his fingers. He held the unloaded pistol with an open magazine in his other hand. "Nice trick, by the way."

"Thank you." Sophia smiled at him with joy over his praise, continuing: "Prof. Benning, you can come out now. The missing bullet is found and all is safe here."

They proceeded on their way up on deck, to find out what had happened to Dr. Stewart, but were stopped just outside in the CIA-corridor.

– 31 –
Meanwhile on Board the Ship

When Dr. Stewart had left the room to search for the cause of the unexpected shots, he had approached the hallway outside the conference room. As he did not hear a sound from there, except some far distant shouts and running steps up on deck, he opened the door, which normally stood ajar.

But the view greeting him outside took him by surprise.

The whole team of CIA agents, the entire armed force of his subordinates on board of this ship, were assembled in the corridor, aiming their weapons at him. He cringed back for a moment, till his natural survival instinct set in.

"What's going on here?" he arrogantly confronted his men, who held their pistols awkwardly, not sure about how best to proceed with their superior.

Dr. Stewart immediately took advantage of this indecisiveness among his men and with authority ordered: "Get back to work. We have much to discover yet, as lagging behind as you are with deciphering Lynford's inventions. It can't be that difficult, coming from 'that' man. Who would have thought he could so easily outsmart you all?"

"But, Sir. – We heard …"

"What? What did you hear? – Speak up, Stanley."

It was another man who answered Dr. Stewart's challenging words.

"Sir, we heard all about you threatening the witnesses. Protecting Mrs. Benning, who …"

"What?" Dr. Stewart interrupted, trying to hide his astonishment that he had been overheard by all, but catching himself immediately. "What is with Mrs. Benning?" he said to gain time. "You can't believe that nonsense they are trying to make you believe. She is our key witness and has proven her loyalty time and again. Do you want to deny that and rather believe that shady Lynford? Think for once. Mrs. Benning brought in the lead to the Russian Velcov family Lynford sold information to. And – the capture of those two proven syndicate henchmen who are currently questioned? That was her doing alone. While Lynford tries to play us and intentionally diverts our investigations away from himself, the real culprit. Don't be stupid, guys. – Now, let me through."

Dr. Stewart shoved his way through the agents as they reluctantly stepped aside. He felt that they were not convinced by his words, but as he outranked all the agents on board of this ship, they did not dare to directly disobey his orders either. They were not certain of their closed ranks against him and he would most definitely not wait for them to ascertain their loyalties.

Stepping up on deck, a new wall of opposition awaited Dr. Stewart.

The marines on board had taken position and tried to block his way to Lynford's boat. They must be aware of his plans of escape as well, he thought. 'Damn, had all the ship heard the confidential conversation down there? How much did they hear?'

With annoyance he righted himself and commanded authoritatively: "Step aside and let the boat down to the water-level."

The captain himself now stepped in his way to block his escape.

"We can't do that, Sir," the captain said in a clipped, booming voice.

Dr. Stewart felt nervous sweat collect all over his back and neck, but outwardly, he tried to present a calm and collected front, as if he was completely unconcerned by their opinion.

As he was the commanding officer and the captain and his ship were ordered to follow his directives, he was surprised that the captain even attempted to step in.

"Of course you can. You are commandeered by the CIA and have to follow my orders."

"From what we heard, you are working with the criminals. We have a duty to stop you," the captain tried again, though his voice no longer sounded so certain.

"Your duty is to follow my directives. You have no idea what is really going on here. Only I have the full clearance on this case and know what is best for our country. And that – right now – is to find the mechanism on board Lynford's boat, as it is connected to his 'dark wood' invention. – Now, get out of my way and let the vessel down, as the mechanism only works when the boat is in the water."

The last statement was a total bluff, but Dr. Stewart expected that none of the marines had checked if the boat was recognizable on their controls while on board of the much larger ship. And as nobody opposed his command any longer, his ruse seemed to have worked.

He approached the boat to be let down to water-level with it. He had no intention of waiting for Vanessa, that sly bitch that had outsmarted him so cunningly. No, she could fend for herself and was a good means to keep his opponents occupied if she did not get rid of them for good. That would give him enough time to escape with Lynford's stealth-boat.

But he had forgotten one further opponent standing in his way of escape, who did not so easily let himself be swayed by Dr. Stewart's words and orders.

Michael had stayed behind on the little boat, secured on deck of the large military vessel.

He had observed, first the marines and then some CIA agents, poking around on the boat trying to find its hiding-mechanism. But Michael was quite certain of the congeniality of Prof. Lynford, so he was not overly worried that they would find anything they were not meant to. If he had learned one thing about Merton over the time of their friendship, it was that he was a notorious over-planner, thinking everything through to the last detail. He would not leave anything he did not want to be found openly lying around, not even when rushing in to save his loved one, the little deary Sophia.

But overhearing the exchange between Dr. Stewart and the captain, he would prevent the corrupt doctor from getting his crooked way. The man who had killed his friend and the innocent girl, no, he would not let him escape with the professor's boat, as that was clearly his intention after his order to kill and the four shots.

Taking up position next to the ladder the marines had put to the hull of the boat, he angrily glared down at the approaching Dr. Stewart.

When the man came up the ladder, as if it was his right, Michael shouted down at him: "Get away. I won't let the murderer of my friend and the little girl on board of this ship."

"You are talking nonsense, good man. Step aside. The boat is confiscated and now belongs to the CIA."

But Michael did not budge, instead waited for Dr. Stewart to get up.

When he tried to set his foot on board, Michael gave him a

punch with his right fist, that sent Dr. Stewart flying back down the ladder onto the deck, where he lay winded, but otherwise unharmed.

"Murder?" the captain now interfered.

"Didn't you hear the shots?" Michael asked back. "He ordered Vanessa to kill them and then the shots. Four of them. They must all be dead."

"Take him," the captain ordered. The marines, without needing any further clarification about which one of the two men their captain meant, took hold of Dr. Stewart, disarmed him and swiftly put him in shackles.

Dr. Stewart screamed and instructed them to be released, but none of the marines nor their captain made the least attempt to heed his commands. Instead they lead him out of sight to be locked up safely.

– 32 –
From Deck Down

Only now fully realizing the tragedy he presumed had happened below deck, Michael felt sadness wash over him like an immense wave. Before, shock had kept him from fully comprehending the significance of the four shots he had heard, but seeing Dr. Stewart attempting to escape, had brought all his emotions out.

A sob involuntarily escaped Michael, at the thought of Merton and the little girl dead, shot and bleeding down below. He just made ready to leave the boat to look for them, when the door Dr. Stewart had stormed through just moments before was thrown open again.

Merton was the first to appear from the shadowed doorway, his arm protectively around Sophia. A man whom Michael did not know followed them and then a group of CIA agents came out, among them a few he had already seen searching their boat. They were all curiously looking around as if searching for something. But as the marines had followed their captain inside to lock Dr. Stewart away, the deck was empty except for Michael.

"You are both alive!" Michael jumped down the ladder and drew both Sophia and Merton to his wide breast in a stormy embrace.

"Well, yes," Merton only now realized what his friend must have thought, hearing the shots even up here on deck.

Sophia on their way up had already explained the shots and her trick with the audio-transmitter to the CIA agents who were following them to search for Dr. Stewart. They had reacted with astonishment, too, to find them alive, after the kill-order and then the shots had alerted the whole ship to what was going on.

Two agents had been left behind down below, to lock Mrs. Benning up in one of their interrogation cells, till they would transfer her to the CIA headquarters in Langley for further questioning, while the other agents followed them up, on Prof. Lynford's suggestion that Dr. Stewart might try to escape with his boat.

But finding the stealth-boat still in place without a sign of Dr. Stewart, made the CIA agents swarm out to search for him elsewhere.

"Where is Stewart?" Merton asked his friend.

"Oh, that louse. He is where he belongs. Locked up by the marines."

The CIA agents hearing this statement, immediately stopped in their search and came back to surround the three.

One of the agents cleared his throat, to get the general attention, before he spoke: "Stanley, my name. Tell me what happened here, good man."

Turning to Michael, he looked at him expectantly and Michael, much too happy to see his friends alive to be his usual taciturn self, gladly obliged, filling them all in on what had gone on here. The most joy he had, when describing the punch he had thrown at Dr. Stewart.

"And the marines arrested Dr. Stewart after that?" Stanley wanted further clarification.

"Yes, after realizing the kill-order he had given, they no longer waited and took him down below deck."

Stanley cleared his throat again, as if a bit uncertain of the reception of his next words: "I'm the next in command then.

Please come below deck with me. We need to file an official report with all your statements. – Lynford, come with me. The others, go with Whitchurch and Stockton."

His fellow agents listened attentively to him and only nodded to his words, while Sophia was not so complacent.

"Mr. Whitchurch, Mr. Stockton? Weren't you among those men at the coast who shot at me? – Can't I go with someone else? I don't trust agents who shoot at innocent bystanders."

"It is just a preliminary procedure. Headquarters will want to see you. They will determine, if you really are just a bystander and innocent," Mr. Stanley explained further.

Sophia huffed in annoyance at this statement, but Merton winked at her, signaling his own calmness and that he did not find anything worrisome about the procedure, and so she complied and they together with Prof. Benning followed the two agents down below into the CIA-sector on board.

There they were separated and Sophia, with a last glance back, had to let go of the reassuring grip of Merton's hand around hers. She was lead into the first room by the one man ordering breakfast from her. The cubicle was empty now and no sign left of the member of the syndicate, who had been questioned here earlier.

The CIA agent introduced himself to her as Whitchurch, before leaving her alone for a moment and returning with a towel and a large ice-bucket, which normally would be used to keep champagne bottles cold.

Glancing at him worriedly, expecting some kind of torture to extract information from her, he just nodded to her and drily explained: "For your cheek."

Gladly, she made use of it to put a cold compress on her throbbing cheekbone, which turned numb in no time.

To her surprise, the interrogation proceeded much smoother and more comfortably than she had expected or overheard with the member of the syndicate. Her interrogation mostly was a retelling of her version of the events leading her to be here, with occasional prompts by Mr. Whitchurch and him scribbling down names and times into a tablet, though a device recorded and transmitted her statement in audio and video back to CIA headquarters simultaneously. Sophia was a bit self-aware because of that fact at first, but soon forgot about the recording, when reliving all the details of her rescue of Prof. Lynford and their escape from the now bombed house on the coast.

When Sophia finished her story, she expected a cross examination and details about when they would be transferred to the CIA headquarters for further questioning, but after an hour, she was released from the confined questioning booth and lead into the larger room, where she had been hiding beneath the conference table before. A plentiful and generous breakfast awaited her, which she gladly partook in. One man even brought her a new ice-pack for her cheek, which by now sported the colorful beginnings of a black eye.

To Sophia's great surprise, only moments after her own release, she was joined by Michael.

As a potential suspect of the CIA, she had thought she would be kept separate from the others till things had cleared up. The two of them easily bonded over their appreciation for the decked-out breakfast.

They stared in wonder when after a few more minutes Prof. Benning and Prof. Lynford came in as if long-time friends, chatting amicably.

"How did it go?" Sophia was the first to ask.

"Fine chap, this Stanley fellow. – Reported to Langley already. They won't need to bring us in, though we need to remain on standby for further questioning," Prof. Lynford informed them, taking a seat next to Sophia, while Prof. Benning sat down across the table from her.

"How are you, my dear?" Prof. Lynford turned to her, for the first time taking in her shiny black eye and the strength of Vanessa's punch at Sophia.

Gently, he touched her abused skin on her cheekbone, before he called out to the CIA agents in the hallway: "Bring an icepack. Hurry!"

"No! No more ice. My face is already half frozen."

"They gave you some ice to cool it already and still …?"

"Yes, yes. But it does not seem to have helped much. I just will have to live with a colorful face for a while." Sophia tried to smile at Merton, but the grimace hurt her and so she immediately stopped the movement of her features.

Seeing her wince, Merton worriedly stroked her cheek, being careful not to come anywhere close to where it could hurt her.

"It is quite all right. It no longer aches so much," she tried to reassure him.

"Brave girl." Merton leaned down and gave her a soft kiss on her unhurt lips.

The clearing of a throat threw them out of their intimate moment quite abruptly and made them take in their surroundings again.

Prof. Benning had intentionally interrupted them, though his broad smile did not indicate any kind of disgruntlement or displeasure about her getting so close to his rival Prof. Lynford. Looking around, Sophia became aware of the CIA agents standing in the doorway. Their presence gave her the reason for Prof. Benning's subtle warning.

She and Merton had been so focused upon each other that they had completely forgotten all about their surroundings.

"Thought you didn't want to have an audience," Prof. Benning clarified in a low whisper.

"Thank you, Benning. Very kind of you. I hope you don't …"

"Of course not," the professor interrupted, cutting off all eventual explanation attempts of Merton with a wave of his hand. "I thought as much, when I first saw you in Sophia's car and you listened to her when she chastised us for wasting time. So this does not really come as a surprise to me." He smiled at them benignly.

"Oh," Merton was rendered speechless by that. Benning was more attentive than he would have given him credit. His rival had recognized his feelings for Sophia much earlier than even he himself had been aware of; that his emotions went much deeper than mere attraction.

The CIA agents in the doorway took in the exchange silently, before the incoming Mr. Stanley addressed them:

"I'm sorry to interrupt you, but we need to separate you again. The Inspector General wants a word with each one of you. He and a team from his Office of Investigations will be here in a few minutes to take over."

The cheerful expression on Merton's face vanished and Sophia felt apprehension creep up her spine. The always so self-assured Prof. Lynford now appeared worried and that could not be a good sign, when the first interrogation had not seemed to worry him at all. What could that turn of events now mean, Sophia wondered.

The agents swiftly put their food on plates for each one of them and tried to lead them out.

Sophia could not help but to turn to Merton: "What is happening now?"

"Don't worry, Sophia. Everything will be all right. You have nothing to worry ..."

But the agent taking Prof. Lynford's arm to lead him away, pulled him out the door with some strength, interrupting their further conversation and emphasizing his authority over him.

At least they did not want to starve them, Sophia thought, finding Mr. Whitchurch standing next to her while holding her well loaded plate like a butler.

He lead her back into the interrogation booth where he had questioned her before. But instead of continuing the interrogation, he put her plate on the table. He raised one of his eyebrows meaningfully, looking at her. "Don't pull any tricks with that door. It won't do you any good, if we have to search for you on board of this ship again." With those words, he left her and locked the door behind him.

Being locked up in a cell with nothing to do was torture in itself for the always active Sophia and she even lost interest in her tasty breakfast. She only nibbled on it listlessly, waiting and wondering what was going on, while she was imprisoned here.

– 33 –
Intimate Inspection

As the booth Sophia was locked in was soundproof, she had no way of finding out what happened on board, while she had to wait. Neither did she hear the one military helicopter leaving with both Vanessa Benning and Dr. Stewart bound and gagged on board, while another one landed only few minutes later, bringing a team of agents and the Inspector General of the CIA. She had no way of knowing, that it was an honor and sign of the importance of this case, that he even took an active part in the investigation and left his headquarters.

Prof. Lynford on the contrary was well aware of that fact, when the Inspector General came into his interrogation booth, as he had worked with the CIA on various cases already. But while he had been rather sure that Stanley was not on the payroll of the Syndicate of his ex-wife and contrary to Stewart would treat him fairly, he was not so certain about the loyalties of the Inspector General, especially because of this man's closeness to politics. Merton had never met the Inspector General, but that he now took personal interest in the case worried him.

Prof. Lynford was the first one the Inspector General wanted to see, sending his team out to take up the interrogations with the others.

The Inspector General swiftly got to the point: "Did you ever work for the Syndicate?"

"No, of course not." Merton wondered about the simple question, answering the man with fervor. He knew that even his tiniest reaction was observed by specialists via the mirrored screen in the room, who were watching him for the least slip in his body language. No lie-detector was needed for those highly specialized experts in reading body language. They were said to be able to see a lie even before it was uttered. He had to be careful with his answers, not to give away too much, but saw his way to freedom slip from his grasp. So much depended upon him and the most pressing for him at the moment was, that he had involuntarily drawn Sophia into this mess along with him. He had to get her and his friend Michael out of this unharmed. Even Prof. Benning's fate now somehow depended on him.

Aware of this burden, Merton sighed heavily.

"Is everything all right with you?" the Inspector General asked, as if he cared.

It took a moment for Merton to nod in answer. He had known that Stanley had been too easy on him with his questions, but that he had let him get back together with Sophia and even Benning and Michael, had given him hope. They could not want to keep them further, if they let them exchange their versions. But immediately being separated again so soon, had made all his worst nightmares reappear.

He must not let the specialists see his fear or they would regard it as a sign of his guilt.

He had to rescue innocent Sophia. She deserved better than to be locked up because of him. He had to get her out of this, even if it meant going back to prison.

The Inspector General continued undeterred: "Did your wife work with the CIA?"

"Ex-wife," Merton automatically corrected. "And yes. She appears to have had the support of Dr. Stewart all along."

"Does your invention 'dark wood' work?"

"Yes, it does."

"Can it get access?"

"Yes."

"Can the access be technically directed to separate the information streams?"

"No." Merton was glad that he could answer this tricky question he had feared truthfully because of its particular wording.

"Why did you sell the invention to the CIA, when, only hours later, you made it available all over the internet?"

"To lure out the head of the syndicate who would try to get close to the transaction, while at the same time assuring my safety against all the secret services and mafia organizations worldwide who had shown an interest in the invention."

"Why the CIA?"

"Because the syndicate had its informants inside."

"How do you know that?"

"How else could the syndicate have even found out about this invention in the first place? My laboratory is still secure and no breach detected."

"Oh, my team will come to that, your secret laboratory hidden away from us," the Inspector General accused angrily, losing a bit of his stoic composure and showing the first tiny sign of human emotion on his face.

"There is nothing to find out. I won't tell you anything about it, otherwise it no longer would be 'secret'."

The Inspector General turned to a member of his team he had brought on board with him, who had intently stared onto the screen of a tablet device during the entire interrogation so far, sending him outside with a short nod.

During the wait, the Inspector General at first had kept completely silent, though he had been staring at Prof. Lynford, as if he thought him to be the worst criminal.

Merton had refused to budge under this treatment. If the man thought that would work on a former prison inmate, he would have to think again. Though Merton had not been imprisoned for long, the experience had hardened him against malicious staring. The criminals tried to determine weaknesses of fellow inmates that way and would use even the slightest blinking of an eye in their favor.

Undeterred by the Inspector General's staring, Prof. Lynford, after a while, came to the decision to turn the tables. Why not get some answers himself? After all, who was the Inspector General to judge him? He should rather keep a better watch over his own 'ship', virtually speaking, meaning the CIA. After all, they had the culprits, creating this whole disaster, in their own ranks. Dr. Stewart certainly was only one of the foul fishes in the pond.

"Are you here to continue your agent Dr. Stewart's work?"

The Inspector General blinked in surprise at this unexpected question from the man he sought to intimidate.

"My agent? – Oh, well, yes, Stewart. He is on his way to Langley."

"Back into the folds of his fellow agents. To supposedly get a recommendation for his bravery in execution of his duty again, I presume," Merton mocked.

"You don't approve?" The man kept his voice absolutely neutral.

Merton could not read anything about his emotions, so he tried to poke further: "Should I approve of him letting me go to prison for something he well knew I did not do, or rather for trying to let my ex-wife shoot me to cover his tracks? Which of those two is more recommendable, you think?"

The Inspector General now looked with clear curiosity at him, no longer trying to hide his interest in the discussion.

"Vanessa was one of our key witnesses in many of the late successes we had," the man to Merton's astonishment finally admitted, no longer holding back from revealing anything, even the most inconsequential of facts, to him. But Merton still did not trust that man.

"Why is it, that you are interested in this case? Why come with a team for internal affairs?"

"How do you know what purpose my team has?"

"Just a pretty guess, but you just confirmed it."

"I undertook no effort to hide it."

"But you are not really interested in me or my inventions or anything I did. Isn't that so?"

"Eventually." The man clearly detested having his motives being found out so easily and now refused to give any more away, looking back into the mirror behind him, giving a sign to the other room with a nod.

Only seconds later, the agent from before came back into the room and confirmed whatever question the Inspector General had posed to him.

Both men now took a seat in front of Merton. Before, they had remained standing, while he had been pushed into an uncomfortable light metal chair.

Much more relaxed, the Inspector General now continued his questioning, mostly letting him retell his version of things, taking especial note of all his contacts in the CIA during all his work for them.

When they were finished and the flood of questions raining down on him had finally stopped, Merton could not help but ask: "Are you working for the Syndicate?"

The Inspector General mirthlessly laughed. "You take the bull by the horns, Lynford. No chatting around things, just right to the heart. – What do you think? Would you have even posed that question, if you still thought I were?"

"No," Merton admitted. "Just wanted to see your reaction."

"Yes, I know. Satisfying, don't you think? As we speak, the members of the Syndicate are being arrested."

"But how do you even know them all?"

"You just told me their names."

"I did? But how can you be so sure all of them were working for …" Merton broke off irritated.

"Initially, not all of them did," the Inspector General explained patiently, now far removed from the stand-offish man at the beginning of the interrogation. "But after a while, around the time when you met your wife …"

"Ex-wife. I can't stand to even think of her, much less call her my wife."

"Understandable. But, your ex-wife somehow got wind about your inventions and wanted to use them for herself. She lured you into marrying her and put all her marionettes in place, to get access to whatever invention you came up with. Her influence in the CIA went high enough, to get whatever she wanted. The one piece missing in my solution was just the head of it all: was it indeed you, as she proclaimed all along, or her with someone high-up, helping her to get whatever she needed."

"But I can't tell you the name of her leading contact inside the CIA. It can't only have been Dr. Stewart. Though she seems to have had him fooled quite thoroughly, he did not appear as if he had been in on her plans. There must have been someone else." Merton could not believe that he even defended Stewart, who had dared to threaten and endanger Sophia.

"There indeed is. But don't sell yourself short. You told us his name already and identified him with Stanley, though you only knew him as her business manager, visiting you for dinner on various occasions, not with his real job-title, as the Director of Operations from the CIA. By the way, your w… – ex-wife does not have a business manager. She does not trust anyone knowing all her business interests. She leads her operations solely on a need-to-know basis, which made it so hard to check her out."

"But you let me rot in prison, knowing all that?"

"As I said, we did not really know. You or her, you were both an equal chance."

"And what pushed the weight in my favor?"

"Your publication of a useless invention," the Inspector General gleefully informed him. "You would not have done it, but would have wanted it kept a secret, to eventually develop it further to get some kind of use out of it, and if only to blackmail someone with its existence."

Merton cringed back in shock about this revelation, but immediately tried to hide the extent of his reaction.

"You don't like to be famous for a failed invention, Lynford?" the man fortunately misinterpreted his reaction completely. "It rescued you from further prosecution."

"Good. And what will happen to Michael, Sophia and Benning?" Merton tried to divert the attention from himself, much too worried that they would detect his lie after all.

"My men are observing them right now. We'll get to them later."

"But they are innocent. They had nothing to do with all of this."

"We'll see."

"You have to let them go."

"Do I have to? Really? What do you promise in return?"

"You are like them then?" Merton commented snidely, too angry to have fallen into that trap so blindly, out of worry for Sophia. But he would give anything to keep her safe.

"Don't worry, Lynford. Your willingness to work for the CIA again on future cases is all the promise I want from you. I'm not an unreasonable man. I see that you are worried about the girl. From what I presume, you would not even be here on board, if it were not for her."

Merton nodded in admission. "What will you do to her?" he now openly asked, when he saw that the Inspector General was already fully aware of his feelings for her.

"Let her go home with you eventually. After all, it should be safe for you two out there, by now."

"Thank you, Sir."

"Nothing to thank me for. Thank you for finally clearing things up for us, after we were lead on fool's errands with our investigations for so long. It is thanks to you that we caught the head of the Syndicate and their corrupt support in the CIA in one grand swipe."

– 34 –
Escape or Release

Sophia was still impatiently waiting in her interrogation room worrying herself sick about Merton, who she was sure would be made the culprit again to clean up all the CIA reports and make their work look impeccable.

Jumping up from her chair every few minutes and walking around, just to recognize the futility of walking in such a tiny space and sitting down again, she was hard pressed not to search for a means to get out of the room she was locked in. She could not stand the waiting, the uncertainty, the worry about her love.

'What was that? My love? – After so short a time?' Could she really be certain about her feelings? But her heart felt sure. Without a doubt, she cared for Merton, the grumpy, arrogant man, who thought to protect her by pushing her away. She did not always agree with his methods, but his heart was in the right place and she cared what happened to him so much. – Yes, she loved him, wanted to protect him and so keeping her locked up and away from him was pure torture for her. She needed to see that he was all right for herself.

Approaching the door, to get a closer look at it, she jumped back in surprise, when it was thrown open, hitting the wall with a loud bang.

"Are you about to try one of your tricks again?" It was Mr. Whitchurch, accompanied by an unknown agent. "Was curious how long it would take you," he added with an ironically lifted right brow.

But he did not seem angry with her, but rather stepped aside to let her go through the doorway and leave the small interrogation-cubicle.

When she came out into the hallway, she saw Merton standing there with a grey-haired man she had not seen before.

Sophia could not help but rush to them, taking Merton's hand. "Are you all right?"

He winningly smiled down at her and introduced her to the Inspector General.

"Sorry I interrupted you," Sophia excused herself. "But I couldn't help but be worried. After all that happened ..." Reluctantly, she broke off.

"It's all right. I understand. You went through a lot for your professor," the man reassured her with an almost admiring glance. "You have nothing to worry about any longer."

Mr. Whitchurch and the other man accompanying him, caught up with her and joined them in the hallway, taking up position behind her. Sophia felt intimidated by their show of strength, as they were at least a head taller than her and built like body-builders. Sophia moved closer to Prof. Lynford and gripped his hand more tightly, as if it were her right to hold onto him.

"You can both leave as soon as we reach the coast," the Inspector General assured them, smiling benignly. "We have no reason to keep you any longer, even after your little escapades, young Miss." The corners of his lips wavered in suppressed emotion, which Sophia thought to be amusement, so she was quite certain that the man was not too angry with her.

"What will happen to Prof. Benning and Michael?" Merton wanted to know.

"Your friend Michael we already let go with your boat.

I thought it too much of a temptation for the Syndicate to risk the boat remaining here, when we as yet do not know the full extent of its reach. Some unknown member might still be on board and could try to get access to the technology. Your man is transferring the boat to your marina right now. We made sure nobody could follow him and as the location of his destination is unknown, he and your boat should be safe for now."

"Thank you, Sir," Merton formally answered the man.

"As far as Prof. Benning is concerned, he will have to stay with us for some time longer. He will come to Langley with me to give his statements against Stewart. – In case we have further questions for you, we know how to reach you both. And, Lynford, regarding the boat's technology, I will get in contact with you personally, as soon as the current situation has been fully resolved."

"So, we are free to go home?" Sophia wanted further clarification to that point, as after all this mess, she could not readily believe that everything was finally over.

"Yes, a car will be waiting for you in the harbor. You are free to go wherever you want."

Sophia smiled up at Prof. Lynford, who had turned towards her and pulled her to his side. Embraced by one of his arms, Sophia felt secure and slowly the realization that it really was over seeped into her being. The worry and fear leaving her tight muscles only made her aware of how tense she had been, her body weakly relaxing into Merton's side.

His reassuring grip showed her that he understood her feelings and gave her strength with his hold and calmness.

Leaning down towards her ear, he whispered: "It is over. I'll bring you home, my dear."

"But don't you need to go home yourself? The first thing I need to do is call my parents, let them know that I am o.k." Sophia whispered back, but she was aware of the CIA men trying to catch their conversation.

"You come first, Sophia. Nothing else matters. Besides, nobody is waiting for me, but you." He accompanied his words with a soft kiss to her temple on her unharmed side of the face.

Bright red crept up her cheeks from the open show of affection and the smile on the Inspector General's face made clear that he knew well what was going on between Merton and her.

"You can have a room, till we reach the shore," he cheerfully told them.

Ashamed, Sophia averted her gaze. Merton, sensing her discomfort, immediately jumped in to protect her. "No, it is all right. Just a bit to eat would be very much appreciated," he successfully diverted the attention from the embarrassed Sophia with the fact that he had not gotten the chance to eat his breakfast earlier.

– 35 –
Driving Home

At a long and delicious brunch as a very much belated breakfast, Merton and Sophia could finally relax after their exhaustive interrogation. The Inspector General had left them alone, leaving with his agents to supervise the arrests on land, taking over the CIA quarters on board as his headquarters instead of losing time by flying back to Langley.

As promised, Sophia and Merton were flown over to the coast as soon as they reached the shore, though the area they were at seemed uninhabited. But when their helicopter landed on an abandoned coastal road, a man was waiting for them, handing over the keys to a rental car.

When they had left the ship, there had been no sign of Prof. Benning and their questions were only answered with the repetition that he was busy right now. Unable to do anything for him, Sophia and Merton left as instructed by the agents accompanying them.

Sophia's apartment could be reached in about a three-hour drive from the place they were put ashore at, while Merton's home would require a much longer journey and they were both tired.

Still, Sophia wondered, why Merton was so eager to accompany her and as he was his taciturn self, she just had to ask: "Why are you driving me home?"

"To keep an eye on you. You need it."

"Ah, what?" Sophia was perplexed by his offhanded explanation and feeling her self-esteem threatened, stubbornly contradicted: "I can take care of myself."

"Yes. I have seen as much. Running head on into an ambush, making a mess of the arranged CIA-support and then trying to rescue Prof. Benning with an unloaded pistol."

"It was not Prof. ... – Damn. I did it for you, you fool. And if you hadn't so rudely pushed me away, I would not have been on the CIA ship in the first place and in need of you coming back to rescue me."

"You say it was all my fault getting you into danger?"

Sophia thought for a while, not willing to reveal her feelings for him, when he criticized her for her rushing in to help him. What else should she have done? Let him be arrested and put away for the rest of his life without anyone helping him? She could not even bear the thought of it, much less consider acting in such a way.

"No, it was not your fault, though, somehow it was."

But Sophia refused to elaborate anymore on her cryptic words, when Merton tried to prompt her again to continue her explanation.

Each caught up in their own thoughts, they drove on in silence for a while. Merton had meant his comments to be more teasing than a real critique of Sophia, because he was more than grateful for every single one of her interferences. Just the worry for her safety had made him utter the words more harshly than he had intended. He loved that girl. How could he find a fault in the angel, selflessly rushing to rescue whenever she thought him in danger? How could he bear the thought of her putting herself in danger for him so carelessly? His thoughts were occupied in how best to court her and make her see, that they were meant to be, though they had only known each other for such a short time. But her blurted-out confession, that she had done it all for him? That must mean something. She had to return his feelings. Why else would she have gone through all this and not just given him up to his opponents?

He racked his brain for a way to start their conversation again and make her see that he was not angry with her; on the contrary.

But he worried for nothing, as Sophia's curiosity came to his rescue.

Her line of thought had gone much in the same way as Merton's, but instead of trying to seduce him, she had wondered about the deepness of her feelings in such a short period of time.

Could she trust the man she had learned to know in the last few days? After all, hadn't he proclaimed back in her apartment that his invention did work, when now it had turned out that it did not fully work?

Merton, during all his interrogations had remained steadfast in his statements that a solution for the direction was not possible and the rumors to the contrary had been false. The CIA had all the available material there was to be had.

Still, Sophia could not help but wonder if the access really was not possible, but she did not know how best to approach that topic without torturing Merton any more than all the CIA interrogations already had.

She tentatively began, forgetting all about the reason for their long silence: "From all the material about the invention I have seen, I somehow got the impression, that an access-directing could be possible. Are you certain there is no possible way?"

"So, it does not leave you in peace either," Merton gave her a smiling glance from the driver's seat, relieved that she did talk to him again.

"I've just heard so much about it, that I somehow got the impression that it would work. I thought you even told me as much, that it does work."

"It does," was all he said, without elaborating any further.

Sophia now almost exploded with curiosity.

"But if it does, and I presume you mean more than just the access to the information scatter via the dark-wood wavelength, then how …? Why? You let them all believe it does not. All the world is searching for a solution now. If it can work, it is only a question of time till someone finds out." Sophia's words rushed out in a hurried blur.

"They certainly will try, and then they will give it up as a hopeless case and everybody will be content that nothing is to be gained by it. That is what had to be achieved."

"You mean that entire thing was your plan all along?"

"May be not the details, but the grand scheme, well, yes. It had to be done; it had to become public domain, so that the fight for the information would stop."

"How could you plan such a thing? And how can you be so sure nobody will find the solution, if there indeed is one?"

"There is one. And the beauty of it is, that the solution is the most unlikely one you could ever imagine. No self-respecting scientist will ever consider the possibility of it. – In a way, the solution safeguards itself."

"But how did you come across it, when the solution is such an unlikely one?"

"Quite by accident, I admit. My key researcher in my secret laboratory, Dr. Ranston, married quite young, right out of high-school. His wife was the one …"

"But isn't your secret laboratory too secret for a wife of one of your researchers to know about it?" Sophia interrupted him.

"No, not so very secret. What would the poor man tell his wife where he is going each day? Besides, she is one of the few approved people allowed on the premises."

"Will I be able to see them once, too?"

"Of course, you will. I'm counting on your support. But now, what I wanted to tell is: While his interests went to science, those of his wife were directed to astrology and all things esoteric. Her latest topics were mind-reading and energy-healing. So, one day, she comes in, her husband quite proud that our penetration-attempts did not work and our research could be successfully concluded, told her about it, while eating the lunch she had brought him. His wife in the meanwhile played around with his headsets lying around on his work desk, intently listening to one. When her husband came back to his desk, he asked her, how she could possibly stand to listen so long to such a muddle of things. She just looked at him strangely and said, if he thought the best-ever instructions about a healing-art she just had discovered to be a muddle, that was his own problem. When he took over the headset, again a wild scattering of sounds met his ears. While when his wife touched the device, she heard the best of information."

"So what went on? Did the device need a medium? Is it that?"

"Well, yes and no. Not a medium per se. It's not alone the person, but also the intent. – Dr. Ranston dismissed his wife's success and had arrogantly discarded her ability to get access. His wife, angry with him, went in a few days later to try again. She wanted to find something revealing about her husband's research, to confront him with it, but to her astonishment, she could not get access that day. – We tried it again and again and found out that she was only able to direct the device, when her intentions were good and her mind was clear of other rivaling emotions."

"That is absolutely astonishing. – A miracle. But could not one of the scientists be an accidental medium as well?"

"That in itself might still be a slight risk, but what makes it rather unlikely to work for anyone else is the reason for wanting access. What scientist solely wants the access to help others, as the slightest attempt at self-gain makes the access unattainable? Do you know a scientist, who does not at least want to further his own reputation? – You see, the likeliness that anyone will ever get it to work is like minus null."

Sophia smiled at that rather unscientific expression from Merton, who was normally such a stickler to correct research procedures.

Sophia found relief wash over her for knowing that the access was safe and she fully agreed with Merton's assumption, that it was more than unlikely that the researching scientists would find out the method to direct the 'dark wood'-device. And even if they were, they could not use it for something bad.

"Now, all the secret services together with all the mafia organizations around the world are preoccupied with trying to get it to work. That at least should reduce crime quite effectively for a while. – With the further hindrance of the good intentions, they won't find it out ever. You are a genius, Merton!"

"Nothing like that. Just a very lucky chap for finding you."

Sophia bent over to him and gave him a kiss on his cheek for this sweet comment, though she could not help but comment:

"As I remember it, I found you."

"For which I am forever grateful."

"Are you?" Sophia was worried. After all, she had known Prof. Lynford only under extreme pressure. And would he think her, a mere student, even worthy of his time? How would they fit under normal circumstances? She could not help but blurt out her worried thoughts to him: "Will we still see each other, now that everything is over? Without all the stress and danger around us?"

Merton looked at her with love in his eyes, though she did not dare to hope that she had interpreted his emotions correctly.

"Yes, my dear. We will. When all the pressure no longer keeps us apart, we can get to explore our feelings for each other."

Though, to the burning flame of his feelings inside of him, those words felt weak and harmless in comparison, even to himself.

He intended to ask her for her hand in marriage and, as nervous as he was about her reaction, he was certain Sophia somehow shared his feelings and would accept him. At least he hoped so.

He would seal the proposal with showing her the love he could give her. Merton racked his brain for the best way to convince Sophia. After all, they had only known each other for a short while, but for himself, there was no doubt that Sophia was the right one for him.

He was planning out all the details in his head, the words he would say, when they arrived at her apartment. He would pick her up and carry her over her doorstep, kissing her senseless. How then could she possibly refuse him?

A victorious smile about the forming image of his proposal washed over his face, which Sophia recognized.

"Pleased with yourself, are you?"

"No," he immediately shot back. "No, not with myself, my dear. With you, only with you."

Sophia gave him a sweet kiss on his cheek again and he could not wait till the drive would end and he could finally fully return the kisses she gave him. For now, he had to concentrate on driving them safely to her apartment.

– 36 –
Unexpected Meeting

Merton planned his proposal in meticulous detail all throughout their way to Sophia's apartment, mulling over and re-arranging his options over and over again. In his mind, he went through all his possibilities and the one he thought most likely to find the most favor with her was to enter her apartment, kiss her senseless and then to sink down onto his knees and ask her for her hand.

He knew he wanted her and failure was not an option for him. Sophia had conquered his heart with ease and was the most important person in his life.

So, when they reached her apartment, he unlocked the door for her with the key the CIA agent, waiting with the rental car, to their astonishment had handed over to them, together with her purse. He swept her up in his arms and carried the surprised Sophia over her doorstep. Inside, he let her down, leaned her against the closed door and kissed her. His hands were roaming around her body and soon he found her a willing and fiery participant in their steamy kiss.

A loud clearing of a throat behind them abruptly interrupted his further plans for his proposal.

Turning around, he and Sophia became aware of the assembled people in her apartment. An older couple, he presumed to be her parents, were sitting on her sofa, while a younger man, standing beside them, was glaring at Merton, but was held back by his arm by the sitting older man.

"Good to see you well and alive, Sophia," the older man greeted her, not having seen her black eye yet, as she was still in the shadows of the hallway.

"Papa, Mama, Marcus! You came all the way here?" Sophia rushed inside and embraced them all, before looking back at Merton, who had remained standing in the doorway to the main living-room.

"Who's that man, dear?" her mother prompted.

"Is he the one who did that to you?" her father fell into the words of his wife, his aggression towards the man in the doorway clear in his stance. Her mother gasped, only now becoming aware of Sophia's bright shining black eye, reaching out for Sophia, to draw her to her side protectively.

But Sophia stepped away, reaching her hand out towards Merton as if to beg him to come in.

"No, of course not. It's a long story, how I got that black eye. – That is …" Sophia began the introduction, but Merton interrupted her.

"I am her fiancé," he said, coming fully into the room now and offering his hand in greeting to her father, who did not take it, but looked him up and down inquisitively.

Sophia took Merton's arm and whispered in his ear: "I want an official proposal at some point, not just the declaration."

Merton smiled at her widely, glad that she had not immediately contradicted his hasty outburst, but her father broke in on their intimate exchange.

"Well, someone who can lure my daughter away on an adventure, with her forgetting all about her family and not letting anyone know where she is, certainly must be the right one for her. Welcome to the family, boy."

Merton looked up in irritation. It had been a long time since anyone had called him 'boy'. But he did not have much time to think, as Sophia's father took his hand and drew him into a hearty embrace, followed by her mother's hug and then a much rougher pat on his back by his future brother-in-law, Marcus.

Her father's question, when he knew that Sophia was the right one for him, was not hard to answer for him.

"Sophia, you, following me and trusting me, when all the world tried to frame me and even I tried to push you away because of the danger we were in, but you still unerringly believing in me and expecting me to do the right thing. That opened my heart and it no longer belongs to me. You are the right one for me and I hope I can be for you."

Sophia stormed over to him and gave him an intense kiss in front of her parents. "Yes," she whispered at him. "That was the loveliest proposal I could ever imagine. Yes, I love you, too."

Though they were tired, they had to retell the story of their adventures in every detail. But before they fully began, Sophia's mother insisted on calling the concierge Mr. Arnestone from across the street over.

When her parents had arrived the night before, he had seen light in Sophia's apartment and had come over to check on her, if everything was all right. He had let her parents and brother know that Sophia had left with the man she had rescued from his house, as she had sent him a note in the mail. The corresponding letter she had sent her parents, must still be on its way or unread in their mailbox at home.

Mr. Arnestone had still been worried by her vague message and when he arrived, was glad to find her and the 'rescued hostage', as he called the professor, all well and healthy and at home again.

The ruffians, who had abducted the professor, had fortunately disappeared without leaving a trace the same day she had left with the professor, he told them. Though that had him worried that they were following them.

But the story of Merton and Sophia cleared things up and Mr. Arnestone was glad, that he did not need to contact the police in search for her, as she had left instructions in her letter, that if she did not re-appear after three days, he should contact the authorities, but not the two policemen, who came in response to her emergency call regarding Prof. Lynford, the two officers Charlie and Leonard. He stayed for a while, but had to go back to his post on an emergency call and so left, before their story had ended.

When Sophia's mother saw her stifling a yawn more than once during her re-telling of their story, she finally had mercy with the two adventurers and prepared them a meal she had brought from home, before sending them to bed. Only now did they become aware that Sophia's apartment was not equipped for all of them, but Merton's suggestion to leave them alone here and take Sophia to a motel, was immediately rejected by her father.

"You think we trust you with her alone, yet, just because you muddle her brain enough to follow you wherever you go? No, marriage first, then you can think of other things. All in good time, boy."

"I assure you, my intentions are honorable."

"Pooh! These young men. Thinking we are from yesteryear. We were young once, too."

"Daddy! We are much too tired to …" Sophia intervened, but was interrupted by her brother, who stepped in between her and Merton, taking on a threatening stance.

"Oh, come on, Marcus. You can't mean to hurt him. I love

Merton. Does that not mean anything to you?" Sophia stepped around her brother and took Merton's arm.

"You need not defend me, Sophia. I can fight for you, if I must."

"I don't want you two to fight. You are both worried about me. There is no reason to fight. – Ma, Dad, you can both stay on the couch, Marcus, I have a spare mattress for you in the attic and Merton and I will share the bed. This way you can watch over us, making sure that nothing untoward happens here." Sophia, short-tempered because of her lack of sleep, laid out the terms and could not help but silently add: "Kindergarten," before a yawn interrupted her further tirade.

Merton embraced her from behind and whispered into her ear: "Is your family always this difficult?"

"No, not really. I always thought them to be extremely understanding. But, you see, they have never seen me bring home a date, so they are not used to … – You know."

"… to share you. I understand. I don't want to share you either. What do you think we go to the justice of the peace tomorrow and apply for a license? Then you can come home with me and I can have you all to myself?"

The joy that suggestion brought to her face was unmistakable. "And avoid all the hustle of a grand wedding? What a dream. Yes!"

"Really? We can still have a big wedding later. I didn't mean to take that away from you."

"No, no! I don't want one. I still remember all the preparations for my older sister's wedding. No. I don't want that. The county clerk is fine and a small church wedding later. But nothing big. What do you think?"

"Sounds fine to me. Your wish is my command."

"What are you whispering, you two?" her mother interrupted them, coming back from the bathroom.

"Planning the wedding," Sophia smiled at her with a big, relieved grin.

"And?" her mother prompted, not content with the information she got, knowing her youngest child all too well.

"Tomorrow, we'll go to the county clerk for the license."

"You know Pater Francis expects to hold your marriage ceremony," her mother reminded. Pater Francis had been her school priest and had married both her older siblings. He was a forward-thinking man and Sophia admired him and his work, so how could she possibly refuse this emotional blackmail by her mother?

"Yes, we can do the church ceremony later. But we want to get it over right away."

"What? How unromantic of you, Sophia. You really agree with that, Merton?" It was the first time her mother or anyone of Sophia's family used his first name and strangely, he only now felt really accepted into the folds of the Warren family, though her father and brother still glared at him a bit judgmentally.

"Oh, Mom. Come on. You saw what Elly did. I can't stand that much chaos again for my own wedding."

"I see. You go on and marry in a civil ceremony, but let me arrange the church ceremony with Pater Francis. You need not do anything, just do a fitting for your chosen dress. And that one's on me. The only thing you have to do is chose a design and appear at the right day and time. – Both of you, understandably." Her mother smiled wistfully.

"Thank you, Mrs. Warren …"

"Hodgepodge." Sophia smiled at hearing her mother's chosen swear-word. "No Mrs. anything to you. You are part of the family now. I'm Elena, like my first daughter, though we call her Elly. And that man still grumbling in the corner about you taking away his little girl is Paul, my husband. No Mr. and Mrs. anything. And no more grumbling, Paul. Merton is a good man. If Sophia chose him, he is good enough for us. Who else would be willing to spend a night with us in the same room. Paul, really, think again. Tomorrow, you will help him get together all documents to obtain the license."

A smile broke out on Paul's face and finally cut the tension, which had reappeared when he had feared for the safety of his daughter. Merton's future father-in-law no longer seemed to want to strangle him any minute, but came over and clapped him on the back, which shook both him and Sophia, who he still held in his arms.

"Thank you, Papa. It really means a lot to me, that you two will get along." Sophia in her usual caring way, looked out for both him and her family members and he loved her the more for that. Merton's grip around her tightened and he never wanted to let her go. But eventually, he had to prepare for bed.

Fortunately, this time around, the CIA had handed him over his clothes and documents from the boat, because he did not think that he could wait any longer to take Sophia home with him. She belonged at his side as he always wanted to be at hers.

– 37 –
The Secret Laboratory

Merton should have expected it. But Sophia kept surprising him at every turn.

They would have a longer honeymoon-trip following their church wedding. But after their civil ceremony, two days after their return home, Sophia's wish for a short honeymoon-trip was to see his 'secret laboratory'.

The wedding night they had spent in her apartment – Sophia's wish, not his. And this time without her parents and brother, who had cheered during their wedding, but now spent the night in a hotel to drive home the next day.

Merton had wanted to indulge Sophia with the honeymoon-suite of the luxury hotel in town. But Sophia, insecure in her sexuality, had begged him to stay at a location where she felt comfortable and at home for her first time. And as it also was the place where he had seen her for the very first time, who was he to tell her no. As compensation, he had ordered an extensive catering with champagne, to indulge her in other ways.

The next day, late in the afternoon, for certain reasons, they were on their way home to his house, where the laboratory was close by on the grounds of his estate, a location his ex-wife had never set foot on.

Merton shook his head in silent wonder on their drive over. He still could not believe his fortune. When he had been in prison, everything had looked so dark and hopeless. His first marriage had been at an end and turned out to have been a farce right from the beginning. At that time, he never would have believed that his life could turn around so much for the better. His heart jumped with joy over having Sophia at his side and being able to call her his, as he was hers entirely. Wanting to see his 'secret laboratory' first of all. That was his girl through and through.

Her parents had let him take away their little girl after the ceremony. They were on their way home now and her mother planned to throw herself into the preparation of Sophia's wedding with their friends and family, inviting Prof. Benning, Mr. Arnestone and Tom, the fireman, so aptly coming to their rescue, as special guests of honor.

Merton would only bring Michael and his researchers from his 'secret laboratory' as his guests. His few close relatives had turned their back on him during his time in prison, one uncle even going so far as to give an interview to the press, that he had always expected something like that of his nephew. That made him in no way feel inclined to invite any member of his own family. But he was thankful, that though they had known each other for mere days, her family had accepted him so readily in their midst. And that her parents and brother were protective of Sophia just matched his own worry about her happiness. Merton wanted the best for her and to make her happy as she made him, and he planned to do his best for the rest of his life.

– 38 –
Postscript

I know you want to hear what happened to Michael. He helped Merton and Sophia so much, though he gave her a big fright in that shower.

But with his warm and helpful way, he soon had a secure place in her affections and she wanted only the best for this kind and gentle man, who for so long had been so misunderstood.

In the end, she did not have to do much. Shortly after their church wedding, which, organized by her omni-potent mother, went without even a glitch, and spending their honeymoon in Venice, Sophia asked Merton to employ a cook and cleaning woman in their new home together, as both mostly stayed in his research labs on the grounds of their home. This was the necessary key to unlock Michael's happiness.

One look at the new employee, Anna Brooks, and Michael's heart was engaged. It was love at first sight for the two and though Sophia had always been a sceptic about this instant attraction, Michael and Anna, their new household fairy, were inseparable from the first day and married only three months later. And not to keep anything from you, their first child, little Mike, was born seven months after their wedding.

Michael never took any steps to reveal the truth about his brother and his wife regarding the death of his father. The CIA had miraculously cleared Michael's records, which Sophia believed had been part of the deal Merton had made with them.

But Michael, though still angry with his brother and former

fiancée for their betrayal, had made peace with them in his mind, because they had two children of their own by now, the girl seven and the boy nine years old. He did not want to rob his niece and nephew of their beloved parents. Though, from afar, he kept a watchful eye on them all, to make sure his niece and nephew were happy and well cared for.

In Merton's laboratory, there was always work for an experienced technician and Michael, without the pressure of having to run a successful car-repair workshop, invented new machines and procedures, which brought him some nice side-income from patents and sales.

Michael and Anna built their own house on the grounds of Merton's expansive estate and continued to live close to them. Their children grew up together and Anna took over the day-care for all of them, even taking on some of the laboratory workers' children. Merton employed a new caretaker and help, to cope with all the extra work, so Anna had her own little home-preschool on the grounds, even taking the educational exams and making Michael very proud of her.

Sophia had two children of her own with Merton, a boy, who had her hair, but had Merton's eyes and a girl, who had the big curious eyes inherited from her mother and otherwise was the spitting image of Merton, though in a lovely girl's way.

And Merton? He had the best of all worlds. He had a family he loved, a wife who at the same time supported and challenged him and who had full understanding for his work. So, after his horrendous first marriage, the life with Sophia was a dream come true for them both.

Sophia loved to work for Merton's laboratory. There she was finally able to finish her thesis topic and with Prof. Benning as co-corrector and constant visitor to the lab, had brought two brilliant professors to work together on groundbreaking research, which she joined with her own unconventional ideas.

Though it took Prof. Benning a while to overcome his astonishment, when Prof. Lynford, after swearing him to the utmost secrecy, had come to reveal the true workings of the 'dark wood'-project to him.

Prof. Benning had thought Lynford had intentionally lied to the CIA to save the world from the effects of the full discovery. But discovering that Lynford had not and still ... – That was just so incredible, that he had stayed away from Lynford's laboratory for two months without a word.

Merton had begun to worry that Benning had run to the CIA and revealed the workings and had somehow worked out a way to circumvent the benign-interest approach. But then, Benning had reappeared with a new research proposal and had offered to combine their efforts on it, as if nothing had ever happened. From then on, they were regularly working together on various projects, among them research work for the CIA.

Prof. Benning never mentioned Vanessa's name in Sophia's or Prof. Lynford's company, though he kept in contact with her. After their interrogations, Dr. Stewart and Vanessa Benning had disappeared for quite a while, before Mrs. Benning appeared again. Dr. Stewart was not heard of ever again, so there is no way of knowing for certain what happened to him after the extended questioning that had followed the first round of CIA interviews with various departments.

Vanessa Benning was put on public trial with lots of media coverage. Her case was treated as the big success of the combined efforts of the police force and the secret services of the nation to fight organized crime. There was never a mentioning of either Prof. Benning or Prof. Lynford and Sophia in connection with her capture and arrest.

Vanessa Benning's sentence was lifelong prison in a high-security facility.

Prof. Benning had repeatedly visited her in prison during her trial and had tried to make her see the error of her ways. But as her prime motive had always been to keep him, her grand and undying love, alive and safe during the whole family-annihilation and continuing fights for supremacy, he could not uphold his judgement over her for long, but instead had to admire her single-mindedness, to which she had subordinated all else.

To Vanessa Benning's surprise, her lover and her daughter stayed by her side during this ordeal and were regular visitors in her prison, where she even learned to know her own daughter, to whom she had kept her distance not to make her a target for rivaling crime organizations or criminals who could have wanted to use her as leverage to take over the Syndicate-lead from her.

Patrick, or rather Patty, Michael's friend from prison and owner of the bombed house by the coast, never had to go back to prison. He got a new house built at the scene as recompense for the air-strike. The caves had mostly remained unharmed from the detonation. The new house Patty then used as a little hotel, which allowed him to fund his family and refrain from further crime.

Michael, his wife Anna, Sophia and Merton and sometimes even Prof. Benning and his daughter, spent their summer holidays there and the children learned sailing at this coast, where their parents had fought for what they believed in.

The End

About the Author

Chris T. Delarmy
is an avid reader, writer and observer of the human condition. From this passion, in order to recompense not being able to see the whole world in just one lifetime, the interest in writing and building own worlds developed and has now culminated in the writing of this first finished novel.

Author's website: delarmy.creative-author.com

Please comment on the book and let the author and other readers know how you liked it.
Thank you!